An American Cage

Ted Galdi

ISBN: 0989850722
ISBN 13: 9780989850728

One

As inmates of Thurgood L. Crick prison funnel out of the library toward the dining hall for eleven-AM lunch, Danny Marsh stays back, hidden behind a rack of books, aware this could be the last hour of his life.

He peers through the small space above the skyline of paperback spines on the fourth shelf of the rack, at the penitentiary librarian fifty feet away, a kind-eyed, plump-gutted man smiling at the felons as they exit.

Five criminals remain by the doorway. Now four. Another smile and nod from the librarian. Three left. Smile, nod. Two. One. Smile, nod, removal of keys from pocket. All convicts are outside. The librarian leaves. The joints of the steel door go *currkunk* as it closes. Danny hears the ding and ping of the key locking up.

Silence.

"We're good," a voice oiled with excitement says to Danny's left. Two other bodies in white prisoner uniforms burst out from behind two other bookracks, one of them the owner of the voice, Monty Montgomery, a lean-bodied black guy about Danny's age, both mid-twenties.

Danny and Monty dash side by side toward the back-right corner of the library, trailed by the third member of the trio, Phil Zorn, a frail-framed, little-legged man in his late forties, whose shorter strides keep him a few paces behind the two athletic twenty-somethings.

Winding around shelves, they move with an erratic hurry in their steps, just as precise as it is crazed, similar to how stagehands might scurry to and fro their places behind the curtains of a Broadway show on opening night.

Danny pushes a desk, its legs screeching as it rumbles four feet to the right. The three inmates stare at the area of cinder-block wall the desk was covering. Four blocks are removed. Monty grips the edge of the gap in the wall, the muscled black flesh of his shoulder exposed as the sleeve of his white prison shirt flops back, and climbs inside, his six-foot-one body wiggling until disappearing.

Phil goes in next, his palm squeezing his eyeglasses to his face to keep them on. Then Danny.

Crouched inside the wall, they're hushed other than the puff of their nervous breath. The only light is the faint spillover from the library, which kisses their stashed stack of supplies. A roll of duct tape. A twelve-inch, battery-run reciprocating power saw. Three large atlases. And ten prison uniforms.

Danny takes a second to absorb the reality that they've come this far, out of the hell of the penitentiary into this forbidden Eden of secret space, then says to Phil, "I'll get you first."

Phil picks up an atlas and presses it to his torso. Danny unravels a two-foot piece of duct tape, tears it with his teeth, and wraps it around Phil's scrawny mid-section, securing the book to his stomach. Phil fastens the second atlas to Danny. The third to Monty. Then they tape up each other's palms.

Danny grabs the power saw, Monty the ten uniforms, Phil the tape. They carry the supplies to a nearby mechanical area, where a ventilation duct runs overhead. Danny flips on the saw, the gentle whir of the blade filling the quiet space. He guides it to the steel shell of the vent, its teeth gnashing through with a high-pitched, metal-on-metal shriek.

While he saws, Monty and Phil kneel around the stack of uniforms. Monty ties a shirt to a pair of pants, then passes the linked length of fabric to Phil, who reinforces the knot with tape.

Danny figures lunch is just beginning now. It ends in a half hour, followed by a standing, in-cell prisoner headcount. No more than ten minutes later the guards will know they're missing. No more than ten minutes from then they'll realize it wasn't some administrative counting mistake. But an escape. And no more than ten minutes from then a legion of hunters across man and beast will pursue them, Texas cops with German shepherds and the legal choice to use lethal force.

The teeth of Danny's saw wrestle with the steel of the vent. *Zeenank, zeenank, thundub, zeenank, zeenank.* Above the noise he tells the other two, "I sure as hell won't miss the franks and beans they're serving down there. That stuff looks like something you'd find floating in a toilet at a retirement home."

Monty, tying the sleeve of a uniform top to the pant leg of a bottom, chuckles and says, "Amen, homie."

"You know what I'm gonna do when we get to Mexico?" Danny says. "Get myself a big ole cheeseburger. Rare. Juicy. Two slices of American cheese. Toasted bun, a little butter on it. Not too much though. Kaiser roll. Side of shoestring fries. Tub of ketchup."

"They even got burgers in Mexico?" Monty asks. "Isn't it all tacos and burritos?"

"Yes, they have cheeseburgers," Phil says, adjusting his glasses. "Our culture, including cuisine, has trickled down there, same as the Mexican culture has found its way up here."

"The professor would know," Danny says. "Cheeseburger it is. Second we get there."

"All right then," Monty says. "I'll have one with your ass. Then I want to see some live music. I missed that shit since I been on the inside. Not like a fancy concert at a big stadium. Local band with some drums. Some guitar. Decent singer. That's all I need."

"I hear you on that," Danny says with a smile, sparks dancing around his face. Growing up on a farm in El Paso, he always saw the world through the no-frills lens of a farm boy. Life to him was much simpler than people made it out to be. Under all the complexities of the socio-economic framework are the same basic pleasures we all crave, like good food and music.

However, Danny has been astounded at how difficult life makes itself to enjoy. It throws curveballs at you, keeping these simple pleasures at deceptively far distances. One of these curveballs got him into here.

"Wheeeee," Monty squeals. He slaps at his thighs. "Nasty ass…"

Danny tosses him an inquisitive look. "What is it?"

"Y'all didn't see that?" Monty asks, his gaze oscillating between the other two. "Rat ran right through here. Damn thing was about to crawl up my pant leg."

Danny laughs, then goes back to sawing.

"It probably wasn't a rat," Phil says. "Either you're seeing things, or it was a squirrel."

"Nah player. Ain't no friendly little squirrel."

"Rat or squirrel, not much of a difference," Phil replies, the sparks from Danny's sawing reflecting on his eyeglasses. "Both of them are mammals of the same order. Rodentia." He speaks with an explanatory friendliness to his voice, like a fifth-grade teacher. "They have a common ancestor going back to the Paleocene period. They're nearly genetically identical. It's illogical how people are scared of one, but think the other is…cute."

"If that thing I just saw snuck its way up your pants, I don't think you'd be calling it cute, no matter what name science people like you give it." Monty shakes his shoulders, getting the willies out.

The black kid from the ghetto and middle-aged ex-professor from one of the nation's top universities continue with their knotting and taping for a few minutes, until the shirts and pants of all ten uniforms are fixed to each other. They drag the white serpent of Texas-Department-of-Criminal-Justice-issued fabric toward Danny, a trail of dust rising from it.

Danny isn't quite done busting through the vent. His eyes are jumpy, hopping between the growing laceration in the ductwork and the gap in the cinderblock wall behind them, fearing a suspecting corrections officer could rear his head into their private Eden any moment.

In thirty seconds he lets go of the power tool's trigger, its shriek dying, and situates it on the floor. He analyzes the slice in the ventilation, then reaches up, clutching the sharp edge of the sawed flap with his tape-padded palms. He jerks on it four times. He surveys the pried-open vent, then delivers one last heave, the hardest yet.

"Is that shit long enough?" Monty asks.

"We don't have time to get it any bigger," Danny says. "Try not to cut yourself. Let's rock." He cradles his palms. Monty sticks his sneaker atop, and Danny guides him through the gash in the two-by-two-and-a-half-foot rectangular ventilation prism. Monty maneuvers inside, carefully avoiding the jagged perimeter of peeled steel. Phil passes him up the power saw and braided rope of prison uniforms. Monty coils the forty-plus feet of white fabric inside, then helps Phil and Danny up.

The tight space smells of metal and sweaty human flesh, an odor that instantly takes Danny's mind to the fourth-period, gym-class locker room at Hoover High School seven years ago.

Behind him in the duct is a path infinitely shrinking and darkening as it approaches some vantage point too shadowy to make out, a view with no exact end or shape to it, a distortion in space-time like the singularity of some prison-borne black hole. Yet, in front of Danny, a mere dozen feet away, is a vent grate in the penitentiary wall, and beyond it the world, exposed through louvers in glorious glimpses of blue sky. Life is out there somewhere. A real life, not the one he's led inside here the last year and a half.

With the mechanical saw, Danny crawls toward the bands of light. Phil follows, with Monty in back towing the rope. Danny squeezes the trigger, and lowers the pumping blade onto a louver, hacking through it. Then another. Another. And another. He twists and pushes the split slats, creating an opening to the outside big enough for a man.

Danny can feel the hot air of the Texas summer on his face. An animalistic urge in his stomach prompts him to charge through the exit now that it's there, but he stops himself. Not yet. Like they planned, they need to time this perfectly to evade the view of the perimeter guard. He'll be circling the property on an ATV. They have to emerge outside exactly after the guard passes, buying themselves the maximum time window to operate before he comes around again.

Huddled on top of each other in the womb of the vent, the three convicts wait. This entire wing of the prison is nearly empty, almost everyone across the property in the dining hall. Silence other than the occasional caw of a bird in the surrounding woods.

Softly at first, mixing in with the quiet of the wing, is the thrum of an engine. As it grows in volume, so does Danny's heartbeat. Soon, about a hundred feet away, the perimeter guard enters Danny's field of vision, riding at a medium clip on his four-wheel patrol vehicle, a rifle strapped to his bullet-proof vest along the spine of his back. The prisoners crouch, making themselves smaller. The guard motors closer.

He passes them.

The felons snap into another equally crazed, equally precise Broadway stagehand routine. Danny jumps through the torn-apart vent grate, descending five feet to the roof of the prison gymnasium, the facility adjacent to the library. Phil does the same, his ankles buckling upon landing. Monty shoves the tangle of tied prison uniforms through the opening, which blasts outside like the innards of a pop-box-snake toy, then leaps down to the gym roof with the other two.

Holding the white rope, they run across the gravel terrain to the border of the building. Monty drops to his stomach. Danny and Phil clench his feet. Monty curls over the edge of the gymnasium with one end of the rope in his hand, stretches his arms three feet down to a caged window overlooking the empty basketball court, and begins twisting the fabric around the intersecting metal bars over the glass.

Per their plan, Monty, the tallest, with the longest reach, is to tie the complicated, yet strong, midshipman's hitch knot, one of the few knots that can hold their weight as they bound down to the ground thirty feet below.

Danny tightens his grip on Monty's sneaker. Letting go means a headfirst plummet to the grave for his friend. He tries to keep all his concentration on his hands, but can't help glimpsing the South Tower guard post, where a rifle-toting marksman hawks over Thurgood L. Crick prison.

His back is to them, however Danny is aware that can change at any moment.

As the trio's escape research confirmed, during lunch the South Tower officer, the only guard with an eyeline to the rear of the gymnasium, keeps his attention predominantly on the dining-hall facility, where the bulk of the population is. Still, a view of the gym is only a mere neck turn away. If the sharp-shooter opts for a cursory glance of his surroundings, or even if a bug happens to buzz toward him causing him to reposition his head, it means a bullet through Danny's.

Danny gulps the humid air, but not much oxygen seems to pass through. His mind dizzies. The treetops spin a bit. Through his hazy gaze, he checks on their other human obstacle, the perimeter guard on the ATV. He's about to complete the first fourth of his oval lap around the premises. Once he rounds two more bends he'll have straightaway sight on them. It'll all be over.

Danny leans forward to assess Monty's progress with the convoluted knot, but can't see over the edge. "You almost done?" he asks.

Silence. A moment.

"Monty?"

Danny's forearms strain, the tattoo on the inside of his right pulsating on top of the muscle. He got it in prison nine months ago, when they decided to break out. It says "No Mad," a double meaning, the first a take on "nomad," as Danny will be permanently leaving his home of America for Mexico. The second is a play on "not mad," since Danny no longer wants to be mad at the world for throwing him so many damn curve-balls, and looks forward to a fresh start in a foreign land.

Danny scopes the perched guard in the South Tower, his eyes still locked on the chow hall, and the mobile one on the ground, coming up on the halfway point of his lap. "What the hell is taking you so long?" he asks Monty.

No answer.

He sees Monty's elbow moving. Then hears him say, "Shit."

"What?"

Monty mutters, "It keeps slipping. I got to start it over again."

Start the knot from the beginning? There's no time for that. Danny feels sweat seep through the pores above his eyebrows, which seems to instantly boil against his skin in the heat.

Monty's elbow is moving again, yet Danny is unable to see if he's making any progress. He checks the guard on the ATV. Now beyond the halfway mark of his lap. He eyeballs the guard in the tower, who shifts positions. His back is no longer to them. His left profile is visible. Danny figures they're just beyond his periphery. If he spins a few degrees more, they're dead.

The weight of Monty's body pulls on Danny, sharp pieces of gravel on the gym roof biting through the thin fabric of his inmate pants and scraping his shins. He assumes the little rocks have drawn blood, but doesn't bother to look. He stays glued on the guard, who remains in profile.

Five seconds.

Ten.

Twelve—

"Got it," Monty says.

Danny and Phil yank him back up. Danny tosses the free end of the rope over the side of the gymnasium, the material arcing past the fiery circle of sun in the sky before meeting with the brick façade of the prison, where it sways, big and beautiful, like a Rapunzelian ponytail.

The South Tower guard is still in profile. Danny has no idea how much longer. The patroller on the ATV is about seventy percent around.

"Monty, go," Danny blurts.

Monty lowers his sneakers three feet down to the top of the cage over the basketball-court window, which juts out no more than six inches from the wall. Laboring to keep his balance on the small, uneven surface, he reaches down, grips the metal bars, then removes his feet, letting them dangle, his flexed arms supporting his hundred eighty pounds of weight.

He clamps the makeshift rope and hops downward against the face of the building to the grass.

Danny is up next. He mimics the dangerous move Monty did to get hold of the window cage and rope. As he pushes himself to the ground the wind tickles the sides of his face, cooling his sun-roasted skin. Monty greets him on the soil with an enthusiastic slap on the back.

The two fit young men peer up at the fragile middle-aged one. With calculated, careful steps, Phil negotiates his way down to the bars over the window.

Danny can hear the purr of the guard's ATV in the near distance.

Phil, his chest pressed against the brick wall, struggles to find his footing on the crisscrossed metal.

"Come on, you son of a bitch," Monty whispers.

Phil slips, his foot shooting off the edge of the surface. Danny watches his body free fall, bracing for the worst, a dead sack of blood and bone right in front of him after a thirty-foot drop. However, Phil only sinks a yard or so, his hands clinging onto the cage, keeping him alive.

"Holy shit," Danny says.

Phil struggles to grasp the dangling thread of tied uniforms.

Danny notices the mobile guard going into the final leg of his lap.

Phil gets hold of the fabric. He begins his descent, his size-eight feet bouncing against the brick wall.

He reaches the earth.

With the ATV roaring behind them, just out of sight of its mounted guard, the three prisoners sprint toward the fence around the penitentiary. Its pattern of metal diamonds trembles as they scale it.

Once at the barrier's peak, they grab onto its spools of barbed wire with their duct-tape-protected palms, then slide over the thorny metal atop the thick atlases fastened to their chests.

They jump down to the terrain on the other side of the fence. The terrain on the other side of society. The side with freedom. And dart into the woods.

Danny feels a thrill in his belly. They're out. Maybe the world is done playing sinister games with him. Maybe it's decided he's had enough and is finally letting him enjoy his time on the planet.

However, the thrill is short-lived. They have a long way to go. Breaking out of prison was only the first part of their plan. Now they have to make it to Mexico.

Two

Danny hurdles over a beetle-covered decaying log, then weaves between loblolly pine and bitternut hickory trees in a dense patch of the Piney Woods butted up to the jailhouse property.

The three escapees are distancing from the prison, but are still far to safety.

After the post-lunch headcount happens, armed law enforcement will swarm this forest. Before then, Danny, Monty, and Phil need to navigate through two and a half miles of brush to the highway, where a pre-arranged ride is waiting.

Phil, the former professor, who's memorized the breadth and bends of this region of woods from a Google Earth photograph he had smuggled into prison, leads the younger two through the thicket. He tears the atlas off his chest and continues ahead with a remnant of semi-stuck duct tape waving under his left arm. Danny does the same, the book freeing from his body mid-stride, opening in the mud to a colorful map of Peru.

"How much time we have?" Danny shouts ahead to Phil.

Phil throws a glance toward the treetops, where the sun shimmers down on them as shapeless blobs of white mixed with fine-formed lasers of yellow. "A little under a half hour."

Danny takes his word for it. Out in the yard, he's seen Phil determine the exact time of day by gauging the position of the sun in the sky. In this last year, since he and Phil have been cellmates, he's seen him do a lot of impressive things with his mind. Phil was the brains behind the entire escape plan.

The greens and browns of the leaves streak past Danny. He summons more gas into the overheating machinery of his legs. His white inmate shirt is suctioned to the film of sweat on his skin. Each of his two lungs feels like it has its own heartbeat, a trifecta of uneven pounding in his chest.

He's been waiting a year and a half for this moment. Freedom. For the last nine months, during escape planning, he'd imagine it every night before falling asleep in his bunk beneath Phil's. But now that he's in this moment, he's disappointed to admit it's not what he hoped.

The inside of his sprinting body is a hotbed of adrenaline and lactic acid. However, buried beneath their burning chemical rumpus lurks a chillingly familiar feeling. The one of prison. He's beyond the penitentiary walls, but still seems inside them. The same chunk of ice sits in the same place in his gut it has since the day he became inmate #4732119.

And he has no idea why.

Phil scurries around the rim of a swampy cauldron of grayish water, his left calf grazing blades of weed. Danny turns over his shoulder to check on Monty. Bushes, logs, trees, rocks.

No Monty.

Danny's feet simmer from a run to a jog to a stop. He spins around and scans the brush for his buddy. In the distance, among a grove of black walnut trees is the whitish outline of a prison uniform, an atlas still on it. Stepping closer, Danny discerns Monty's face above the white fabric.

"Come on," Danny shouts, flailing his arm. When Monty's speed doesn't pick up, Danny hollers, "What are you doing, man? Hurry up."

No answer. Danny notices a trace of a hobble in Monty's gait. He flips his upper body a hundred eighty degrees, cups his mouth with his hands, and yells toward Phil, "Hey. Stop. Professor. I think he's hurt."

Danny rushes toward his buddy Monty. A transposed déjà vu of scenery erupts in his periphery as he covers ground he just crossed in the opposite direction. Nearing Monty, he hears the on-and-off of a groan. However, glimpsing Monty's expression, he sees nothing but optimism, two exuberant eyes in the center of a shaved head.

"What's the matter?" Danny asks.

Monty waves him off, continuing on at his poky pace. "You're going the wrong way, homie. Turn your ass around. Don't mind me."

"Tell me what happened."

"Turn your ass around, I said."

Danny notices a red splatter dotting the rear of Monty's right pant leg around knee level. Above the red dots is a tear-shaped rip in the fabric. Through it Danny sees a crimson glaze all over Monty's black skin, an angry wound screaming among it, its lips half-inch-thick flaps of pink flesh.

"Son of a bitch," Danny says to himself. This is bad. This will slow them down. Possibly too much.

Danny kicks the bark of a tree. He hears a loud noise nearby. He anxiously turns toward it. A cop? No. Just a branch falling. The muscles around his left eye begin quivering. A tic he picked up in jail.

Just when he thought the world was done toying with him, it slices his escape partner's leg, exponentially chopping their chances for success.

"Don't wait back here with me," Monty says. "Go dammit. Keep running."

"Fuck you. I'm not leaving you behind."

Monty winces. The propped-up optimism on his face deflates. "I can manage."

"No, you can't. The back of your knee is shredded. You must've caught it on the razor wire going over the fence."

"I'll push through it, yo. Get to the van. Tell our ride I'm just a little behind."

"You'll never make it. The three of us got this far together. And we're getting to Mexico together." Danny slides Monty's arm behind his neck. "Let me help you."

"You're slowing yourself down."

"I don't care." With Danny's aid, Monty moves about thirty percent quicker than he did alone. However, still considerably slower than a healthy man.

Phil approaches. His gaze examines the tandem march of the other two, then angles upward and analyzes the sun's position in the sky. "That's as fast as you can go?" he asks.

"Should've seen him before," Danny answers.

"Just a nick on my knee," Monty adds. "Can hardly feel it. I'm straight."

"You can hardly feel it because of your spiked levels of adrenaline," Phil says. "From here we've got about two point one miles left. Impossible to cover in time at this rate."

"I'm aight. We're gonna get there. I know it, yo. I *know* it."

"I'd say you two are going a little over three miles per hour. Which means you'd arrive at the pickup location around twelve twenty PM. Lunch is already over. Headcount is in progress *now*. They'll know we're gone any second. A hundred fifty cops will be in these woods by twelve twenty."

Silence other than the rustle of leaves as Danny and Monty's feet pass over them. "Stop, just stop," Phil shouts, a high-pitched femininity in his tone. Danny, who's never heard his old cellmate raise his voice, quits moving. Monty unhooks his arm from Danny's neck. They stare at the smaller, older man. "Even if you increase your speed, our margin of error is simply too low with..." Phil points at Monty's leg. "*That* in the mix. We can't go on like this. We'll all be goners."

Danny's breath shortens. He walks in circles.

"Daniel?" Phil calls.

Danny doesn't acknowledge him, still going in circles.

"You're having a panic attack," Phil says. "I need you to stay strong. We all need to stay strong right now."

"That's a little difficult with only minutes—" A noise. Danny's ass clenches as he looks toward it. Not a cop. Just an animal scampering between bushes.

"You're getting paranoid," Phil says. "A textbook panic-attack side effect. Remember what we used to talk about in the cell when you'd feel like this? Logical statements. Just keep repeating logical statements to yourself. The guards don't know we're out yet. We're fine. We just need to manage around this... obstacle with Monty's leg. And we can't panic or else we'll lose focus." Phil lays a hand on Danny's shoulder. "Be strong for me."

Danny takes a deep breath. Phil's words, as they've had for the last year, are able to get through to him and soothe him. "If we can't go on like this," Danny says, "what the hell do we do?"

Brainiac Phil runs his fingers through his graying-blond hair. "Let me think." He peers at the forest stretching in all directions. He sits on a rock, holding his soft-featured, chipmunk-cheeked face in his hands. "Just...let me think."

Three

The blood blotches on Monty's white pant leg widen as he and Danny stare at the ex-professor on the rock. Whatever is in that head, Danny reasons, is their only chance of survival.

A minute passes.

"The map showed a small town about a half mile to the east," Phil says. "At the rate you were going, we should be able to get there by noon. I'm not positive what we'd do once we arrived. But at least we'd be out of the woods, the first place they'll look."

"What about your friend picking us up?" Monty asks.

"We'll…we'll have to deal with him later. It's not a perfect plan. But—"

"It'll only be a matter of time before the cops drive through every nearby neighborhood," Danny says. He rubs his brow, the tips of his fingers moistening from the accumulated sweat. "We'll be sitting ducks as long as we're in the general area."

"Not if we can get inside," Monty says. The other two turn to him. "One of the houses. In town."

"Who in their right mind is gonna let three prisoners through their front door?" Danny asks. "We can't just…break in either. It's Saturday. Nobody's at work or school. They're home."

"We don't tell them we're prisoners," Monty says. "Ain't you ever ducked out in someone's crib for a little when the pigs were patrolling the streets for you?" His partners offer blank stares. "Hell, I should've figured with you two white boys. It's simple. You lie. Say your car broke down or something. Need a phone. They let you in. You play nice. You call a homeboy to pick you up and get you the hell out. In this case, the professor can call his friend and have him scoop us up in the van."

Phil pinches the fabric of his white top. "How do we lie our way out of these outfits?"

Fifteen seconds of quiet.

"I have an idea," Danny states. He removes the duct tape from his palms, takes a handful of muddy earth, and slaps it across his chest. Confusion sweeps across the others' faces. "Don't just watch me," Danny says. "Do it too."

"You losing it, Danny?" Monty asks.

"This'll help us get inside a house. We don't have much time. Hurry. Grab the dirt. Get it all over."

Phil and Monty look at each other. A moment. "Fucking shit," Monty mumbles, then undoes his atlas and tape and joins in. Phil too.

Over the next two minutes, Danny explains his idea as they slather the white of their getups with clumps of brown dirt and black mud, shivers of weeds, and fragments of pebbles. Danny isn't certain this will work. If it doesn't, and they all go back to jail, it'll be his fault. And he'll have to live with that. It's a risk he's willing to take. He already has to live with a lot. What's one more bad memory? To him, the past doesn't matter much. Life is about the future. It's about movement. Looking back is for senior citizens.

They embark on the half-mile hike east, Danny assisting Monty as he did before. By the time they exit the woods, the sun has nearly climbed to its noon apex. It beams down on a tiny trailer-park community, cooking it in ninety-nine-degree heat. Danny lets go of Monty and stoops at the waist, setting his palms atop his knees, surveying the sight before him.

Thirteen mobile homes jacked up on cinderblocks are scattered across eight flat acres of dust without regard to rows or any other uniformity of layout, toward the front an oblong patch of dead grass punctured with the stakes of a yellow sign holding moveable red letters that spell "Big Oaks Trailer Park," toward the back a procession of power lines with drooping wires and rusty transformers that extends over the azure sky to the horizon.

Dust whirls from the ground through the hot air, a few specks clinging to the sweat on Danny's skin beneath his eyes.

"That one," Monty says. He points at a singlewide, tin-walled mobile home, out front an old pickup truck, new pink bicycle, and two beach chairs. An inkling of a grin blooms on Monty's face. "Jesus would open his door for three men in need, wouldn't he?" he asks his escape partners, alluding to a "WWJD?" bumper sticker on the pickup.

"Fine by me," Danny says. "Professor, you're the most well spoken. You do the talking."

Phil replies with a nod.

They pace toward the trailer, Monty bringing up the rear with a limp. The sun bears down on the mud on their shoulders, giving it the tint and texture of placenta. They pass the pink bicycle, shiny on its kickstand in the glow of the day. Phil walks up the three-step, plywood staircase to the cream-colored door. Danny and Monty wait beside the pair of beach chairs.

Phil knocks.

Four

The trailer park wheezes as a strong wind passes through. Phil knocks on the door again. A few moments. It cracks open, the sound of Saturday cartoons spilling outside. A mid-thirties man about six feet tall stands in the entryway, the ajar door slab hiding half his face. A green eye looks Phil up and down. Then again.

"Sorry to interrupt you, sir," Phil says. He gently steeples his hands and signals to Monty. "We've been hunting in the woods. When hiding down in the mud, my friend cut his knee on the edge of a rock. We'd be eternally grateful if you could let us in, for just a few minutes. Spare some bandages so I can patch him up, and let me use your phone to make one quick call."

The single green eye stays on Phil for another moment. It moves to Danny and Monty. A playful, trombone-led score emanates from the cartoon program on the TV inside, soon accompanied by a character's voice shouting, "Not again Mother Hen."

The green eye watches them for a couple more seconds, then the half a mouth exposed below it opens to ask, "Which one?"

"Excuse me?" Phil replies.

"Is hurt. The black one or the white one?"

A moment. "The black one."

The green eye moves back to Phil. The door opens some more, revealing the full of the face, which has classically handsome features yet set on a landscape of leathery, sun-worn skin. "He bleeding?" the man asks.

"Some."

"Well, I don't want him inside if he's gonna bleed all over. He can wait out here on the stairs. You and the other one can come in, you knock that mud off your shoes first."

Phil's shoulders deflate an inch as he says, "Thank you, sir. God bless. God *bless*." Stomping his feet on the plywood staircase, Phil motions for Danny to join him. He does, chunks of dirt and of grass freeing from his sneakers. They enter while Monty takes a seat on the top step.

Danny looks around the trailer's interior. An area rug sits on the vinyl floor and on that a belly-down young girl no older than eight watching the cartoon he heard outside, so engrossed in the show that she doesn't notice, or care to peek at, the visitors. Behind her, sewing a quilt on a loveseat, is the mother/wife, a woman with an appearance opposite her husband's, bland features on perfect skin, who pays Danny a quick, flirtatious glance before returning to her needle and thread.

The man crosses the den into the kitchen, where he opens a cabinet beside the microwave, revealing three shelves of general-purpose supplies, from glue to matches to roach spray to dozens of other containers and packages. His back to everyone else, the tour dates of his KISS tee shirt on display, he roots through the cabinet, soon fishing out a bottle of hydrogen peroxide, a box of gauze, and a roll of Scotch tape.

He sets the goods on the counter beside his half-drank mug of coffee and folded-open Saturday newspaper. "Have at it," he says to Phil, who lingers in a part of the trailer not quite in the den, not quite in the kitchen.

"You're a true saint," Phil tells him with a smile, then collects the first-aid gear and heads back toward the entrance, cutting in front of the TV screen, not snapping the little girl from her trance. He sits in the open doorway, one foot on the vinyl trailer floor, the other on the top plywood stair, and unscrews the bottle of hydrogen peroxide.

Danny, in the corner, gazes at the three family members. The heels of the child, wigwagging to the rhythm of the cartoon theme song. The hand of the woman, pulling the sewing needle up through a partially completed design of a teddy bear's face on the quilt, a brown length of string extending from the end. The eyes of the man, perusing the op-ed section of his newspaper.

Monty moans as Phil pours the hydrogen peroxide on his cut. The man peeks up from his paper and asks Danny, "Your friend decent out there?"

"He'll be fine."

"I can call an ambulance for him, won't be no trouble at all."

At this Phil's hands freeze. He and Monty both look up at Danny. A moment. Danny replies, "No need for that. Thank... thank you though."

Phil's hands begin moving again.

The man lifts his coffee cup and has a long sip. He takes a good look at Danny's face and outfit. "What were y'all hunting out there anyway?"

Danny, who's never hunted a day in his life, hesitates, his mouth opening a bit, yet not a bit of noise coming out.

"Rabbit," Phil announces, unraveling the roll of gauze.

"Is that right?" the man asks Danny.

"Yes sir."

The trailer's patriarch has another sip of coffee, his eyes locked on Danny's. He places the cup down, stare still focused. A few moments. He returns to the newspaper.

On the TV the voices of two animated trees argue about the location of a Princess Beatrice. Danny's attention travels to the lady on his right, her careful hand inserting the sewing needle through the cheek of the teddy bear, light flooding onto her through the large window above the loveseat.

Then Danny hears something he dismisses as an auditory mirage, some trick his paranoia is playing on him. Yet, as the sound builds, and his mind processes more of it, he comes to the realization that it's likely not a hallucination, that its presence is perfectly possible right now, even probable.

Phil stops wrapping the gauze and angles his ear upward. Monty looks straight ahead, breathless. Danny knows they hear it too.

A police siren.

As it loudens it grows more complex, different tones blending with the original. More sirens. More cops. Danny glances out the window above the loveseat, through it a view of three other trailers, and in the distance behind them an empty strip of road. The head of the woman, unfazed by the noise, obscures part of the glass. She continues looping her thread in and out of the teddy bear's face.

Danny sees the black-and-white nose of a police car shoot onto the edge of the window, its spinning red lights emerging a split second later. *Vuswoon*, another cruiser zips by. *Vuswoon*, another. Two more tail, appearing to the left of the woman's head, disappearing behind it for a moment, then speeding on and exiting Danny's view past the right rim of the glass pane.

He shifts his gaze to the other two criminals. Monty, still breathless, stares at the dusty lot. Phil remains motionless for another two seconds, then continues circling the gauze around Monty's knee, his hands quicker than they were before.

"I'm a hunter myself," Danny hears from inside, the unexpected arrival of the voice in his ear poking at something sensitive in his overheating brain, causing all the muscles in his shoulders and arms to tense.

Danny turns to the man, who's risen from his kitchen stool and is strolling toward the coffee maker. "I mostly keep it to white-tailed deer," the man says. "November and December they're in season. Way colder than this." He slopes the pot's spout over his cup, a smoky, brownish-black stream soon adjoining the two receptacles. "I gotta ask. Them outfits you're in...look almost like pajamas. That some summer thing y'all rabbit hunters wear on account of the heat?"

"Exactly," Danny says. "They may look like pajamas, but they're not priced like them. Wish they were. Highly engineered to breathe the right way."

The man, still standing, guides a sip of the hot liquid through his lips, and asks, "What kind of weapons you use on a rabbit? Gotta be careful, I reckon, you don't employ too much firepower, blast the sucker wide open into a zillion little pieces. Then you don't got much of a trophy to stuff and hang on your wall."

Phil chimes in, "Lever action twenty-two." He enters the trailer, the first-aid supplies cradled in his arms. "I have a Henry."

"A Henry." The man grins. "My first rifle when I was ten."

"I had a good feeling about you the second I saw you," Phil says as he crosses the den past the TV, which turns to commercial. He arranges the hydrogen peroxide, gauze, and tape on the counter. "He's all bandaged up. Once again, thank you for the hospitality. Now, if you wouldn't mind letting me borrow your telephone for just a moment to check in with my wife. Then we'll be out of your hair."

"Hey, before y'all go, would it be all right if I had a quick look at that Henry? Haven't held one since I was a boy."

The trailer is hushed aside from the brief sound bites from the television as the little girl scans through the channels. "Saving for retirement shouldn't be a—" from an infomercial. "When two bull elephant seals square off—" on National Geographic.

"Actually," Phil says, "the rifles are locked up back in the truck. With our cell phones. No service out there. Which is why I'm kindly asking if I could use that landline."

The man puts the bottle of hydrogen peroxide back in the still-open cabinet. The hand of his daughter clicks the channel-down button on the remote control. The hand of his wife runs her sewing needle through the quilt.

A new noise bleeds into the atmosphere, emanating into the trailer from the open entryway, where Monty's elbow pokes through as he waits outside. *Thunt. Thunt. Thunt.*

Danny, unsure what it is, looks toward it over his shoulder, where he sees Monty's partial profile through the doorway. When Monty's head goes backward and his gaze upward to the sky, Danny realizes what the sound is from.

A helicopter.

"Sure you can use it," the man tells Phil, nodding at a cord phone on the wall beside the refrigerator.

"Thank you," Phil says, his chipmunk cheeks arching into a smile. He meanders on his little legs around the counter in the kitchen, removes the phone from its mount, and drifts down a hallway, out of earshot from the family, the cord stretching with him.

Thunt. Thunt. Thunt. A small pool of sweat swells on Danny's hairline. It bunches unevenly, a bead of moisture breaking off. As it oozes down the skin of his forehead, snaking toward his eyebrow, he zeroes in on the dynamics of the chopper noise overhead, the way it trails off, then crescendos as it boomerangs back toward them.

He watches Phil punch the numbers on the phone's keypad. He presses his fourth. Then his fifth.

"Don't change the channel," the woman screams.

Danny whips his eyes toward her, the bead of sweat propelling off his forehead, fracturing into smaller droplets in the air. She's pointing with her sewing hand, her elbow locked. Danny's eyes follow the direction of the needle extending from her grip to the TV screen.

His mug shot is on it. So are Monty's and Phil's. "Alert: Prisoners Loose" is heralded in bold letters along the bottom of the local-news broadcast.

Time seems to slow in Danny's field of vision as he watches the heads of the woman and girl turn to him, and the heads of the man and Phil turn to the TV, the details of each expression, and the muscles in each pivoted neck, pronounced.

"We've received word they've been missing no earlier than this morning," the newscaster reports, "and are likely on foot, putting them in a radius of Crick no more than..."

The man's cup of coffee steams beside him on the counter as his green eyes pass from Danny to Phil to a set of kitchen knives in a block holder about four feet away.

Stillness for three seconds.

The man lunges toward the knives. An accompanying gasp from his wife. Phil lets go of the phone receiver and hurls his body shoulder-first at him. The top of Phil's head rams into his hip just before he grabs a knife. The phone bangs on the floor, and a moment later the entwined bodies of Phil and the Good Samaritan.

Danny, on the other side of the counter, can't see them wrestle but can hear them, their rolling bodies slamming into the cabinets beneath the sink. He scurries to them. One is fighting for the protection of his family, the other the preservation of his freedom, both drives equally as primal and powerful. Yet, the trailer owner is larger and stronger than Phil, and seems to be edging closer to the knives.

Danny's mind spins as fast as the chopper above. What can he do? He has a clear path to the knives. If he gets to them, then what? He'd never use one on the man. That's not in his nature. He knows it's not in Phil's nature either. However, the man, naturally terrified, would likely use one on them. Danny figures he should take the knife block and simply clutch it, play defense, shield it from the owner.

As he steps to the blades, he feels a semi-soft, though heavy object smash into his head. His vision goes black for a half-second. When his eyes open, he notices strips of gold and brown thread among the dry mud on his chest, an over-turned sewing basket at his feet, thimbles and needles scattered about. Screaming, the woman of the home charges at him and begins smashing down on his head with the base of her fists, the lavender smell of her perfume filling his nostrils.

Danny absorbs the blows without countering. Hitting a woman isn't in his nature either.

"Run to the Brauns' trailer and tell them to call the police," the mother yells to her daughter.

The girl, eyes watering, rises from the rug.

The door slams.

Monty stands in front of it. The child shudders. He twists the lock. Then runs across the trailer, favoring his right leg, and seizes the block of knives before anyone else. He unsheathes the largest one.

"Enough," he yells.

The two men on the floor stop grappling. The woman stops swinging at Danny. The little girl squeezes her mother's hip. Everyone stares at the big black man with the big blade.

He holds it at an upward angle in front of him, like a rhinoceros horn.

"You," he barks to the man. "Up."

Hands raised in submission, he climbs to his feet. Phil, with a bloody nose, ascends from the floor as well.

"Shut the curtains," Monty tells the woman. She doesn't. "Shut them," he says louder, nostrils flaring.

She does. With no bulbs on, and the natural light drained from the trailer, a shadow drapes everyone and everything.

"Da…da…ad…daddy…wh…a…what….what's happening?" the child manages to push from her shaky voice box.

Her father doesn't have an answer for her.

"Professor," Monty says.

"Yes."

"Your nigga on the way?"

"I never got a chance to dial."

Monty nods at the helicopter sound above. "We can't wait around for him to pick us up here. We gotta get out of the area. Now. Cops be coming door to door soon. Call that motherfucker up and tell him to meet us somewhere at least five miles from the prison. Somewhere secluded."

"How will we get that far?"

With the hand holding the knife, Monty snatches the truck keys from the counter and jiggles them.

"Understood," Phil says. He retrieves the phone off the floor, takes it into the hallway, out of earshot, and begins dialing.

"What do we do about them?" Danny asks. He scopes the family, then the sharp blade in Monty's grip. "We can't…hurt them."

A moment. "I don't want to hurt them," Monty says. "But I don't trust them either. They call in the license plate of that truck when we're on the road, we're fucked."

Danny peers at the three frightened faces, man, woman, and child.

"We gotta tie them up," Monty says. "In here. Once we ditch the truck and go with Phil's friend, we'll call the cops, anonymously, and tell them to untie them."

Danny doesn't like the idea of roping these innocent people up, but knows Monty is right. If they just drove off, someone would call the police right away. Every cop in the county would be scouring the streets for the vehicle.

"Yeah," Danny says, unable to make eye contact with the family. "All right."

"Check for stuff in there," Monty says, pointing at the open cabinet with the general-purpose supplies.

Danny digs through it. He soon unearths a package of zip ties. "Sorry," he whispers in the man's ear as he grabs his wrist.

"Tie them to...solid shit," Monty says. "That won't move."

Danny is as gentle as possible as he binds the man's wrists to a pipe beneath the sink. In the background, the voice of the TV newsman says, "...Monty Montgomery, African American, twenty-five, six one, serving nine years for grand theft auto. The second, Dr. Philip Zorn, five foot seven, whom you may remember from news coverage in 2004. One of the world's leading neuroscience researchers. Sentenced to twenty-eight years for aggravated sexual assault. And Daniel Marsh, five eleven, white, straight brown hair, brown eyes, twenty-four, serving..." Danny doesn't listen. He hates his association with that crime.

In a couple minutes the two females are restrained, the mother to the showerhead in the bathroom, the daughter to the dinner table.

Monty emerges from the master bedroom with three pairs of men's jeans and three tee shirts. He passes the fresh clothing to the other two criminals, then tosses Phil the truck keys and one of the two cell phones from the counter. They strip out of their muddy jailhouse attire into the new outfits.

The sight of the bound-up family, especially the child, nauseates Danny. He vomits into the garbage can in the kitchen. Phil encouragingly pats his back while Monty peeks through the blinds, studying the chopper in the sky.

"Not yet," Monty says. A half-minute of indoor silence passes. "*Now.*"

He pushes open the door, summer daylight surging in, along with the amplified sound of the overhead blades. He locks the knob from the inside, lets his two escape partners follow him outside, then slams the door shut behind them. They scramble toward the pickup truck. Phil unlocks it and they dive inside, just out of view of the circling helicopter.

The engine turns on. In a trail of dust, the fugitives pull away from the mobile home. Danny takes in the lemon scent of the tree-shaped air freshener bobbling from the rearview mirror. The crisp, clean smell feels unnatural to him in this moment, like it's trying to wash out the notion of the in-progress manhunt going on less than a mile away.

They're no longer on foot, which is helpful. But they're no longer off the radar either. The authorities know what they did. And the pursuit will widen until they're out of the country.

Getting out of the country rests on the shoulders of Phil's friend, an ex-convict Phil met at Crick years ago, before Danny was an inmate. This plan just got even more complicated. If Phil's friend botches his new instructions, the manhunt will eat the escapees alive.

Five

A 2002 Ford F-150, a "WWJD?" decal on its back bumper and cracks like spider-webs on its maroon paint job, rides north on a sleepy, rural road. Danny is aware the sleepiness will soon morph into wildness as the manhunt expands north, with all its squad cars, choppers, and rifles. They don't have long to get to Phil's friend before the law gets to them.

Phil drives fast, however not *too* fast. Getting nabbed for speeding would assure their capture. Their restrained rate makes Danny anxious. He wishes they could just blaze ahead. He lies in the backseat, hiding his body from the view of passing vehicles. Monty does the same, reclined in the front passenger seat.

Danny looks out the window, trying to take his mind off of the sandstorm of problems in his head. He observes the flat green fields, most of overgrown, ignored grass. Among them is a self-proclaimed "Fishing Outlet," a shack with three rods decoratively poking out from the lawn by the sign.

Up the road a half mile, a vinyl banner wrapped around two trees announces "Dry Goods." A mile farther up is a white house with a sled leaning against its mailbox post, "Propane Refills" spray-painted onto the wooden planks in orange along with an arrow directing toward the side of the home.

Danny keeps seeing that little girl. Her little eyes overflowing with tears. Her little hands clasped together around a table leg. He puked in the trailer, yet his stomach doesn't feel any better now that his breakfast is out of it.

He tells himself to just block the thought. It's part of the past. And the past is over. He needs to focus on movement. Movement means moving on.

Danny slips his hand under his stolen shirt and frees from the band of his underwear a folded piece of paper, which has been there all day. He'd kept it under his mattress in jail the last year and a half. It's the only item he wanted to bring with him when he escaped, something he sketched in prison off of a childhood memory. Nobody knows he has it, even former bunkmate Phil.

He unfolds it and stares at it, a penciled duplicate of an ad for cough medicine Danny remembered seeing in a magazine when he was just nine years old. It's of a moon with a cartoonish face, wearing a sleeping cap, peacefully snoozing in a big bed in the night sky. The copy below says, "Drift for the Night, Just Right." When he drew it, Danny recalled the image in perfect detail in his mind and rendered it in perfect detail on the page. He has a rare skill for sketching things out of memory.

Danny's not sure exactly why he recollected the visual of the magazine ad one winter evening early in his sentence, but he did, and when he brought it to life on paper, it calmed him.

Afterward, he'd often pull it out and look at it on the hard days. There were a lot of them.

"Hey, professor," Monty says. "I don't speak a lick of Spanish. That gonna be straight down there?"

"Of course. A lot of people speak English. But I'd recommend you learn Spanish for the long term."

Monty pivots, turning to Danny, who hastily stuffs the sketch between his back and the seat. "You don't know that shit either, right?" Monty asks.

"Nah."

"I'll teach you, Daniel," Phil says with a smile. "Both of you. Once we get there. After, of course, our dose of cheeseburgers and live music."

Danny likes Phil, despite his nerdiness. Over the last year Danny began viewing him as a father figure. Danny hasn't spoken to his real father for two years, since the night of the incident that got him thrown in jail. His old man offered him money for a top attorney, but Danny refused it and went with the public defender. He doesn't plan to talk to him ever again.

"You sure your homie can hook us up with a place to stay down there?" Monty asks Phil.

"He's already mailed me photos of the apartment complex. It's lovely."

"You think it'll be tough to get a graphic-design job?" Danny asks.

"Ah, your calling," Phil says. "Until our fake IDs and papers are prepared, we'll want to work off the books. Cleaning dishes, anything. Once our documents are in place, we can do whatever we please."

The summer of 2014, when Danny was arrested, he was working in the graphics department at Amogo Studios, a digital firm in his hometown of El Paso that specializes in virtual reality.

During high school Danny had friends, but wasn't in a defined group. He wasn't unpopular, but not popular either. He played baseball freshman year, but was never considered a jock. He got good grades, but was never a star student. His friends came from a variety of social circles. Among them he never quite had a best one. He never spent enough time with any to forge a strong enough bond.

After a while his buddies would piss him off with typical teenage drama and instead of talking it out, Danny wouldn't call them for a couple weeks. He wasn't trying to be mean. He simply didn't mind hanging out by himself, spending a weekend doodling in a sketchbook.

He worked on his father's farm high school summers, then year-round for two years after graduation. He was being groomed to one day take it over. But he wanted to try something else, something creative, something with art.

So he enrolled in a graphic-design program at a community college. He interned at Amogo Studios after his first year and accepted a full-time job offer when he got his associate's degree.

The CEO of Amogo, Buddy Chaplin, a well-known tech entrepreneur from Texas, told Danny one day in the office he had the "it factor" managers wish for in designers. Danny loved Buddy and his co-workers. They were creative. And social, though they tended to beat to their own drum. Just like him. He quickly grew close to three guys and one girl, who became his first real group of friends.

He finally belonged somewhere. Life finally felt stable.

Then it threw him a curveball. And he was no longer Danny Marsh, promising graphic designer. He was inmate #4732119.

Danny hears the cough of a muffler from a passing vehicle. He's reminded other cars are on the road. And their drivers can see Phil at the wheel. Surely there's a chance a nearby motorist caught his photo on the local news. If the person makes the connection, the cops are called and the escapees are shot dead. Or back in prison. Danny is certain he wouldn't survive much longer in jail. That place was killing him from the inside like a tapeworm.

"Hey, we getting close?" Danny asks.

Phil's eyes meet his in the rearview mirror. "Shouldn't be much longer, Daniel." Then Phil's chipmunk cheeks force their way into a reassuring smile.

The pickup rolls along for the next three miles in silence. Then it fills with a loud blast. Startled, Danny for a second can't make sense of the noise, then notices Monty's hand on the radio and learns it's just the electric guitar of a song. "Green River" by Creedence Clearwater Revival.

Monty, staying low and out of view in his seat, scans stations to a mid-chorus Rick Ross rap, which he takes in for a bit before stopping on "Cupid" by Sam Cooke.

When the song ends an announcer comes on with highlights from the in-progress NBA Finals between the Cavaliers and Warriors. "That's another thing I want to do when I get to

Mexico," Monty says. "Go to a sports game. I don't even care if it's gotta be soccer. A pro athlete is a pro athlete."

"Pass," Danny says. "Athletes are winners of the genetic lottery. They get everything they want from an industry subsidized by millions of everyday Joes. The players don't give a crap about the fans. They live on a different planet than them."

"Are you a little sore 'cause you got snubbed asking for an autograph when you were a kid or some shit?" Monty jokes.

Danny chuckles.

"You'll hit the beach with me though, won't you?" Monty asks.

"Hell yeah," Danny says.

"That's my boy. I'm looking forward to that more than any of the other stuff. You know I ain't never seen the ocean? You ever see it in person?"

Danny nods.

"Of course you did, you a white kid who comes from some money. Probably went on vacations and shit when you were growin' up. Not me. Tryin' to see the damn ocean. That's what I was doing, you know, the day I got busted."

"For stealing the car?"

"I met this girl at a party. Hot. Let me tell you. Ass, but not too much. I don't like too much. And I'm talking her up. Real smooth, you know. Like how I always did it. And she tells me she ain't seen the ocean. Barely even ever left the ghetto. And I tell her I didn't see it either. Then I say let's go tonight. I'll drive through the night, we'll be there as the sun is coming up. Real romantic. All that. She don't own a car. I don't own a car.

So I go to a parking lot and hotwire one. We get in. She's lovin' it. I'm lovin' it. I got as far south as Snyder."

"What happened to the girl?"

A grin pops onto Monty's face, as if accompanying an image of the girl popping into his mind. "When the cops got me, I told them she don't know the car was stolen. That I boosted it before I picked her up. Why should we both get in trouble? What's the good in that? You know…" His arms cross. His chin tilts to the right. "I never even asked her her name."

He exhales audibly through his nose, a gesture with the spirit of a chuckle yet lacking the throat noise to officially be one, then goes on, "I'm no angel. I've stolen stuff before. For money. Money to eat. Nobody ever gave me anything. Never met my dad. My moms is a junkie. I had to snatch shit from time to time. But I never stole anything *off* of somebody. I'd pick up things nobody in particular happened to be watching at the time. Never got caught once. Then the one time I borrowed a car, not for money, just to see the damn ocean, is the time I get lit up. Hell, I wasn't even planning on keeping the thing. I would've brought it right back to that parking lot I found it the next day." He pauses. "God's kind of funny like that, ain't he?"

Nobody answers.

"Please Mr. Postman" by The Marvelettes flows from the radio at low volume. Monty turns to Phil and says, "I admitted to my crime. And I know Danny's admitted to his. Seems like him and me were the only two guys in Crick who did. I got to ask you, man. I known you for nine months and I hadn't asked you. What they accused you of, did you do any of it, any at all?"

Phil shakes his head and says, "Of course not."

"There was DNA though, wasn't there? That's what some niggas back in jail said anyway."

A moment. "Evidently, there was DNA. But how they got it, how they attained a sample of *my* DNA, especially in *that* format, is far from clear."

"You mean the cops?"

"No. The people who framed me. The people who put my DNA on that girl."

Danny, who already knows Phil's story and knows how uncomfortable the events make him, leans forward and in a soft yet assertive voice says to Monty, "I told you he was set up. We don't need him to repeat it all."

"No," Phil says, "it's fine. The three of us are partners. If he wants to ask me something, he has the right."

They're quiet for a half mile. Then Monty asks, "So...who framed you?"

"I have my suspicions, but you can never be sure."

"Who are you suspicious about then?"

"Rivals."

"You in some old-man gang in Austin I didn't know about, professor?" Monty asks with a laugh.

"*Academic* rivals. They can be just as vicious, if not more so, than gang rivals. In my world, it's about getting to a discovery first. Then it's yours. Your name is on it forever. And everyone else, the slower ones, are forgotten. I'm sure you've heard of Darwinism, named after Charles Darwin. Another scientist, Alfred Russell Wallace, came up with a nearly identical concept, independently of Darwin, around the same time.

But Darwin published his first. Which is why they don't teach Wallacism in biology class today. At the turn of the millennium I was working on a theory that would've redefined neuropsychology. All of psychology in fact. A dozen years ago my research was well beyond what's considered the most cutting edge today. I was on the cusp of tying it together. Which would've proven the lifework of many other practicing neuroscience researchers void. They knew they couldn't beat me in the lab. So one of them, or a group of them, decided their only hope was to keep me out of the lab entirely. What better tool for that than a prison."

Monty scratches his shaved head above his right ear. "That's terrible. Wow. Sorry that happened to you, teach."

The summer sun comes down a cloudless alley of sky through the windshield, covering the pickup's interior with light so bright it sucks the color and texture out of the seats and dashboard, while permitting their shape, almost like a white bed sheet laid atop everything.

Monty squints. He holds his hand to his brow, like a visor, and says to Phil, "Why didn't they just kill you? Seems a lot simpler than going through all those steps to frame you."

Phil eyeballs him for a second, then moves his attention back to the road. With a sigh, he says, "I suppose it's much easier for a conscience to take away a man's freedom than his life."

Monty keeps his gaze on Phil, keeps his hand on his brow. Then he nods and turns up the volume of the radio.

Phil merges into the right lane and slows, preparing to exit.

Danny has a scary thought. Their ride is coming from the original pickup point, not far from the prison. Would the cops have put up roadblocks there already? Even if Phil's friend is reliable, he could be trapped, unable to get to them. He's apparently in a big van, with enough space in the back to conceal the three criminals during the eight-hour trip south of the border. There's no way they'd make it that long in this F-150. Not with its wide windows putting the driver on full display.

It's possible this guy is stuck. A lot is possible right now. Most of it bad.

Six

Phil takes a two-lane county road east for three miles. He makes a left at a fifteen-foot billboard made of wood, barely imprinted on its weather-worn paintjob the cornflower-blue words "Splash Paradise," below them a smiling, adolescent boy in swim goggles and trunks engulfed in a wave.

The trees bordering the truck's path thicken in density and lengthen in height, soon masking the street behind it, and soon after masking the circle of sun in the sky ahead of it.

"It's safe to sit up," Phil says. Danny and Monty rise from their reclined positions.

Cast in a shadow, the stolen vehicle enters an empty parking lot labeled "A," and traverses pavement with weeds growing out of it and the occasional piece of trash sitting atop it.

Danny soon sees a hut with a "Tickets" sign on it, and beyond it a squiggling, soaring, sloping network of interwoven tubes and slides, a collection of dirt and branches on the crests and in the valleys of the dry fiberglass.

Monty nods at a medley of graffiti on the wall of the ticket hut. "If nobody comes here no more, who's doing all that spray painting?" he asks Phil.

"My friend said it's been closed for five years. I'm sure a stray teenager sneaks in every now and then to smoke marijuana and clown around. I assume we won't run into any in the light of day."

"You assume, or you're positive?"

"I'm not *positive* of anything right now. We didn't have many options. Let's just…stay calm. The last thing we need is to start bickering with each other."

Monty huffs and looks away. Phil puts the truck in park and flips the key, stifling the sound of the radio and engine, leaving them alone with the quiet of the condemned water park.

The trio exits the vehicle. The humidity crawls into Danny's mouth. They walk past the ticket booth to a row of turnstiles. Monty heaves his hip into one of the revolving bars. *Clanick.* It doesn't budge. "I'll be…" he grumbles to himself, rubbing his hip, then shimmies past the entry barrier. Danny squeezes through next, followed by Phil.

The trees in the park are much shorter than the ones in the parking lot so maximum sunshine could spill down without blockage onto frolicking children and lounging parents, which now, as it's been for the last five years, spills down only on the disgraced fiberglass corpses of the attractions that failed to keep that crowd.

Monty limps along the semi-circular curve the walkway takes, crossing a diagonal of pavement where shadow meets light and turning the corner into the core of the park. Danny, about a dozen feet behind, does the same.

He studies his surroundings. In a few seconds he spots the rendezvous spot. A big map of the park. Monty stands beside it, hands on his hips, a perplexed look on his face.

"Where'd Phil's friend go?" Danny asks.

Monty peers ahead, then to both sides. "*I* didn't see him. *You* see him?"

Danny swings his head over his shoulder, glimpsing Phil, who's just turning the corner, a halo of sunlight around him. "Hey," Danny shouts. Phil stops walking and tilts his chin up. "You said he'd meet us at the big map in the front, right?"

Leaning left, Phil peeks around Danny's body at the map. Then gazes down at the asphalt by his feet for a few seconds, a contemplative bend to his brow. With slow paces, Phil makes his way to the other two and says, "There are multiple lots. He likely came in through a different one. There must be more maps. He's probably waiting by one of them."

"Multiple lots maybe, but just one entrance," Monty says. "Didn't he tell us to meet at the map right by the *entrance*? How could he go anywhere else?"

"I'm not from this area. He is. I never heard of this place, before. He has. Maybe there's a second entrance, for employees or whatnot, with another sign just like this one near it. Who's to know? It's a big park." Phil reaches into his pocket and pulls out the cell phone they took from the trailer. "I'll call him and see exactly where he is. Okay?"

Monty holds his stare on him for a second, then dabs some sweat on his forehead with the back of his hand.

Phil keys the number on the cell and holds it to his face. Danny and Monty watch. Five seconds. Ten. Fifteen. Phil lowers the phone.

"He's not picking up?" Monty asks, a discordance of sarcasm and surprise in his voice.

Phil doesn't reply.

Monty rolls his head from shoulder to shoulder a couple times, the sort of gesture an athlete makes after a referee's bad call. "Are you shitting me?" He steps closer to Phil. "All he had to do was drive from one place to another. All *you* had to do was make sure he did it." He steps even closer. "How did you fuck that up?"

Danny, fearing Monty may sock the frail professor, steps in the middle of them, separating them with nudges on their chests. "Guys, stop," Danny says. "Just...just chill out."

Monty backs away. He clenches his fists and takes a long breath.

A few moments.

"My friend is reliable," Phil says. "When he was still locked up, he used to help me smuggle things into Crick all the time. He's been helpful even after getting released. The power saw, the one we used this morning, got to me through *his* connections. He won't let me down."

Monty spits on the ground. "Looks like he already did."

"I'll find him," Phil says in that comforting fifth-grade-teacher manner. "Wait here. Maybe he'll show up by that map. In the meantime I'll take a lap around the park and see if he's somewhere else. Possibly his phone gets bad service out here, which is why he's not picking up." He turns and begins striding deeper into the park.

"Professor," Danny calls. Phil stops. He spins his head. "The family in the trailer. Now that we're off the road in the truck we should call the cops and have someone untie them. Do it anonymously from that cell phone. Say you're a neighbor or something and you heard a noise."

With a grin, Phil wiggles the phone in his hand. "You're right. I'll give the local precinct a buzz while I'm making my lap." He walks off.

Once Phil's out of hearing range, Monty asks, "You really think we can rely on this friend of his to get us all the way to Mexico, then set our asses up down there?"

Danny sits on a bench. "I don't know."

"The guy's an ex-con. Typically us felons ain't a dependable bunch."

"I got my doubts too, man. But he did get a power tool into Crick for us. You know how hard that is? Anyone in Texas who's that good a smuggler must know a person or two in Mexico. I'm sure he's legit."

Monty leans against the map and spits on the ground. "I just don't have a good feeling about this."

"Stay positive. All we can do at this point."

With a snap of his shoulder muscle, Monty pushes himself off the map and begins pacing. He closes his eyes and holds his face and palms up to the daylight. He lets the rays wash over him. "It's sunny every day in Mexico. It doesn't rain at all I heard."

"Not *never*."

"Maybe once a year. For the plants and shit to grow."

"Maybe a little more than once."

"You ever see a picture of Mexico with rain in it? Ever?"

This isn't an argument Danny feels like having. So he just smiles and says, "Glad I didn't drag along an umbrella."

Monty laughs. So does Danny. While Monty continues basking in the sun, Danny puts his elbows on his knees and his face in his hands. He thinks about the free world around him. And wonders why freedom hasn't felt better today, hasn't been what he thought. He ponders that chunk of ice still in his gut, that sensation of the penitentiary.

Maybe it's America, he reasons. He's physically free, but he's still wanted here. A fugitive. He's not welcome here anymore. In Mexico he'll be liberated. All will be better once they cross the border.

"Guys," he hears from a distance.

Danny flicks his head up, noticing Phil under the faded orange piping of a water slide about a hundred feet away.

Smiling, Phil motions them toward him. "I was right," he yells. "Different map. Back here." He disappears under an archway labeled "Lazy River."

"Ahh haa," Danny cries in elation.

"Well shit," Monty says with a smile.

Danny gets off the bench. Monty slaps him on the back. They walk in Phil's direction. "Mexico amigo," Monty says in a bad Hispanic accent. Then begins singing "Guantanamera," swaying his hands like a salsa dancer.

Danny chuckles. "You're a crazy son of a bitch, you know that?"

"I wouldn't say crazy. Silly, maybe. Sexy, though. That makes people forget about all the flaws." Monty shakes his hips to the hum of the song.

"You'd have to do about a thousand crunches a day to get sexy enough for anyone to forget about all *your* flaws. Just too damn many."

Smiling, they pass the tall wooden legs of a lifeguard stand, then a vacant PVC rack for inflatable tubes, then a garbage can with the Splash Paradise logo on it. Danny hears a chirp above. He assumes it's some forgotten park sound effect from some forgotten park sound maker. Then he sees a flash of blue streak over his head, which shapes into three pieces, two wings, one body. A bird. A real bird. In the real world.

Danny strolls under the "Lazy River" archway, Monty a couple steps behind.

A hand crashes onto Danny's face, its thick thumb pressed to the bridge of his nose, the nail digging into his skin.

A blast of adrenaline shoots from Danny's brain and courses through his body, from his groaning throat to his flailing arms to his stiffening legs.

However, he is unable to fight or flight. The hands that hold him, one on his face, another on his shirt, are too powerful, pinning him at an angle where he can't get off a step or a punch.

He lets out a scream. The palm over his mouth muffles it.

Danny notices a white cloth in his attacker's grip. He feels its scratchy fabric on his skin. The hand holding it is attached to a meaty forearm covered in tattoos.

Something chemical leaps into Danny's nose and lingers in his lungs. Soon the adrenaline that gushed into him seems to surge out as fast as it came in. He loses energy. Then feeling. The world before him, the real world, becomes faint.

Then disappears.

Seven

Black. More black. Gray dots among the black. More gray dots.

Danny's eyes open. He blinks. Consciousness emerges. He blinks again. The gray dots fade, clearing his field of vision, revealing his surroundings.

Wood planks above him. Concrete beneath him. Cinderblocks around him. All of it made visible, faintly, by strips of sun squeezing between the slats of plastic blinds over a square window.

He tries to stand. He can't. His shoulder joints are yanked on, sending trains of pain down his tricep and trapezius muscles. His hands are locked behind him to his aluminum seat. Glancing down, he notices a tangle of chains around each ankle, keeping them tight to the chair legs.

His mind, still hazy after its unconscious spell, guesses he's been arrested. However, the hypothesis dissolves as he soaks in more details of the small room. Its odor of rotting milk. Various scatterings around its dim perimeter. A lawnmower engine, a sock dotted with dry blood, a hammer, a stack of *Hustler* magazines, an unopened crate. This is no holding cell.

Danny notices a human figure in the space with him. The body, farther from the window than his, is veiled in shadow. It sits chained in a chair like Danny, its head tilted downward in stillness, chin to chest, an air of peace to it. Like a corpse. For a closer look, Danny leans as far to his right as his shackles permit. It's Monty.

Is he dead?

Danny tries to talk. But his tongue butts into a wad of grainy cotton. A gag, something his muddled mind didn't notice until the apparatus became functional.

His pulse picks up. His breathing, isolated to his nostrils, becomes heavy and hearable. The pace of his heart and his lungs, not intentionally, fall into lockstep, each thud in his chest accompanied by a hiss of air. He sits in this state, doing nothing but thudding and hissing, for over a minute.

He turns right and screams at Monty. No words, just sound. He shouts for about ten seconds. Then catches his breath. Then shouts for another ten. A note of motion in Monty's neck. Then his shoulders. As Monty's head lifts, a feeling of relief lifts inside Danny. His friend is not dead. Life, despite whatever grim condition it may be in, is still there. Yes, for both of them, life is there.

Monty, also gagged, communicates with only noise. But his eyes, frightened and surprised, say enough. Like Danny, he doesn't know where the hell they are.

They make mouth sounds and eye gestures at each other for a bit longer, and soon quiet and still. An aura of dejection fuses with the room's stench of spoiled milk.

They stare down at the floor for fifteen or so minutes.

Hinges squeak above and behind them. The sound of an opening door. Light floods the room. It burns Danny's eyes. In the newfound brightness he gets a good look at Monty's face, noticing a lump near his left eyebrow the size and shape of an egg's bottom half, as if he was struck by a blunt object.

Footsteps. The wood stairs groan as if the body descending them is a burly one. Danny tries to look behind him but can't turn his head far enough. The moan of the steps is replaced by the thump of boots on concrete.

Danny sees the body. Yes, it is a burly one. It stands about six foot four, with two hundred forty or so pounds hanging from its broad-shouldered frame. Danny takes it in from the floor up.

Black motorcycle boots lead to long-ascending denim, a hint of a white undershirt, over it a leather vest with a motorcycle club patch ("Lost Circle MC" beside a pair of stitched-shut eyes), and protruding from the sleeveless top two bare arms, muscular and powerful, yet not ripped and defined, a layer of fat weaved in, and on their surface an assemblage of tattoos, a swastika on the shoulder the most prominent, mixed among serpents and stars and other symbols, many with the polish of a professional design shop, others with the blotchy look of prison ink.

Danny notices an eight-ball tattoo on the man's forearm. Something in his misty mind sparks. He remembers the image. From the water park. He remembers hands on him. A cloth. A chemical. Chloroform, he thinks. Must have been. This asshole chloroformed him.

Staring back at Danny with pale blue eyes set on a middle-aged face set among a nest of shoulder-length, reddish-brown hair is a man without love or hate in his expression, without anything in between, just a tinge of awareness tinged by a vague sense of want, like the look on the face of a predator gazing about the landscape of some African plane.

The man reaches behind his leather vest and digs into a jean pocket. When his hand comes back around, it reveals a metal object about nine inches long, its tip glinting in the light streaming in from upstairs. Danny's mind takes a second to process the image.

Scissors.

The sight of the long blades, no more than a foot from Danny's face, launches him into panic. His gag absorbs shouts of terror. He jerks at his chains. As he thrashes, the steel restraints patter on the skeleton of the aluminum chair, filling the cellar with a calypso-like jangle.

The man steps closer, the twin triangular daggers only three inches from Danny's flesh. Monty looks away. Danny clenches his eyes. Each thwack of his heart sends a shockwave through his internal tissue. Amid the pneumatic pumps of his nostrils, he hears the sliding open of the scissor blades. He feels a hand grasp his forehead, as if to steady it.

He listens to metal scrape metal. Again. And again. He braces himself for pain, for a foreign object puncturing the skin of his face. But it doesn't come. Instead, he feels a delicate tickle on his cheek, nothing more. Another. And another.

The scissors keep snipping. He raises one timid eyelid. Then the other. He peeks down. Locks of his hair checker his lap. More brown strands flurry down from his head. The deep whacks of his heart calm to milder jabs. The piston-like blast from his nostrils cools to a crisp wind. Monty's eyebrows collapse in confusion as he observes this peculiar scene.

Within five minutes most of Danny's hair is hacked off, his head now blanketed by an uneven brown fur that shows through to the scalp in some places and extends over a quarter-inch in others. The large barber returns the scissors to his pocket, pulls electric clippers from another, and takes the short fur even shorter, homogenizing it all around.

He exits the same way he came, leaving Danny and Monty with the thump of his boots on the concrete, the groan of the staircase, the squeak of the hinges, then the darkness of the closed door.

The rays of daylight coming through the window are feebler than the ones Danny saw at the water park. At least a couple hours must have passed since they were there.

Pangs of starvation and dehydration commingle inside him with the sear of anxiety and uncertainty. Danny and Monty, each with a shaved head, one voluntary, the other involuntary, sit side by side in silence for the next twenty-odd minutes.

Creak. The cellar door opens. Illumination. The cellar stairs groan. More than before, four footsteps on them now versus two. The big barber treads the alley between Danny and Monty's aluminum seats, then turns around, towering over them and looking down at them like a sentinel.

A softer patter of shoes trails his. Another body, shorter and narrower, splits the space between the two chairs and stops beside the sentinel. Danny throws a hasty eyeballing at this second figure. Leather loafers. Tan slacks. Beige blazer with elbow pads. The face, within a second of initial processing, appears familiar, but the hairdo prevents Danny's subconscious from completing a snap association.

A moment later, when Danny's full faculty of observation takes over, he realizes the identity of this second man. The hair, dyed jet-black, is a departure from the graying-blond strands Danny is used to, and the attire a deviation from the white monochrome Danny's always known. But it's him. It's him.

It's Phil.

Reflexively, Danny signals SOS at this familiar face, screaming and gesturing as much as the gag and shackles allow. *It's Danny, your partner. And Monty, your other partner. We're tied up. You're not. Help us. Help us.* When Phil doesn't react right away, Danny assumes he didn't see him or hear him. So screams and gestures with even more ferocity.

The helping of house light from the open door illumes a colony of dust particles diffused through the cellar, most wafting at a slow rate, while others appear frozen, suspended in an exact position by something with a precision that seems beyond the interplay of gravity, kept in place by nothing short of the complete stoppage of time itself. Amid this colony of dust, Danny stares at Phil, and Phil at Danny.

Then Phil dips his head, a splash of shame on his down-turned face. "I am so sorry for this," he says. Danny doesn't know what he's talking about. Doesn't know where he is. Doesn't know what happened to the prison escape. Doesn't know what happened to his life.

Phil nods at the sentinel. The large man steps to the rear of Danny's seat and undoes his gag. Though leaves Monty's on. Danny can now physically speak, but doesn't, the hush not a product of his mouth, but mind, his brain at a complete loss for words.

They remain this way for about a half-minute. Then Danny, in a croaky yet fiery voice, says, "Get these chains off me."

Phil steps across the concrete in the opposite direction of Danny, his new loafers landing on a patch of newly sheared hair, then places his hand on the shoulder of the sentinel and says, "I'd like you to meet Wade. This is his home. He was responsible for smuggling the power saw into Crick for us. And he'll be responsible for assuring our safety south of the border."

Wade, smirking, waves.

"Are we in Mexico?" Danny asks this new stranger in his life.

"Nope," Wade says through his sustained smirk.

"Why the fuck am I tied up?" Danny blurts, tugging on his wrist chains, turning his attention back to Phil. "Get me out of these things."

"The chains are just a temporary...security measure," Phil says. "Again, I deeply apologize. Wade had to restrain you and Monty so we—"

"I thought *Wade* was driving us to Mexico?" Danny shouts.

"We're still going," Phil says with an optimistic uptick in his voice's pitch. "But the plan always had an extra step to it. One I couldn't reveal before now. Since you may not have agreed with it..."

Danny's mind tries to make a connection between this basement, these chains, and their escape plan, but shakes out nothing. Silence for a few seconds.

Phil points at Monty and says, "Monty cutting his leg added some complications to matters, forcing Wade and I to improvise quite a deal over the phone before. But the plan...the actual plan...always remained the same. After the jailbreak, Wade and an associate of his would conk you and Monty out, not to harm you, simply for logistical reasons...and take you right here."

A moment. "This whole time you, Monty, and me were planning the escape, you were communicating with your friend here about *chloroforming* us?" Danny asks, the croak still in his voice but not the fire.

"Technically it was a mixture of chloroform and diazepam. But that makes no difference at this point. I apologize for any shock the events at the water park might have caused you. As mentioned, Wade doesn't want to harm you. He simply needed to get you in a condition where—"

"We're wasting valuable time," Danny yells. "Do you have any idea how many cops are looking for us right now? What the fuck are we doing down here? We need to get to Mexico."

Phil glances at Wade, tightens his lips, then gazes at Danny and asks, "Do you think getting to Mexico is *free*?"

Danny squints.

"Sneaking a power saw into a maximum-security prison," Phil says. "Safe passage across the border. Forged IDs and documents...quality ones...for three fugitives. A place to live. Did you assume Wade offered these to us because he woke up one morning and was feeling particularly generous?"

Danny's squint deepens as his mind pieces this together. He peeks at Wade and asks, "So you want money?"

Pacing, Phil says, "Not only did my academic rivals damn me to a twenty-eight-year prison term, but in an even more Machiavellian maneuver, they drove me to near bankruptcy. The civil suit from the first alleged *victim* in Austin clawed away most of my savings. A lot of my remaining money was spent while I was in jail, on contraband lab equipment Wade's associates snuck inside for me. Basically, I'm broke." He clasps his hands behind his back mid-stride and goes on, "Monty admittedly is not a man of means either. But you…you Daniel…" Phil stops, locking eyes with his former cellmate. "You're in a unique position to alleviate our financial obligation to Wade."

Danny's brow furrows. "I don't have any money."

"I know. But your father does."

The word "father" travels from Phil's mouth through the dusty air, through Danny's flesh, and razors into his heart. The cellar is quiet for a while.

"He's dead to me," Danny says. "You know that. I won't ask him for a thing."

Though Danny resents his dad, he feels an unexpected protective instinct brewing in him. He asks Wade, "Are you trying to extort my family?"

"Wade is a man in a unique line of business," Phil says, returning his hand to his friend's beefy shoulder. "Who has a unique set of connections valuable to people in our situation. Like any other keen businessman, he is only trying to obtain a fair price for a scarce service."

"You'll call your parents from here," Wade states, "and tell them to round up two hundred and fifty thousand dollars of cash in a duffel bag. You and Phil will drive to meet them in

El Paso. I'll stay here with the nigger as an insurance policy so you don't try to pull any shit on the road. Once you get the money in El Paso, I'll have a friend from the cartel to pick you and Phil up and drive you over the border. I'll meet you down there with the nigger, get y'all your documents and set y'all up in your apartments."

Danny's spine, like his spirit, wilts, his body sinking a few inches on the aluminum seat. Ten seconds pass. "My parents aren't giving you a dime."

"The choice is yours," Wade replies, scratching the rim of his nostril with his thumb. "You can make a phone call to your folks and ask them to part with some loot, which we know they have plenty of. And you and blackie go to Mexico and start your new life. *Or,* you don't make the phone call. And I leave both of you chained down here. Without food or water. At a certain level of dehydration, insanity will kick in and you'll wish you were dead." He smirks. "Then I'll start force-feeding you just enough water to keep you alive, but not enough to quiet the voices in your head. That's when it'll get fun."

Danny glimpses Phil, hoping his former bunkmate will intervene, will tell his friend Wade to calm down, will make this better somehow, even if just an iota. But Phil is mute, head hung in the shadow of the bigger man, timidity touching every feature of his chipmunkish face. Phil is no tough guy, Danny reminds himself. He's a nerdy professor, likely petrified of this brawny biker-gangster. Though unchained, Phil's hands are just as tied in this situation as Danny's.

"Your asses need to be on the road soon," Wade says to Danny. "I'll get a phone. You calling your parents or not?"

Danny's mind tries to shape the two sides of this choice. On one end, he doesn't make the phone call. And he, and Monty, remain locked in this cave without a plate of food or a glass of water until they go insane. Danny's health, both physical and mental, will be in ruins. Or he calls them and grovels for two hundred fifty thousand dollars of his father's hardearned money, a man he swore to never associate with again.

He needs to vomit. His mouth opens and his insides spasm. Yet nothing is in his stomach, so nothing comes out. He dryheaves. The blood vessels in his face tingle.

After everything with his father, if Danny asks for the money, he'll lose his pride. And when you're a nomad whose only possessions are pride and a sketch of a magazine ad, pride is practically all you have.

His heart rate accelerates as he deliberates. He doesn't know what to choose. Sneering at him, Wade steps closer, his body heat wrapping Danny, and asks, "Your decision?"

Eight

Lieutenant John Ramos lifts his coffee mug to his lips, sips, and sits it beside a framed photo of his wife and two little girls. He lets the hazelnut mouthful seep into his taste buds for a couple moments, then swallows and picks up his paperwork slog where he left it, writing the DOB of a perpetrator on an arrest form, a datum he gleans from an image of the man's driver's license imprinted in the center of a sheet of printer paper as a fuzzy-edged rectangle of bleeding black ink, a product of the police station's copy machine, which has been on the fritz.

Ramos tries to remain concentrated, however the conversation to his right keeps drawing his ear.

"That's a normal length, where…France?" a husky officer in his forties asks a deputy about twenty years his younger.

"Times have changed," says the deputy, a tall white boy with a bulgy Adam's apple that shifts in a unique way upon each uttered word, like a gymnast's body during a regimen of warm-up stretches. "Besides, I don't wear them for the look. I wear them 'cause of the heat." He nods at the beige uniform slacks on his colleague. "You telling me you're not hot in those on a day like today?"

No response other than an eye roll.

The young deputy points at his thighs, the vast majority exposed, the rest covered by the fabric of a short pair of police shorts, and says, "These breathe. I can be outside patrolling on hot days and feel fine." He runs a finger across the skin of his knee. "Dry as a bone. Didn't break a sweat all shift."

A second middle-aged officer leans over and studies the kneecap. Feigning surprise, he states, "Wow, not a single dab of moisture. You're right."

The deputy, not registering the sarcasm, offers him a courteous grin in return.

In a booming, bar-room voice, the older cop says, "Looks like you didn't break a sweat today...you just broke your hymen."

Laughter erupts through the small-town station, not just from the two officers doing the teasing, but the five others spread across the room. Lieutenant Ramos included.

As the deputy's face reddens, the joker notices Ramos chuckle. He says, "Lieutenant, you got to weigh in here. We can't let him represent the town of Rene in those things."

Ramos rotates in his swivel chair to face them. He folds his arms, the tan complexion of his forearms pressing against the blue of his Rene Police Department polo. He tells the deputy, "They are a little short, Noah."

"They're for the *heat*, sir." The deputy stares at the far wall, where a scribbled-upon whiteboard of open cases is framed between US and Texas flags, above it a photo of state governor Greg Abbott.

"So it's all about heat…you don't think your legs look good in them at all?" the joker inquires.

The deputy takes a deep breath, looks down at the early-Eighties linoleum floor, looks back up, and says, "I wouldn't say they're necessarily *nice*. I wouldn't call them ugly either, though. They're somewhere in the middle. Legs. Just normal legs."

The older cop lets out a quick but strong laugh, which sounds like a paper bag ripping in half. He composes his expression and asks, "Well, if they're not ugly, it means they must have at least one decent feature. Which is your favorite?"

"All right," Ramos interrupts with a smile. "He's had enough, Hawkins. Let him get back to work."

The middle-aged cops, chuckling, wander off. The deputy sighs.

"Pull me our arrest file from the week before last," Ramos tells him.

"Yes sir." The deputy walks toward a monolithic, metallic filing cabinet in the back corner, his long, white legs on parade.

Ramos drinks his hazelnut coffee. He pens a few figures onto lines of his form. A door swings open, the wood slab smacking into the wall, sending a reverberating whump through the little station. Ramos and the other seven officers in the room freeze, gazing toward the open office door, a "Chief of Police" placard fixed to it.

A man with white hair and a white moustache, older and bigger than the rest, stands in the doorway. A convoluted expression, one part unease, one part urgency, is strewn across his face. "I just got off the phone with the county sheriff's office," he tells the others. "They have reason to believe the three convicts who escaped from Crick this morning may be hiding out in Rene." He claps his hands. "Let's move."

The chief strides toward the exit. Cops scrabble for their guns and keys. Amid the commotion, the deputy drops a fistful of folders, papers flying all over. As he kneels to pick them up, Ramos says, "Christ, just leave them."

All the officers file out the door, the heavy patter of their feet on the linoleum floor like a war drum seeing them off as they go to their squad cars.

Nine

The dust in Wade's cellar is having its way with Danny's lungs. He coughs. Then holds his right hand, which Wade recently unlocked, to his mouth and coughs again.

Phil, his back to the wall across, is anxiously rocking his weight from his heels to the balls of his feet, the fabric of his new blazer nearly touching the cinderblocks at each backswing.

Wade, a shadow enmeshing his upper body, is bent forward, digging through a cardboard box on some old shelving in the corner.

Monty, both hands still chained to his chair, gag still mashed in his mouth, is gazing at the blinds over the single window.

Wade's back straightens, the black of his leather vest emerging from the black of the shadow. He steps to Danny and extends a silver cell phone.

Danny takes it with his one free hand. Then takes a deep breath. Using his thumb, he keys ten digits and clicks "send." He lifts the receiver to his face.

He decided he'd be willing to gamble with his own physical and mental health by staying imprisoned in the basement, however felt wrong rolling the dice with Monty's. If Danny didn't call his parents for the cash, Monty would remain locked down here too, forced to withstand the same withholding of food and water.

"Mom," Danny says into the phone.

The first few things out of her mouth he doesn't pay attention to. He's so comforted to hear her voice that the individual words fade to nothing in its wake, like puddles in the ocean. That voice flows through him. As does everything it reminds him of. Nothing else like it. Mom.

"Yeah, I know," he says to her. "Maybe you should turn off the news, then." A moment. "I'm not hurt...Promise... Mom...*Mom.*"

He listens. He nods. He listens some more. "I didn't tell you," he says, "because you'd worry too much about me. Just like you're doing now." A pause. "Yes ma'am...Uh huh... Well." He's silent for a few seconds, then in a soft tone says, "I needed to get out. You knew that. You knew." He darts his gaze away from the other three men. "You knew how I was doing in there."

A nod. Another. He says, "Mexico." He listens. "Yes...Yes... No...I'm coming home." He sighs. "Not coming home like that...The police, no...Then Mexico." He nods. "I wish. I wish."

The feeling of comfort that's been cascading through him begins drying up. He knows what he needs to ask next.

His eyes drop to the floor. A twitch encircles the left one. He says, "I need a favor from you...and dad."

Gripping the phone with four fingers, he scratches his newly shaved temple with his pinkie. "Money," he tells her. "Two hundred fifty thousand." His empty stomach hollows out even more. "No...no. It's not for me." He scowls at Wade. "It doesn't matter who it's for. It's a long...too long...I just need it." He glances at Monty. "I do...It's the only way I can get to Mexico." He shakes his head. "I don't know. I really don't know at this point."

He listens. A head scratch. He says, "I'm in a town in East Texas called Rene...Ten hours away...Soon...Yes, two hundred fifty thousand...No...Hard to tell...I'll explain...Not now... It doesn't matter...El Paso, to meet somewhere, not the house, the cops will look for me there...Not long...To pick it up, right. No...*No.* I don't want to talk to dad. Ask him for me...No, just, please. Uh huh...I'm in trouble...I'm not hurt, mamma...Yes... Trouble...I need it...Cash, yes." His eyebrows slant downward and inward. His sealed lips part a bit, then a bit more. "Ah...I understand...That's true...Oh...Oh...Hold on, let me ask."

Danny lowers the phone from his face and tells Wade, "She says they have about seventy thousand in cash stashed at the house. Even if my dad agrees, they still won't be able to come up with the full two fifty today. It's Saturday. The banks are closed. Tomorrow too." He hunches his shoulders and asks, "Can we spend the next day or so hiding out here, then meet them on Monday, when they can get the rest of the money out in cash?"

Wade laughs. Then says, "Do you know the size of the manhunt that'll be against y'all if you're not found by *Monday*? Every town, county, and state department in Texas will be involved. You need to get to El Paso tonight, and out of America by sunrise with my money."

Fuck, he's right. Danny's gaze hangs on Wade for a moment. Then he moves the phone back to his face and says, "No. It has to be tonight." He closes his eyes, inhales audibly, then exhales even louder. "I don't know…No…Try to think of something…Anything…Not sure."

Danny listens to his mother's reasons why this task, in this timeframe, is absurd, and why his father probably won't agree anyway.

"He's letting me have a phone," he tells her. "To talk to you…The man…Whose house I'm at…it doesn't matter…Call or text me on this number after you speak to dad. I'll coordinate with you from the road."

She guarantees him, between tears, that she'll do everything she can to help. He's not sure if he should apologize to her or thank her. So he does both. "Thanks, mama, for this, thank you, thank you," he says in an energetic voice, then in a deflated one, "Sorry for…the money…for everything really… for what you're seeing on the news." A moment. "I love you." She says the same to him. And he hangs up.

Danny can't believe he has to now bring the contents of this murky cellar, its entangled criminal lives and their ensnarled criminal motives, to the pure pastures of his hometown and family farm. He sits on the chair, three of his limbs fastened to it, the fourth dangling at his side, digesting the decision he just made. His pride is gone.

"Food and water," Phil tells Wade. "We owe it to them now that Danny agreed." Wade nods. "I'll go fetch it," Phil says with a grin, then scurries to the stairs. On his trip up, his gaze catches Danny's. Phil has a spring in his step, as if he's relieved Danny made the call, as if Wade had some twisted punishment lined up for him too if Danny opted against it.

Danny reflects on their year as cellmates. Danny wasn't cut out for life in a maximum-security prison. It couldn't have been further from what he was used to, the warm bed in the farmhouse, the home-cooked meals, the loving family.

Overnight this all transformed into a bed of metal, food like feces, and daily scoldings from armed guards. The "fancy white boy," as Danny was often referred to, lived in constant fear of getting a dick shoved into his ass or a shiv shoved into his rib just because a lowlife with no incentive to care about the consequences might find it funny.

He lost ten pounds his first month at Crick. Twenty his second. And the non-stop psychological grinding left his mind just as depleted as his body.

Then, a half-year in he got a new bunkmate. Not some seamy bruiser like the majority of inmates. But a mild-mannered, soft-spoken professor, similar to ones he recalled from school. Even better, this was a master of psychology, with the easy, yet intellectual demeanor of a therapist.

Phil was kind to Danny from day one. By day two Danny began opening up to him. Phil wasn't only a good listener, but a well-placed commenter, absorbing Danny's words, offering pithy feedback always with a question at its tail, which showed he not only got Danny's point, but had a new way of looking at it, one Danny should consider.

They talked about Danny's family. His past. His crime. His fears and hopes. Phil, like him, wasn't cut out for maximum-security prison. Yet he'd been locked up for over a decade already and survived. He gave Danny hope. Soon Danny began eating normally again. He had Phil to thank.

And a year later...this? Though Phil is at Wade's mercy too, Danny can't help but feel betrayed by him. All those days in the prison library when they were chipping away at cinder-block mortar, Phil knew Danny would be chloroformed and chained after the escape, not to mention strong-armed into picking up the six-figure tab. The knowledge of the subterfuge stings, yet Danny tries not to grow angry at Phil.

After all, it was Danny who was naïve enough to believe Phil had some saintly friend on the outside who'd risk getting fugitives into Mexico for nothing in return. After all, it was Phil who figured out the space behind the library wall led to an air duct that led to the gymnasium roof that led to a short dash to the woods. After all, it was Phil who invited Danny to be a part of the escape, without which Danny would still be trapped in jail, a much worse fate than being stuck in a basement in the real world, soon on your way to freedom in Mexico.

Fine, then. Danny can look past Phil's deception. In net, Phil has helped him much more than hurt him. This isn't Phil's fault. He simply wanted his freedom, and had no way to pay for it on his own. It's not Danny's fault either. Not anybody's. It's the world's fault. It's playing yet another cruel game with Danny's life.

This current game has horrifying consequences. Danny's dad, who obviously hates him, won't agree to fork over a quarter million dollars. Then what? If things go bad with the cash Danny could ditch Phil in El Paso and reach Mexico, a short trip away, on his own. But Monty, the insurance policy, can't claim the same. What is this Nazi Wade capable of doing to Monty when Danny doesn't pay up?

Ten

Hands on his hips, Lieutenant Ramos stands at the intersection of Dixie Street and Schilling Avenue in downtown Rene, surveying the faces of passing pedestrians, smiling and nodding at ones recognizable.

Nearly four PM, the sun is still bright, yet off its apex westward, trapped behind the crisscrossed metal bars of the oil derricks that have been a fixture of the Rene skyline since the 1930s.

Well below the A-frames of iron are the strips of storefronts on both sides of Dixie, the town's main street, which have an Old West vibe to them. All businesses are brick with a rectangular window hooded by an awning, none rising above two stories, all butted one next to another without a sliver of an alley, none for a chain corporation (except for a local insurance salesman operating under the State Farm umbrella, the logo painted in shoe polish next to his name on the glass).

Ramos watches one of his patrolmen through the window of Benedict's Drug Store about twenty feet away. The officer, standing at the counter, shows a photo to a man in a white lab coat. The man shakes his head. The officer holds up another photo. Another head shake. A third picture, a third denial. With a polite wave, the policeman exits, then enters the store next door.

"What do you think?" a voice asks behind Ramos.

Turning, he notices the young deputy. A pile of paper about thirty sheets thick is wedged under his right arm, a stapler in the hand, a dispenser of Scotch tape in the left. The deputy shifts the tape to his mouth, shimmies a piece of paper from the stack with his free hand, and presents it to his boss.

Ramos stares at the full-color mug shots of Monty, Danny, and Phil, heights, ages, and weights beneath, "WANTED" above. "Nice work," he says, then begins walking north on Dixie.

The deputy performs a clumsy transfer of the stapler to the back pocket of his shorts, the tape to one hand, the posters the other. He paces up to Ramos and asks, "Where do you want 'em?"

"Everywhere."

"Just public property or private businesses too?"

"Everywhere."

"I reckon I may have to print some more in that case."

"Then print some more."

"Yes sir."

They tread up the sidewalk. Ramos grins and waves at a woman driving by in a minivan.

"Any more news from the county?" the deputy asks.

"Not yet."

The loose gait of the lanky deputy contrasts the tight, crisp steps of Ramos, a man about five foot nine with a compact yet muscled frame, the tight skin and lean striations typically owned by someone younger than his thirty-eight years.

"How does the sheriff's office know they're in Rene, anyway?" the deputy asks.

"Nobody's certain they're in Rene. Their vehicle was found about nine miles away, so it's safe to assume they're nearby. A police chopper spotted their pickup at that water park in Kanton that closed a few years ago. Splash...this or that."

"Paradise."

"That's it."

"I used to go with my little niece. Well, she's not too little anymore. Shame that place went out of business. Their Devil's Drop waterslide was really something."

Ramos shoots him a quick look, then gazes ahead. "It was odd. The Ford they were in had about three quarters a tank of gas. No damage to the body. Engine in fine shape. They just, apparently, left it there. I can't figure out why."

"How do we know it was even theirs?"

"They stole it, around noon, from a family that lives right outside Crick. The mother's mother, seventy-seven-year old lady, comes over to babysit the little girl. The parents had a cookout to go to. Anyway, grandma knocks on the door. At three o'clock. As scheduled. No answer. Knocks a couple more times. No answer. Tries going in. Locked. Sees the truck out front is gone. Gets suspicious. Goes around back to get a look through the window. Shades are drawn. Family apparently never draws them on a sunny day. So she goes to the nearest neighbor's trailer. Tells this fella she thinks something's wrong. They call the phones. Landline and cells. No answer. The neighbor gets his toolbox and pries open the front door. They find the family tied up inside. The little girl too. They were like that for over three hours. Thank God grandma was coming over. Who knows how long they would've been stuck there."

The deputy purses his lips. "Geesh."

"There've been no other stolen-car reports since. There's a strong chance they're still in the vicinity. Stay on your toes, Noah. These boys seem the crafty type. You hear how they escaped from Crick?"

"I've been making copies this whole time. Didn't hear nothing."

"There'll be a full investigation. They only have bits and pieces now. But from what I heard so far, it seems like quite a bit of planning went into this. For the last few months, during recreation time, the three of them went to the library while most other inmates played basketball. Only one librarian was on watch in there. Over time they carved away at the mortar between four cinderblocks and pushed them back into the wall. Covered up the growing hole with a desk. I'm guessing two men were on lookout while the third dug. Did it with little screws. Imagine the patience. The guards found the screws and rubble inside hollowed-out books in the Classics section, old Greek texts you don't get many prisoners thumbing through."

"No hammer or chisel? Just screws?"

"That's what I said, wasn't it?"

"Why go through that trouble?"

"Picking at the wall with a screw is quiet. A hammer would've grabbed the attention of the librarian. They went through hundreds of them."

"How do prisoners get a hold of that many screws?"

"One of them had work duty in the woodshop. Another in the laundry. Probably where the uniforms came from to make the rope they climbed down on. Guy must've worn a second uniform on top of his own into the library a few times, stripped a layer off, then hid it in the wall."

"They don't have cameras in the library? They didn't see him doing that? Didn't see them chipping away at the wall with screws either?"

"The first thing the guards did was check the camera footage. These boys nudged the desk over enough where a big bookcase was blocking the view of the desk. The camera caught none of it."

The deputy takes a deep breath. "You weren't lying when you said they were a crafty bunch."

"Even more impressive, they also got a power tool into Crick somehow. Used it to cut through an air duct."

"How in the heck did they manage a stunt like that?"

"Guards aren't positive, but have some ideas." Ramos stops at his squad car, parked at a paid meter. Even though he's the lieutenant of the town's police department and no cop would dare slap a ticket on his windshield, he still puts change in the meters. "At this point, Noah, how they escaped prison doesn't matter a whole lot. Our job is to put them back in."

"Yes sir."

"I've got a man at every highway onramp in Rene, and another on every road leading out of town. We're checking every vehicle looking to leave city limits." He cracks his cruiser door. "I'm going to take a spin to each checkpoint to see how they're doing. Radio me if you need anything."

"Yes sir."

"If these sons of bitches are in Rene, they're not getting out."

Eleven

A slew of condiment bottles lines Wade's kitchen counter. The tops are popped on a handful, lost on a couple more, the bottoms resting on a lime-green tile surface dotted with the crusty and sticky reds, yellows, and browns of the spillover that's accumulated since the last time the counter was scrubbed, which Danny guesses was a while ago.

The sound of the TV drifts in from the adjoining den. The clink of a door lock mingles with it. Then the swoosh of a door screen. Danny feels the heat of the outdoor air on his skin.

Wade exits his house into the backyard. Then Phil, who motions Danny to follow. Danny's wrists and ankles ache as his arms and legs move. The chains are gone, but their bite on his flesh and bone lingers.

The backyard is plain, no flowers, no fences, no furniture. But big. Wade's house sits on a lot of land, the neighbor's to the left barely visible, to the right not at all. In the distance, above the encircling trees, are the peaks of Rene's oil derricks.

Wade approaches a black Buick Lucerne with tinted windows parked fifty or so feet behind the home. Phil follows, hands in the pockets of his new slacks, Mozart's overture from *The Marriage of Figaro* humming out his lips. His face beams with a childish giddiness Danny's never seen on him in the year they've known each other. Phil's been locked up for over a decade, Danny remembers. For a crime he didn't commit. With freedom only a few hours away, he has reason to sing.

"A client of mine is a mechanic," Wade says, patting the Buick's nose. "Buys and sells beat-up cars at his garage. I traded him a bag of ice for it. A steal if you consider what I get meth for wholesale." He runs his fingers over the rust-flecked grille, two of its slats dented toward each other almost forming an "X," then looks at Phil and says, "She's a little banged up. But she'll work just fine getting you from here to El Paso."

Phil's eyes fight the glare of the sun, which stripes the roof of the Buick in three narrow strips, its hood in one chubby one. "The tail lights?" Phil asks Wade.

"Checked 'em."

"The plates?"

"The car was never stolen. Had one previous owner. Retired fireman with a gambling problem. Hard up for cash, so sold it to my client at the garage. Plates and VIN number are both clean."

"The tints?"

"Within Texas regulation. This thing won't raise a single eyebrow when you drive it across the state."

Humming the overture again, Phil circles the vehicle, his eyes drinking in various physical details, wheels, lock pins on the doors, hatch on the trunk. "Well done, Wade."

The big man nods. "I loaded the trunk with a bag of food and drinks."

Phil graciously bows his head, then turns to Danny and asks, "Ready?"

Something doesn't feel right. Sure, Wade might do something terrible to Monty if Danny doesn't produce the cash in El Paso, but who's to say Wade wouldn't hurt him regardless, just for fun? Danny gestures at the house and asks Phil, "How do I know he'll be safe once we leave?"

"Who?"

"Who do you think?"

A pause. "The nigger," Wade interjects.

"Ah," Phil says.

"I ain't gonna hurt him," Wade tells Danny, leaning against the hood of the Buick. He spits. "I'm just babysitting him."

"Maybe so. But I want proof."

Wade smirks, revealing tobacco-tainted teeth, which aren't the typical yellow hue of most smokers', but orange, almost like a light pumpkin skin. Danny wants to hit him in those ugly chops. But that'd be a bad idea. Danny isn't a fighter. He'd never been in a fight in his life before prison. And all the ones in there he lost. Badly.

He feels powerless. Shoulders shaking, Danny steps away from the other two. He kicks the ground and shouts, his voice reverberating through the big Texas landscape. Eyes closed, he walks in a circle. The sleeves of the tee shirt he's now wearing, one of Wade's, two sizes too big, droopily sway past his elbows, the right one nearly reaching the "No Mad" tattoo on his forearm.

"You're having a panic attack," Phil tells him. "Remember, logical—"

"Cut it with your psychobabble advice. I'm not in the mood."

"So you're not having a panic attack then?"

He is. Of course. But doesn't want to admit it in front of Wade. "I'm not leaving here until I know Monty is going to be okay."

A half-minute passes, Danny continuing in circles, the panic attack persisting.

"Photos," Phil calls out.

Danny stops circling. "What?"

"That burner cell phone Wade gave you to communicate with your parents on. It can receive picture messages I'm assuming." Phil turns to Wade, who nods in confirmation. "While we're on the road, Wade can periodically send you a photo of Monty. Say, every half hour. To prove he's fine and well."

Danny considers this for a few seconds. A bird squawks somewhere in the surrounding woods. "How do I know he's not going to just take a bunch of pictures of him now, then beat on him and send me the photos from before he's hurt?"

Phil's brown eyes glance upward in thought for a couple seconds. "We can timestamp the pictures…in a way. Monty can put up fingers to indicate the hour. Say, at eight o'clock he'd hold up eight. The half-hour marks can be shown with his tongue. At eight thirty he'd display the fingers and stick out his tongue. For the hours of eleven and twelve, he'd show all ten digits, then rely on the closure of his eyes, one shut for eleven, both for twelve. Monty would have to willingly engage in multiple poses through the day. Wade wouldn't be able to just quickly snap several photos of him now. If the pictures keep coming in, and Monty continues looking okay in them, your doubts about his safety should be allayed. Work for you?"

Danny marvels at how quickly Phil's brain came up with this outside-the-box proposition. It seems to check out. "Fine."

"Wade?"

The big biker spits, then nods in agreement.

"Off on our journey then," Phil says, his face with that childlike giddiness again.

Wade hands him the car key and a burner phone of his own. Then reaches behind his leather vest and removes a pistol from the waist of his jeans. "Just in case you get into a jam."

Phil grips it in an awkward fashion, pinching the handle with two fingers, as if it's the first time the neuroscience researcher ever held a firearm. He stows it on his hip, in his slacks. Then unlocks the car and opens the passenger door.

Danny looks back at the house where his buddy is confined, then climbs into the car. The picture-message thing has calmed his rambunctious nerves, at least a bit. He realizes he has some leverage in this dynamic. He's the money guy. And because of that he got Wade to agree to take the photos, which should guarantee Monty's safety while Danny is on the road.

However, Danny's leverage will be leveled the moment his parents' cash is a no-go in El Paso. Between now and then he needs to come up with a plan to protect Monty if the quarter million never comes to fruition. Unfortunately, what that might be is a mystery to him.

Phil gets in the driver's seat and turns the engine on. It doesn't sound terrific, but good enough to get them to El Paso.

As they pull off the property toward the street, Danny checks his phone. No word at all from the actual money guy, his father.

Twelve

Danny's father lifts a bottle of Macallan whisky from his kitchen counter and refills his glass. He doesn't sip it right away. He stares out the window at the rows of ruffled greenery reaching across the fifty-two acres of his farm. His family's farm.

He raises the drink to his silver-stubbled face, his reflection on the windowpane watching him as he eases the liquor down his throat. He hears his wife behind him. In the adjoining living room. Not tears. Not anymore. She stopped crying about ten minutes ago. She's fidgeting now. He doesn't turn to look at her, but can imagine what she's doing. Crossing her legs. Then uncrossing. Adjusting the couch cushion. Checking her phone. Leaning back into the cushion. Sitting still. For only a moment. Adjusting the cushion again. Back to the phone.

He has another sip of whisky.

The men out the window in the field are finishing up for the day. Danny's father watches one of them, a short worker with deep-brown skin, cargo pants, a sweat-soaked blue tee shirt, and a white fishing hat with a strap looping around his chin. The man, unlike the others around him, crosses the farm with a hint of resistance pushing against his steps, almost as if he were wading through water.

Danny's dad, who came from nothing, worked hard his whole life. Even today, the day his son was all over television for escaping prison, he managed to put in a half-day in the field, leaving some grass stains on the knees of his jeans. He never let Danny take anything for granted. And his boy never did. He was always proud of his son. Still is. Even after everything.

"Please, Ben, tell me *something*," his wife says.

He watches her adjust the couch cushion. Then check her phone. She flips it facedown on the coffee table, then places her elbows on her thighs, puts her fingers over her mouth, and rocks. He swirls his cup and glances down at the whirlpool of whisky.

"He hasn't spoken to me in two years," Ben says. "And now he wants a quarter of a million dollars?"

She peers at him from the living room. Behind her on the wall is a wooden cross flanked by framed family photos. One of Danny in a tuxedo with a bubbly brunette at senior prom. Another of his older sister, Kayla, on a high-school church mission trip in Nicaragua. Danny, at eight years old, in laser-tag gear. Kayla and her husband smiling with their baby girl among the flickering light from a "1" candle on a cake.

"He's in trouble," Danny's mom says. "The money isn't for him."

"Sounds like a line."

"Our Danny may be many things, but he's not a liar. You know that."

Ben does know that. He finishes his drink. He sets the cup on the counter. All around him are knick-knacks his wife collected from markets over the years to give the kitchen a quirky, homey ambience.

"He doesn't even have the decency to call me?" Ben asks. "We'd both be giving him the money, but he only gets in touch with you?"

"Me and him have a different history. He's comfortable with me." She softens her voice and says, "With you, he has his reasons not to be."

"Don't give me that, Hannah. I was the one who did the right thing then."

"On paper it was the right thing. I've told you that a thousand times. But still. You turned Danny in. You expected him to just let that go?"

Ben leans over, his forearms resting against the edge of the counter, and picks up the whisky-bottle top. He slowly rolls it between his thumb and middle finger. "I'm a Christian. I have principles. Breaking them means I'm no better than any heathen on the street. When I saw what I saw that night, I was supposed to just go back home and forget it ever happened? All because my son was responsible?"

"Danny made a mistake. I'm not denying that, but—"

"I remember when he worked on the farm with me. He'd do anything I told him. With a smile. He was my best man." Ben flicks the whisky top. It bangs on the marble counter, hits a spice rack, and spins by the sink. "But all it would take was something small to throw him completely off. When he was sixteen he planted a crop for me. And a rabbit ate a bunch of it up. Things like this happen. You acknowledge them and plant again. Not Danny. He took it personally for some reason. Didn't show up to work for two days. Slept over the Hallington brothers' house. Something went wrong and instead of dealing with it, he ran from it. He was like that his whole life. I never understood it. That night two years ago I wasn't going to let him run from reality."

The husband and wife are only fifteen feet apart, yet the distance feels deeper. The curtains are drawn in the living room, a gray-scale sheath hanging over the photos, turned-off TV, and tower of DVDs from the late Nineties and early Two Thousands Danny and his sister amassed as stocking stuffers over multiple Christmases.

Her eyes water. "He's still your boy, Ben. Both of ours." She nods at the kitchen counter. "Remember when you'd bring in corn from the farm when he was six and he liked me to put all those spices on it? One day I mixed them all in a shaker and wrote 'Danny Flakes' on it in marker. I'd season all his food with it. I've been mixing Danny Flakes ever since. Even after he…went away…I still keep a shaker of them in the cabinet." She wipes an eye. "Through it all, through everything that happened, I still think of him as that six-year-old boy. He was so sweet." She cups her neck with her right hand and wraps her left arm across her chest. "He knew everyone's birthday. In the whole family. Even second cousins on both our sides who he never met. He'd always remind me a few days before to send a card. He was our boy then, and he is now. He's in trouble. He's terrified. I heard it in his voice over the phone. He needs that money. He needs his parents. Now."

Ben picks up the whisky top from the counter and inserts it into the Macallan bottle. He peers at their fifty-two acres. All the men are gone. The wind rolls a ripple through green leaves growing around wooden posts. Far back, on the road, he sees an El Paso police cruiser. They've been looping the property all day.

"How much cash was it again?" Ben asks.

"We had sixty-eight thousand in the attic. So a hundred eighty-two more. By tonight."

He lets out a long breath. His son hates him. All because Ben stood by his Christian principles that one summer night in 2014. But he doesn't hate his son. Hate has no place in Christianity. Jesus didn't hate the enemies who crucified him. And if Danny is really in as much trouble as his wife thinks, leaving him hanging would be an act of hate.

"Fine," he says. "I'll help him. But only if he asks me himself."

Thirteen

The black Buick Lucerne Wade gave Phil motors along a road through the southern tip of Rene, a no man's woodland between residential areas.

Other than the mesh stretch of chicken-wire fence along the dusty path, the vehicle is the only manmade object in the area, bordered on one side by a field, the other side oak trees, and above a pinkish-blue sky. The sun's intensity dims as it dips west, casting a long black shadow behind the vehicle that appears not a separate thing but an extension of the car.

A quarter of Danny's newly shaved head is captured on the glass of his side-view mirror. The haircut reminds him of childhood. The last time he buzzed his head he was eleven.

The car is quiet other than the radio. The ex-bunkmates haven't said a word to each other in the ten minutes they've been on the road.

Up close Danny notices Phil not only colored his blondish hair black, but threw a coat of dye on his eyebrows for consistency. Maybe due to lack of a proper applying implement, maybe due to lack of time, maybe due to lack of something else, the whole of the brows isn't black, spots of original, pale hair poking through.

The look, which has a cheap, vaudevillian flair, is a contrast to the dignified air Phil always had about him in jail. Danny recalls a constant professorial elegance, from the way Phil cuffed the too-long prison pants just so on his short legs, to the way he always tucked a napkin into his collar at meal time, which would've cost him a beating if he weren't a smuggling customer of the Aryans, and thus earner of their protection.

Soon the dirt road turns to pavement and the Buick turns into a business district. A billboard shows the smiling face of a baby girl about three years old. "Sign Up for the Fifth Annual Lindsay Lancaster Memorial 10K" is written along the top. "All Proceeds Go to Cancer Research" below, along with a website URL.

Danny assumes that little girl is Lindsay Lancaster, and that picture is one of the last taken of her. Cancer. Just a baby. Her parents must have coordinated an event in her memory. Which is nice, he thinks. But the whole thing is just so sad. The nice part is so overwhelmingly outweighed. Why does the world give some babies cancer and let others grow up to be star athletes?

In middle school Danny tried to right some of the world's wrongs. He was never religious, but used his father's connections at their church in El Paso to organize a fundraiser for victims of Hurricane Katrina. What did those people do to deserve to have their homes demolished by a natural disaster? He collected eight thousand and seventy-seven dollars for those poor souls. And used the local branch of a national charitable organization to deposit the funds and dispatch them to the sufferers.

A year later the charitable organization got into hot water for mismanaging money. It was paying its executives exorbitant salaries while only donating five percent of contributions to victims of its causes. Danny hopes the same thing doesn't happen to Lindsay Lancaster's parents.

"Isn't that a shame?" Danny asks, nodding at the billboard.

Phil peeks at it as they pass it and asks, "Is what a shame?"

"Little girl dying like that. It doesn't seem fair."

"What do you mean by fair?"

"A baby can't hurt anyone. It never did anything wrong. Then it drops dead. Where's the fairness in that?"

"Fairness by whose hand?"

Danny's nose scrunches in confusion.

"When I hear the word fair," Phil continues, "I think of someone, or something, choosing one side over another in a biased way. Who in this case is biased?"

Danny folds his arms.

"The medical industry?" Phil asks. "Society?" A moment. "God? Who's the biased one making it unfair?"

Danny doesn't have an answer.

"Nature is nature," Phil says. "There is no fairness, or unfairness to it. It simply is what it is."

Danny envies Phil for this notion. Life would be less painful if you could deem any event "is what it is." Danny recollects one night in jail he and Phil were talking about regrets. Phil told him it's illogical to beat yourself up too much over regrets because ultimately they're the result of activity in neurons, little cells thousandths of a millimeter in diameter in your brain. A regret isn't something wrong with *you*. But tiny neurons that short-circuited momentarily.

The explanation felt cold, but Danny found it oddly comforting. Just like this one about the baby with cancer. However, he can't bring himself to fully accept it.

A quarter mile ahead, standing in a bed of overgrown grass beside the street, a girl with a suitcase at her feet flashes a hitchhiking thumb. As the fugitives approach, her features become more apparent. About five three. Late teens, early twenties at most. Shoulder-length black hair with a purple streak through it. Soft-edged square face, at its center two pleading blue eyes.

The Buick gets closer. A yard or so away, through the windshield, she makes eye contact with Phil, then Danny. Phil blows past her. In the side mirror, Danny sees a gust of dust kick up behind the car, covering the girl with a sepia tint before wafting away into the open air.

The chain of consecutive songs on the radio ends, the drawl of a local disc jockey replacing the music. After a brief bit on the weekend weather, he informs his listeners, "The manhunt for three felons who escaped Thurgood L. Crick Prison this morning is still ongoing. If you have any information at all, contact your local law enforcement precinct or call nine-one-one. These men are assumed to be armed and extremely dangerous. Photos of the three criminals are on the radio station's web page. They were convicted for…"

As the DJ details their crimes, Danny's mind drifts to that dark summer of 2014. When it happened. He'd been two months into his full-time graphic-design job at Amogo Studios. His team just wrapped a three-week project mapping the user flow for a space-shuttle-simulation app. Danny, working alongside the creative director, suggested a change that streamlined the app's navigation. The higher-ups loved it.

The night they finished, the eight-person project team went to a gastro pub to celebrate. Tham's Corkscrew it was called. Danny found the name weird (What was Tham? The owner's first name? Why corkscrew? It wasn't a wine bar, rather an alehouse.).

They certainly celebrated. Buffalo wings. Three plates. Spicy. Asian. Honey glazed. Nachos. And pitchers of beer. They had a table in the back. Cups and plates nearly blanketed the full of the surface. They were loud, but not in an obnoxious way. A jovial one. No other customers were close by. Passing staff members smiled at them, sometimes giggled at an overheard joke. The Amogo team worked hard the last three weeks. And the client applauded what they did. They deserved to have some fun.

The waitress, a pigtailed girl right out of high school too young to drink herself but old enough to serve, paid the crew a lot of attention. Each time she came over she'd pick up the pair of pitchers at the center of the table and top off all eight glasses. When a pitcher hit empty, she'd return with it refilled her next visit.

Danny was enamored being in the company of these older men and women, these established professionals in the field he craved to have a career in. They respected him. After his work on the space-shuttle app he was one of them. He saw his future that night. And he liked it.

They stayed at that back table of Tham's Corkscrew for over two and a half hours. Eating and drinking the whole time. Buddy Chaplin, the CEO, paid for everything on the company credit card.

The team said their goodbyes as they scattered out the doorway into the night. Most everyone else lived in their own places close by the bar, which wasn't far from the office. Danny, fresh out of school, was still staying at his parents' house on the farm, a thirty-five minute drive away.

As he approached his car in the parking lot, he felt the alcohol in his system. But he didn't feel drunk. He'd been drunk before. Many times. He knew what it was like. This wasn't that. This was something milder. But it was still something. He wasn't sober. That's for certain. He tried to gauge how many beers he had. But couldn't. Sometimes the waitress topped him off when his glass was almost empty, other times when it was practically full. There was no running count of full-to-finished drinks.

Most people in the group had more than him, though he couldn't put a number on their consumption either. The tally was meaningless anyway, he thought. He felt fine. That's all that mattered. So he got in his car and headed home.

At 9:29 PM, thirty-two minutes into the ride, only three blocks from his house, he slammed into a Toyota Tercel.

Danny's car was flipped. His collarbone fractured. His mind fried. He was among farmland at nearly ten o'clock on a weeknight. Nobody was around to help. After squeezing out of his toppled vehicle, he rushed over to check on the other driver.

The man, Robert Patrick Flynn was his name Danny would later learn, was unconscious. But breathing, his chest slowly puffing up and down. His body was mashed between his seat and the smashed-in front of his car. Danny mustered up all of the strength left in his battered muscles to free the two-hundred-plus-pound man from the compromising position, then leaned his passed-out body against the Tercel.

Still no other cars. No other people. Danny knew medical attention was needed. He also knew he wasn't sober. If he called nine-one-one on his phone to help the other driver, it could incriminate him. Though his automobile would be found at the scene, to make an effective case police would need proof he was the one actually operating it. So he reached into the Tercel and called from the other man's phone, which was flung on the wrecked vehicle's floor, though still functional.

Once the dispatcher confirmed an ambulance would come, Danny felt his only option was to run. He saved this man. Now he needed to save himself.

He ran home, went inside, and screamed. His parents stormed downstairs. They found him sitting in the kitchen, the cuts on his neck from broken windshield glass bleeding all over the stainless-steel refrigerator door, red streaks that looked like his finger paintings his mom used to hang on the same spot years before.

His dad saw the windshield glass on him and smelt the glasses of beer in him. He gave his son a quick inspection to assure he wasn't seriously injured, then became infuriated and inquired where the car was. After dodging the question for ten minutes, Danny finally told him. When his dad drove to the intersection, he encountered El Paso Police among the EMTs, and was informed of the other passenger's critical state.

Within minutes two officers, accompanied by Danny's own father, knocked on the Marsh family's front door. The patriarch affirmed that the son was in fact driving the vehicle, and was likely over the legal limit. Which a breathalyzer soon proved. Danny was handcuffed and carted away.

His record was clean prior to that night. Fleeing the scene of an accident for a first-time offender typically would be met with some leniency. Less if the victim suffered serious injury, which was the case. But paired with a DUI conviction leaves a judge no room for sympathy. So Danny was charged with a felony.

Yes, Robert Patrick Flynn survived, partly thanks to Danny pulling him out of the car. But also thanks to Danny he lost a leg. The left, amputated from the knee down, something he would've kept if Danny just took a damn cab that night. Like he should've.

The Buick turns off Dixie Street onto a busy straightaway road leading to the highway onramp two and a quarter miles away.

For the first time the whole ride, Phil's expression breaks from neutral. His brow furrows. He leans forward, as if for a better view of something. Looking ahead, Danny sees it too. The black and white of a Rene cop car.

Phil eases off the gas. The Buick slows. Then stops on the side of the road. An old Cadillac convertible zips by them.

Then a truck, the force of displaced wind slightly shaking their sedan.

A row of cars is queued up at the highway entrance. A police checkpoint.

Danny gulps. He gazes at his old cellmate. Phil swings the nose of the Buick a hundred eighty degrees, the screech of the wheels rattling a flock of crows out of a nearby tree. As the birds flap toward the clouds, the Buick rolls the way it came.

Phil veers back onto Dixie, then makes a few more turns through town. Eight minutes later the onramp for another highway comes into view.

Another checkpoint.

The chill and moisture on Danny's neck build.

Phil pulls over, parks, and says, "They know we're in town."

"How?"

"Unclear."

"What the hell do we do now?"

"Unclear." Phil strokes his chin in thought.

Fourteen

The hitchhiking girl with the purple streak in her hair still hasn't had any luck roadside in Rene. The tall, untamed weeds at her feet enfold the bottom half of her cheap suitcase, a banged-up box of brown cloth, the teeth of its zipper track askew in a few places.

Her blue eyes widen when a Mercedes appears on the horizon. She steps forward, her sneaker toes meeting the edge of the pavement, and pops a thumb in the air. The sun stretches the shadow of her five-three frame across the street. The car nears. She adds a jiggle to her raised hand.

But it's no use. The Mercedes, its interior tight with a family of four, ignores her, its tires stamping the girl's shadow as it cruises along. She blows out a breath of disappointment, her lipsticked lips flapping.

She reaches into the rear pocket of her denim skirt and pulls out a watch. A man's. An expensive one. A sleek steel band with a yellow-gold face. A sharp contrast from the look of her suitcase. She checks the time. 6:33 PM. Then sticks the watch back in her pocket.

Her foot taps in the thick grass. She peers over her right shoulder. Then her left. Her foot speeds up. The sun, though milder than it was a few hours ago, is still strong. It comes down on the exposed, tan skin of her shoulders, the tad of stomach peeking beneath her halter-top, and the length of her legs. Her forehead is a dash damp with sweat. And though the heat may be in play, it seems like the perspiration has inspiration in something else, something inside her, some thought, the same one causing her foot to tap.

Another car. A black Buick Lucerne.

She strikes her pose. The vehicle approaches at forty or so miles an hour. She wiggles her fist. The sedan slows to thirty-five. Then thirty. She goes up on her tippy toes in a jolt of excitement.

The car decelerates to five miles per hour, then desists moving entirely, its nose hovering over the edge of the girl's shadow on the asphalt. The passenger-side window rolls down. She scuttles to it, leaning over to make eye contact with the two travelers.

Directly in front of her is Danny, then Phil manning the wheel a couple feet away. Danny gazes at the glove box, the muscles in his face taut, while Phil, with a forced game show host's smile, looks at her.

Phil devised a plan to get past the police checkpoints, one involving the hitchhiking girl with the purple hair they passed earlier, one he explained to Danny about five minutes ago. It shocked Danny. The boldness of it was uncharacteristic of the mild-mannered professor. However, with sixteen years to go on a sentence for a crime he didn't perpetrate, Phil is obviously willing to leave his comfort zone to achieve his freedom in

Mexico. This plan is well out of Danny's comfort zone too, yet he agreed to go along with it due to zero alternatives.

"Howdy," Phil says. "Where you heading?"

"Anywhere but here," she replies. A moment. "California. Eventually. But I assume you're not going that far." She glances over her shoulder, then situates her attention back on Phil.

"No, but we are heading west. Hop in. We'll take you as far as we can."

Her lips glide apart, revealing a smile that's just as adorable as her face. Danny can't help but peek up at her for a moment. "Thank you, thank you, thank you," she gushes, then opens the rear door. "Ahh...suitcase." She scampers through the grass, retrieves her bag, and climbs in.

As she settles into the backseat, Phil studies her in the rearview, remnants of that awkward grin still clinging to his expression. Danny, with stiff shoulders, stares into the mirror too. Phil puts the car in drive and they begin cruising.

"Jane," the girl says, her voice with a trace of a Southern accent.

A couple minutes ago Phil stressed that someone who's spent the day hitchhiking outdoors likely hasn't caught the TV news and seen their photos. He was right. This chick seems totally unaware of who they are.

"So what's in California, Jane?" Phil asks.

She crosses her arms atop the suitcase on her lap and says, "A change."

"From what?"

"Nobody in my family, at least that I know, ever made it out of Georgia. I figured I'd be the first. California always seemed right to me. At least what it's like in movies." She looks out the window at the colorful meadow they pass, a boarded-up house toward the back with a rusty swing set next to it.

"Georgia is quite a beautiful place itself," Phil says.

"Beautiful, sure. But it wasn't for me. Not anymore. Let's just say certain people, no matter how hard you try, can never see the world the same way as you. What's in their head will always be different, even if you explain something to them till you go blue in the face. I left three days ago. No car. Eighty dollars in my pocket. Time to go." She pats her suitcase. "Time to go."

"That's some road trip for a young lady to take without a friend."

"It's not a road trip. It's a move. A *permanent* one. Every material thing I own is in this suitcase." She leans forward, her head entering the space between the front seats. She no longer addresses Phil in the glass of the rearview, but looks right at him. "You rely on friends for the little things in life. For the important things, you can only count on yourself."

She retreats to the rear, her back meeting the leather seat. The bobbing zippers on her luggage send a soft chime through the quiet car. Danny glimpses her in the mirror. A twinkle in her blue eyes. A grin on her red lips. He imagines she's thinking of California and her new life there.

A one-two of anxiety hits Danny's breadbasket and chest when he pictures what they have to put her through. She doesn't deserve this. But what else were they supposed to do? Be spotted at a checkpoint and go back to jail? She'll eventually get over what happens, but Danny could never get over a return to prison.

The anxiety subsides, giving way to that queasy feeling Danny had this morning when he tied up that innocent family. He's tried blocking the image of the mother, father, and daughter from his mind, but it's kept bubbling back through the day. He wonders if he's a bad person. He's wondered for almost two years.

But what even defines "bad?" It's not like the world has a cosmic dictionary that lists the answer. "Bad" is a human invention. Though there's no objective meaning, "bad" still exists, though. Danny is sure of that. But not sure of much else about it.

He turns his attention from the girl in the mirror to the scenery outside. Wood signs for nearby businesses are nailed to the wood barks of trees they drive by. The first for "Mary's Room Furniture" in red paint. Another saying "Bat Cave Tours: Experience Something New." The next some sort of PSA Danny guesses, a picture of a brain in a vat of a bubbly green substance, "Your Mind" scrawled above, "on Meth" below.

"So what about you two?" Jane asks. "What's your story? What's west?"

"We're salesmen," Phil answers. "Client visits."

She scans his business-appropriate outfit, then the old jeans and loose tee shirt on Danny. Her black eyebrows curve down toward her blue eyes. "You're a salesman too?"

Danny faces her. He nods.

"I never met a salesman who didn't talk." A moment. She smirks.

He gazes at her for a few more seconds, then turns back around. "I talk when I need to."

"Don't let his reticence fool you," Phil interjects. "He's a very promising new hire in the organization. It's his first business trip. I've taken him under my wing. I've been showing him how things are done."

"Aren't you just a doll?" she says through a grin.

"And you?" Phil asks her. "Los Angeles? Actress?"

"I can barely remember my phone number, let alone lines." She chuckles.

Phil chuckles too.

She runs a hand through her dark hair, the dyed purple streak lifting, then lowering across her forehead, and says, "One thing at a time. Get there first. If it is what I think it is, and…my soul feels right there…I'm sure a job and all the rest will fall into place."

They stop at a red light. A man on a Yamaha motorcycle pulls next to them and peers in their direction.

Even though Danny and Phil changed their outfits and hairstyles before hitting the road, and even though tints are on the Buick's windows, their faces are still their faces and the windows are not, by law, fully opaque. Danny's heart rattles as this man's glance lingers on them. The light turns green. The biker disregards them, looking ahead, revving his engine, then bulleting off.

The Buick continues toward the highway. "Your tattoo," Phil says to Jane. "Was it a mistake?"

She takes a gander at her left arm, where a blue rose extends from her shoulder to her elbow. "What do you mean?"

"I'm not sure if you're aware, but there's no such thing as a blue rose. No gene in any species carries the pigment delphinidin, which makes flowers that shade. Some breeders have tried to sidestep nature by artificially creating a blue rose. Inserting the blue gene from a flower such as a pansy into a red rose, then using an enzyme to switch off the red gene." He grins. "But the humans never quite succeeded. The red could never be completely turned off, resulting in a flower that isn't a true blue, more of a purple."

She takes a few moments to absorb this scientific speech from this supposed salesman. Then replies, "I know blue roses don't exist. That's why I got the tattoo."

Puzzlement streaks across his face. "I don't see the point. It just looks...forgive my candor...a bit comical."

She sweeps her index finger up and down the rose stem on her skin. "The point is that only one exists. Right here. The only one in the world. And if someone in some lab somewhere does wind up figuring out how to make another one, then well..." She glances out the window, a church whizzing by in the opposite direction of the car. "Then I guess I'll just have to have the blue petals colored in black. No such thing as a black rose either. But when I got the tattoo I thought blue was a better choice. A black flower is just...sort of gloomy. Life is too short to be gloomy."

Silence.

They go another half mile. Phil makes a left. "The highway is back there," Jane says in a befuddled voice.

He doesn't respond.

A touch of nausea begins spiraling in Danny's stomach. He takes a deep breath.

Quaint houses line the street they're on, tucked among a wooded expanse. Jane's head, holding a confused expression, swivels between the windshield and both back windows. She gazes at Phil's face in the rearview. No remnants of that game-show grin anymore.

They pass a concrete slab on the ground, "Grover Avenue Elementary" etched on it. Phil turns into the school's parking lot, vacant on a summer Saturday. He winds past the corner of a one-story brick building, blackness on the inside of its windows, trickles of paling sun the outsides.

He parks.

Jane's expression no longer shows confusion. It's contaminated with fear. "What are we doing here?"

Phil spins around. Accompanying him, aimed at Jane, is a black Sig Sauer .45 caliber pistol. "You're going to do exactly what I tell you to."

Fifteen

A chain in the Marsh family's basement shakes as Danny's father pounds a right hook into a heavy bag suspended from it. His face is covered in sweat, which smells like the whisky he was drinking upstairs in the kitchen. A lot of people don't like exercising after they have a few glasses of alcohol in them. Not Ben Marsh. A good drink and a good workout are his two outlets for stress. On the most stressful days, like today, he has to do both to stay sane.

In his fifty-seven years, he's come to understand there's a lot out there that can drive us mad. We're fragile creatures. Even rugged farmers like Ben who never cried a day after infancy are delicate in their own ways. The key to managing the delicacy is recognizing what your breaking points are. We all have different ones. You build personal principles around them. And you never, never cave in the face of those principles. Because they'll suffocate you in the rubble.

This can be tough. Which is why God invented booze and boxing.

Hannah, Danny's mom, opens the door. She watches her husband throw two jabs into the Everlast bag, followed by a big right.

"I texted Danny," she says. "I told him you want a phone call."

He lets his hands down. "What did he say back?"

"Nothing."

This room of the basement, which Ben converted into a gym twelve years ago, has mirrors on all four walls. The image of him beside the wobbling heavy bag surrounds the husband and wife from a different angle on all sides. Ben remembers seeing Danny in these mirrors. He taught his son how to lift weights down here.

"He's headed to Mexico?" Ben asks, throwing a punch.

"How many times do I have to say it?"

"To *live*?"

"It's where he'd be safe."

The links in the chain of the bag jostle and jingle against each other as Ben slams it with his taped fists. "I don't understand," he says, sweat seeping into his eyes. "The judge gave him five years. He's put in one and a half. And according to you his behavior inside was as good as any. They would've let him out in three. He's already halfway done. I just...I don't know what he's thinking, Hannah."

"He wouldn't have lasted that long. I saw the look on his face when I'd visit. It wasn't him anymore. It was someone else." Due to overcrowding in West Texas penitentiaries, Danny was assigned to Crick, all the way across the state. Despite the ten-hour drive, Hannah visited religiously.

Ben stops hitting the bag, grabs a towel draped over a squat rack, and dries his silver-stubbled face. "To avoid suffering for just a year and a half more," he says, "look at what he has to give up. The rest of his life. He's a fugitive now. And will be until the day he dies. He always has to hide. Always needs to look over his shoulder." He throws his long arms in the air, the white towel flapping. "This home. All this. It's gone. He won't be able to come back to America. He'll be in Mexico. Forever. Living some watered-down version of the life he used to know."

Danny's mom tears up. Ben, who didn't mean to make her cry, looks away. "I asked if he'll live somewhere close to the border, by El Paso," she says. "He told me yes. We can visit him there. It'll be easy." She forces an optimistic smile, its corners lacquered in tears. "Kayla, Ian, and the baby too. We can all go. It'll be fine. Really. It'll be just like old."

Ben tosses the damp towel into a basket. "No it won't."

The optimistic grin is wiped from Hannah's face. She gazes at dumbbells strewn across the floor mats. Ben knows it won't be the same. And he knows she does too.

"A long time ago I went to school with a boy named Jimmy Nash," he says.

Hannah doesn't look at him, her eyes still on the scattered weights.

"Early Seventies," he continues. "We were fifteen. I was never friends with him per se, but friendly with him. You know how it was when you were a kid. Your buddies would have other buddies, then they'd have other buddies, and at football games, or dances, or in the cafeteria, or what not, you'd congregate. And that would be your group, even if you knew some better than others. Jimmy Nash was in my group. As it was. He thought he was a real outlaw. Always bragging about how he'd broken into some car and stole a radio. Or even a house. We didn't really believe him at first. He used to get on my nerves if I'm speaking honest. Seedy fellow. Didn't smell, but had hands and skin that always looked sticky, like he didn't take more than a shower a week."

Ben sits on the cushion of the bench press. He goes on, "Jimmy brought this necklace into school one day. Looked expensive. Said he stole it from a lady late the previous night who was walking home from the train station. Way it went, Jimmy and his older brother, who was nineteen then, wore ski masks. The brother held a gun to her, told her to do what they said. Made her take off the necklace and give it to Jimmy. He said he was on his way to a pawn shop after school to sell it and split the cash with his brother. Jimmy didn't come from money. His mamma couldn't afford something like that. We didn't know any other way he could've gotten it besides robbing it. That day we started believing him. Maybe he really was a thief."

Hannah wipes the corner of her eye and tilts her head in curiosity, as if unsure where he's going with this.

"A few weeks later," Ben says, "a story is in the paper about a local woman, the mom of a mom and pop shop near Fort Bliss. A customer found her on the floor. Her forehead was split open like a pistachio." Ben illustrates by tracing with his index finger the vertical axis of his skull down to the bridge of his nose. "Cash gone from the register. No witnesses. Cops had no clue who did it."

Hannah slightly cringes.

"Jimmy doesn't show up in school the next day," Ben says. "Or the day after. Comes in that Thursday. For the first time ever his skin looked clean. Like he showered ten times since we saw him last. But he didn't look good. He was pale. Eyes were red with black bags under them. He didn't brag about robbing that store with his brother. Never mentioned it. And none of us asked. But we knew it was him. Nobody had proof. There was nothing to turn him in on. But people in the group were convinced. Jimmy never talked about stealing ever again. Wound up graduating high school. Got a job at the Shell station right around the time the oil crisis ended. Worked his way up. Now he owns two stations of his own. I run into him from time to time in town. Beautiful wife. Three kids a little older than Kayla. Jimmy looks great."

He peers at the floor mats. He shakes his head. A dab of sweat falls off. He says, "Not only didn't Jimmy spend a day in jail, for that crime or any of the others, but his conscience is free of it. When you see that man in town, with his family, smiling, he doesn't look like a person carrying a burden on his shoulders. He was shook for a couple days afterward in school, but that was that. Like he flipped a switch in his head and just put it all behind him. And now he's cleansed of everything."

She's quiet for a while. Then, in a non-offensive tone, asks, "What's your point?"

"Danny isn't like Jimmy. I don't think he's able to flip a switch in his head and forget he robbed that man of a leg driving drunk. He was able to *run* from the problem, sure. The night he did it his instinct was to run away. Come here. And now his instinct is to run to Mexico. It's the same thing. The boy has been running from problems his whole life. Even if we help him out and give him this money, and he makes it to Mexico, he won't be saved. It's going to take a lot more than that. He's the only one who knows what."

"He's not religious like you, Ben. He doesn't think like that."

"No, he's not spiritual like me. Which is fine. But he's just as principled as me. Especially when holding himself to a standard. He needs to stop pretending principles don't matter. Or else his own will get the best of him. In a way much worse than any prison ever could."

Sixteen

Jane Pilgrim sits in the backseat of the Buick gazing out the window at the vacant schoolyard. The man in the front seat with the strange-colored eyebrows, aiming the pistol at her, has just finished explaining his intentions, and she's just begun processing them.

She catches her reflection in the rearview mirror. The lines crossing her brow indicate worry, while the muted blue of her eyes don't imply surprise. In her twenty years she's dealt with a lot, much of it rooted in the depravity of humans. The shadows of people's dark sides have always had a knack of shading her path in this world.

Maybe it's because she was born in a bad area. Maybe it's because of bad luck. Or maybe it's her own fault, brought upon her by some bad trait. She doesn't know. What she does know is that she's landed in shit again. And though she's startled, she's not surprised.

"Let's get going," Phil says.

She complies, opening the back door, exiting the car.

Danny rubs his temples, sighs, and gets out too.

Phil pulls the key from the ignition and steps onto the blacktop. The sun, a couple hours from setting, is a blood-orange ball low in the sky. It projects a long silhouette behind him, which moves like a marionette as he approaches the Buick's trunk, the lengthy limbs joggling off the joints.

He unlocks the hatch. Danny, per Phil's plan, gets in the trunk, nuzzling against the paper bag of food Wade packed. Craning his neck, Danny peers at Jane through a valley of space between the metal of the lifted hatch and the glass of the rear windshield.

She is emptying the contents of her suitcase into the backseat, also per Phil's plan. As she tosses a pair of leggings out of the luggage, her glance meets his. His big brown eyes have an apologetic flicker in them. She holds her stare on his for a moment. Then turns back to her task.

A sympathetic look means nothing to her right now. As the one with the gun recently detailed when he revealed their true identities, both are criminals. Both need her to do this so they can evade the police. Though the younger one appears more reluctant, it makes him no better than the older.

As she spills more clothing onto the mounting pile on the backseat, she notices the older fugitive peering at a dumpster near the schoolhouse. Something there has attained his attention. He saunters over to the overflowing bin of trash, which is stuffed with busted supplies from the school year that recently ended, like desk chairs with cracked backs and bookracks with shoddy shelves. Atop the pile of garbage is a cardboard box of broken microscopes and other science equipment. A brilliant burst of color glistens inside it. Which Phil reaches toward.

He extracts some object from the box and strolls with it toward the Buick, his face attentively fixed on it as he plays with it in his palm.

Danny, from his crouch in the trunk, asks him, "What is that?"

Phil lofts the three-inch-long piece of glass above his head, intercepting with it a ray of setting sun, a small rainbow emanating around it. "This, Daniel, is one of the most important items in the history of science. One of the edges is cracked, which is why they're discarding it I assume, however, it still works perfectly. Do you see that spectrum of light it's producing?"

"Yeah, so what?"

"Isaac Newton used a glass prism just like this to conduct what's known as a crucial experiment. He proved that color is not a property of the things we see. Color, like the brown of your hair, doesn't live *inside* the hair itself. Rather, color is simply a property of the light that *reflects* from things. This of course raises greater questions about the truth of the world around us versus how we perceive it. Is your hair itself actually brown if nobody were looking at it, or is the brown merely an illusion the human brain conjures up? Can we humans ever harbor truth, actual truth, about the world, or are we damned by nature to forever be deceived?"

Danny peeks at the prism, then Phil's face. He doesn't offer a reply.

Phil underhand tosses the sharp-edged glass object to him. As Danny cradles it in his interlaced hands, Phil says, "My gift to you." Danny grips it between his thumb and index finger and gives it a once-over. "Hopefully it'll remind you that the truth is an elusive concept. Never take it for granted." Danny, who doesn't seem excited about his new gift, dismissively tucks the prism in his pocket.

Stepping to Jane, Phil watches her clear out what's left in her luggage. From over her shoulder, he observes the heap of jackets, jeans, shirts, socks, and bras in the backseat and nods in approval.

He takes the hollow case, carries it to the rear of the vehicle, and inserts it into the trunk. Danny nudges over to make room. With a grunt, Phil rams the luggage with his shoulder, wedging it inside. Danny ducks his head. Phil slams the hatch, a metallic echo resounding through the school grounds.

Phil hands Jane the car key and climbs through the back door. He curls his narrow, five-seven body into a fetal-like position on the carpeting behind the driver's seat. "Okay," he says.

As planned, she begins cloaking him with her clothes. She uses the larger items first. A denim jacket splayed wide, a sundress opened like a tent top, a baggy sleeping sweater flattened out.

Before his body is completely covered, she sees him place the nose of the pistol against the bottom of the driver's seat. She stops for a moment, consuming the sight and the bevy of possibilities stemming from it, takes a deep breath, and continues dumping articles of clothing on him.

Soon he's fully masked by her possessions. As he instructed earlier, she scatters the remaining items all about the Buick's back, creating a consistent feel of messiness versus a stand-alone mound behind the driver's seat, helping hide the outline of a hidden human body.

Jane closes the back and gets in the front, sitting in the driver's seat, sticking in the key, sliding the selector into gear. She pulls off school property, soon turning onto the residential street they came in on.

The automobile is silent other than the purr of the air-conditioning vents which, despite their volume, emit just a bit of a chill. The AC, like other components of the Buick, which shows over 100,000 miles on the odometer, lacks power and precision. The tires don't seem to grip the road well when she turns, as if the treads are worn. She assumes the criminals stole the car. Whoever the real owner is, she thinks, didn't take great care of it.

She's hot. But doesn't roll the window down, fearing the winnowing in of outdoor humidity could potentially worsen things. So she remains walled inside this airtight shell. It smells like her in here. After all, all her belongings are all over. Her own scent is tainted with the stench of a second body, the sweaty one behind her pointing a weapon at her tailbone.

Soon a new aroma enters the atmosphere. A delicious one, smoking brisket from the backyard of one of the nearby houses. She loves brisket. Yet her mind is too occupied to enjoy the smell. She's busy debating her options.

Is there a way out of this? She's not restrained with a rope, chain, or any other implement. She figures she can make some sort of a move. What would that even entail? She could stop, get out, sprint screaming to one of these houses, and bang like mad on the door.

Hopefully someone opens up right away. Even if not, her knocking at a doorstep could be enough to spook the man with the gun behind her. He'd know the door could open at any second, know he'd be spotted, know the police are only a quick nine-one-one call from the homeowner away. He'd probably get in the driver's seat and race off, let her be.

Eyeing a white home with a manicured lawn, she notices through the front window the lights are on. Someone looks home. This is a perfect target. She eases on the gas, slowing down.

Then a cold dose of reason sprays her brain. Making a run for it would be too risky. The moment she stopped the car the man with the gun would become suspicious. For all he'd know they were at a traffic light, however he'd still be leery. The moment he heard the driver door crack there'd be no more suspicion, but certainty of her fleeing. From that instant she'd have to get the door open in full, get her feet on the asphalt, and get her body out of the Buick before he could react. And by react, she means pull the trigger.

Impossible to do. A simple squeeze of his index finger is all it'd take, a fraction of a second. She couldn't out-hustle that.

The timing of his reaction is too formidable an obstacle, but what about the likelihood he reacts at all? Sure he has a gun, but that doesn't make him a murderer. A lot of people have guns. Every man she knew in Georgia had a gun, and over half the females. But then she recalls that this isn't every man. This is an escaped convict. He could even have slain before.

The chances are low he has the conscience to kill, but there's still a chance. She imagines the pistol. Mere inches behind her. Level with her coccyx, angled up at her spinal column. The slightest possibility of him pulling that trigger keeps her obedient. If he did, the bullet would make a short trip, ripping through her, likely killing her in an instant. Even if it missed something vital, it'd still probably burst through vertebrae, paralyzing her. And if it didn't hit bone, it'd still tear up her womb, rendering her childless for life.

Though no one watches her, she shakes her head, a visual expression of the final decision made inside it. No, she won't make a move.

The branches of the overhanging elm trees on the street double in reflection on the Buick's windshield as she transports the prisoners toward the highway as she was told. The heat is getting to her. Between the seat leather and skin of her legs is a film of sweat, which her right hamstring slips slightly upon as she tenses and un-tenses her foot muscles in operation of the pedals.

She sees herself in the rearview. A bit of a quiver to her bottom lip. She realizes her teeth are chattering. Though none of this surprised her, it still worried her. She thinks about the ludicrousness of her present situation and how she ended up in it.

The trucker she hitched a ride from in Louisiana yesterday morning took her as far as East Texas, dropping her off in this town called Rene. She spent the whole day in some bar, thankful of the aging local cowboys nice enough to buy her beer and two full meals. Then last night. She grimaces when she thinks of what happened last night. But it doesn't compare to this predicament.

Maybe this is what you get, Jane, for trying to start a new life in California. It's possible you'll never escape Georgia and the mess you left behind. Possible you're nothing but white trash like your mother. And always will be.

She shakes her head.

Her attention drifting from driving, she hits a pothole. The Buick spasms. Behind her is a distinctive ding she believes to be the brass button on her denim jacket banging against the metal of the pointed pistol. Her throat muscles contract. The little sound heightens the reality that a loaded weapon is aimed at her. That there's a job she must do. No time to brood on Georgia.

Focus, Jane. Focus.

Soon, as she was instructed, she makes a left onto Mabius Boulevard, the street leading to the highway onramp. The police checkpoint emerges.

Ahead, a line of three cars waits behind a row of orange cones. Two officers, an older white guy and a thirty-something Latino, run the operation. The elder speaks into his radio while the younger converses with the driver of the lead vehicle, a late-model Mustang.

Jane slows. Soon stops, hers the fourth car on the queue. Behind the other automobiles, she has a partial view of the policeman's exchange with the man in the Mustang. Though she can't hear their words, she assumes the cop is asking questions by the way his face pauses in expectation after his mouth stops moving. This goes on for another half-minute. Then, with a point and a nod, the officer permits the car to continue on.

What will he ask her?

A utility van is next. Jane is just two away. Though she's been nervous since the schoolyard, she feels the onset of anxiety, a different type than the former. The original, a fear for life, left her frozen. The latter, anticipation of what the cop might do or say, does quite the opposite, igniting her insides into a tizzy.

The van gets the signal to pass. One more, then her.

Peering into the rearview, she tries to relax her expression, to appear natural. But it's difficult. Like the inverse of an uncoiled spring, her facial muscles keep snapping back to their wound state when she tries to push them loose.

The Chevy Silverado in front of her gets the okay. Her breathing slows, then speeds. She frees her foot from the brake, inching ahead to the officer. He wears a nameplate on his polo that says "Lt. John Ramos."

He makes eye contact with her through the windshield. He holds his attention on her for a moment, then strides to the right, around the nose of the vehicle. Stopping opposite the juncture of the driver-side front and rear doors, he peeks into the backseat, through the tinted glass, at the clutter of clothing.

A few moments go by. He takes two steps forward, lining himself with the girl at the wheel, bends a bit, and spins his index finger, gesturing for her to roll down the window.

She does. "Hi officer."

His eyes stop on her with curiosity. He glimpses the purple rope in her hair and blue rose on her arm. "Good evening, miss."

She smiles that good smile.

"Where you heading?" he asks.

"Nowhere in Rene. Just passing through."

Though the gun isn't touching her, she can feel it on her body. It's pointed at the base of her backbone, where a delta of nerve endings condenses. A poke of pressure the diameter of the weapon's barrel presses into these nerves, creating a tingly chill that zings up her back and wings across to each shoulder.

"Passing through to where?" the cop asks.

She considers telling him the truth about California, but it seems too personal, too real. She wants to keep herself distanced from this once it's over. If the prisoners eventually get caught, she doesn't want to get wrapped up in the aftermath. Not to mention, after what happened last night, the less the local police know about her, the better. So she lies, "Staying with some friends for a few days. In Houston."

He watches her face. She assumes she looks nervous to him. He points at the backseat and says, "That's a lot of clothing for a few days."

She laughs. Like her smile, the giggle has a charm to it, yet seems forced. "I never know what I'm going to wear until right before I step out of the house. It's the worst feeling to be at someone else's place getting dressed, then you have an idea for an outfit and remember you didn't pack it. So now I just stuff almost everything I own in my car before I spend the night away from home. Better to bring too much than too little. You cops are lucky. You don't have to deal with that. You wear the same thing every day. Can't say I'm not a little jealous."

Again she snickers. Again it sounds false. He doesn't react with a word or gesture.

Looking into the eyes of this officer of the law, she deliberates making a move again. Things are different now that he's in the mix. Maybe she can signal to him somehow.

He paces toward the rear of the car, assessing various pieces of it on the way. Wheels. Roof. Tail light. He looks through the back windshield, taking in at another angle the mess of dresses, shoes, shirts, and undergarments. A cloud of dirty air rises from the exhaust up the height of his body.

Jane ponders strategies for communicating her distress. A note? There's no pad or pen in the Buick. Possibly a typed note on her phone? Then she remembers the man with the gun, the man pointing that gun at her right now, confiscated her phone back at the schoolyard. Forget writing. How about mouthing a message?

With slow steps the cop returns to her at the driver's window. She smiles, then looks at the steering wheel as thoughts whizz through her head. There's risk in mouthing something. Unless he has lip-reading experience, which she doesn't think is part of police training, he'd have no idea what she's getting at, and might even say something like "Why are you talking without making sound?" and grab the attention of the armed felon.

"You don't like suitcases?" the officer asks.

She peeks up at him. She could of course just be honest. Tell him out loud fugitives are in the car. He and the white cop, two guns versus one, would apprehend them and haul them back to jail. Justice would be served on these scumbags.

But if the man behind her is a maniac, as he very well could be, he'd pull the trigger on her for ratting. He'd probably shoot at the cops too. Sure they'd eventually subdue him, if not these two then their backup units, but the damage would be done. She'd be childless, paralyzed, or dead.

She's no martyr. She's just a twenty-year-old girl who wants to get to California.

"I was in a rush," she says. "Didn't have time to pack. I was supposed to be there an hour ago."

He has another look at the clothes, then at her. A moment. "Enjoy your trip, miss."

A smile and a wave from Jane. She rolls up the window, steps on the gas, and ascends the sloped asphalt of the onramp.

Her exhales are crisp and loud. Adrenaline trembles her fingers around the steering wheel. She merges with the flow of traffic on the highway. She zooms to seventy miles per hour. The speed feels like freedom, like she's a bird flying out of a cage.

Phil rises from the pile of her belongings, a polka-dot sock on his head. He brushes it off, then leans forward, sticking his face in the space between her seat and the empty passenger's. "You performed well," he says. Then juts his neck forward and gently kisses her on the right cheek.

She swallows hard. Then wipes his lingering saliva off her face. Though his gesture disturbs her, her brain is too drained from stress to think much about it. She drives toward the horizon, where a light-charcoal sky meets a chocolate-colored tree line.

They go a mile. "Where do I pull over?" she asks.

"What do you mean?"

"Where do you want to drop me off?"

He doesn't respond.

She glances at him. "Hello?"

"Why would I drop you off?"

"I just...*what*...I...are you fucking with me?" She rakes a hand through her hair. "I did exactly what you told me to. I got you onto the highway."

"Yes. And like I said...you performed well."

Silence as the Buick continues another mile.

She moves toward the shoulder.

"I wouldn't do that," he says.

"I'm pulling over. I'm getting out of this car."

He lays the gun on the center console, doesn't point it at her, just finesses it into her view, reminding her, as if she forgot, that he has it.

She gazes at it. Then back at the road. She doesn't pull over.

"See," he says, "my friend in the trunk and I have a journey ahead of us across Texas. I'm not technically in the clear, so to speak, until I retrieve something in El Paso and am on my way to Mexico with it. If I let you out of the car now, sure, there's a chance you'll put this behind you, hitchhike out of the state, and be on your way to California." He pauses. He holds up a finger. "Or. Or...there's a chance I let you out of the car now, you find the nearest police officer, and tell him, or her, two escaped prisoners are in the area in a black Buick Lucerne. I, my darling, am a man of science. And we men of science don't like operating with a low margin of error. Letting you out now greatly diminishes my margin of error."

"I won't tell the cops a thing. I swear. Please…please just let me go."

"I will let you go. Just not now. Once I have what I need in El Paso and depart for Mexico. It won't be long. Just a few more hours on the road."

Her breathing weakens as her mind spins. A tear builds in the corner of her right eye, not quite falling down her cheek, hovering on the rim of the lower lid.

"Isn't it intriguing?" he asks. "How reality works?" He has a dreamlike look on his face, as if so consumed in wonder by the question he posed that all of this, his felon accomplice in the trunk, his civilian hostage in the driver's seat, the manhunt for him, appears to mean nothing in the moment. "If I let you free now, you'd go down one of two paths. You'd immediately continue on toward California. Or you'd look for the police in Texas. Only one is real. Yet since I am not you I don't know what the reality would be." He grins. "Even more fascinating, if I *don't* let you go now, which I won't, neither of those two paths matters. Even the real one. A new reality engulfs the original, making it just as meaningless as the one stemming from the path in your head you planned to *not* choose." He leans back in his seat with the weapon. "Just magnificent…"

She looks at him as if he's nuts. Then takes a deep breath, and like he wants, keeps driving.

Seventeen

Between the suitcase and bag of food, Danny doesn't have much elbowroom in the trunk. But he still manages to slide his hand to the band of his underwear and slip out his sketch of the cough-medicine magazine ad with the cartoon moon. He's able to free his burner phone from his pocket and use the screen light to illuminate the advertisement in the pitch-black trunk.

For some reason it doesn't calm him like it used to. He sets the crumpled sheet of paper down.

On the road before, his mom messaged him about calling his dad, but Danny was so preoccupied with the police checkpoint and their ignoble strategy to duck it that he hasn't made the call. Or maybe he hasn't done it for another reason. A deeper one than preoccupation. Fear.

He admits to himself this is likely. He's avoided his dad since 2014. He had every right to. What sort of a father turns his own son in to the police? It was too much to deal with. So he didn't deal with it. He simply stopped acknowledging his dad's existence. Even that one time his father visited him in jail, Danny just stared through the plexiglass divider as he spoke, then walked back to his cell.

But he can't walk away now. He *must* call him, which scares him. He wonders what's so frightening about it, a simple phone call. After a couple minutes he determines that his dad's opinion may be too much to bear. Danny always respected his father's judgment. Their whole El Paso community did. Hearing a man you admire explain how big of a screw-up you are never loses its toxicity. Even if you've already swallowed the speech in the past your body doesn't develop an immunity.

However, if Danny doesn't call there's no money. Without the money Monty's safety falls into jeopardy, presided over by a racist overlord, Wade.

Also, without the cash, Danny can't count on Wade's connections to set him up with a new identity in Mexico. If Danny were able to break away and make it down south solo, he'd have to find a fitting place to live and forged papers to work, direful deeds with no money or Spanish competency. Worse, Wade's cartel associates would be looking for him down there. In this case, not to help him...quite the opposite. He'd have his freedom, but wouldn't really be free.

Danny is positive his father will say no. But he still needs to make that call. It wouldn't be fair to himself or Monty if he didn't try.

He takes a few deep breaths. It must be a hundred fifty degrees in this damn trunk. His lungs feel like they're sweating. He looks at the phone's lit-up keypad. He still remembers his father's cell number after all these years.

Thinking of it jogs memories. They used to talk all the time. Danny especially liked when he worked summers on the farm in high school, and sometimes his dad would signal him aside at noon and eat with him. Just him. The other men would have lunch among themselves while he and Danny would munch on burgers side by side sitting on milk crates, the sun shining on the back of their necks.

Those were some of the few moments Danny and his dad were ever alone, without his mom and his sister Kayla around. His dad would loosen up. He'd laugh. He wouldn't spout fatherly advice or quotes from the Bible.

He even told a few stories from when he was in high school that surprised Danny. His dad apparently liked pulling pranks back then. Hilarious ones. He could've gotten into a lot of trouble with the principal if he ever got caught. Those stories were a father-son secret. His mom and Kayla had no idea about them, and still don't.

Danny presses the first digit on the keypad. Then the second. His chest muscles harden. He types in the rest of the number. He lifts the phone to his face. It rings.

Ben's voice.

"Hi," Danny says.

Then neither Marsh man says anything for a while.

"I need your help, dad."

Ben tells him he knows.

"Can you help me?"

Ben tells him he can.

"Okay," Danny says. "Bye."

Ben tells him bye.

The call ends. Danny couldn't endure an exchange any longer. His whole body tremors. Not from fear. Something else. In his head he doesn't hear the voice of the real father he just spoke to, but the one of his fill-in father figure. Phil. On nights they were in their cell at Crick, chatting about nothing in particular, just passing time. He doesn't know why his mind went there. The emotions in him are complicated, a webbing of relief and regret and mental reflexes he can't name.

The hotness of the trunk intensifies. With the phone not in use, its screen goes dark, blackness encapsulating Danny once again.

The Buick travels a couple more miles. His shaking finally dissipates. He's not sure what the hell just happened inside him, but now that it's over he feels different. Lighter, but more vulnerable at the same time, like a foot with a callus scraped off, the newly exposed skin healthier but more delicate.

He's always played down the significance of the past. But how could he react in such a strong way to this two-year-old grudge with his dad if the past hardly mattered? He still believes life is about moving ahead. An idle body goes nowhere. Staring back doesn't seem to make sense.

However, in graphic-design school they taught that a point is just one spot in space. It takes two points to make a line. And without a line you have no path. To build a better path forward, maybe you have to peek behind you every now and then and look at the path you've already walked.

This moment of reflection burns off when he remembers what his mom said about the cash. His parents may have both agreed to help him, but it doesn't mean they will. Danny is due in El Paso before sunrise. How the hell will his mother and father scrape together the two hundred fifty thousand by then, on a Saturday night with all the banks closed?

Eighteen

All of Rene's experienced cops are out monitoring onramps and streets on the outskirts of town for the felons. Others are scouring the woods and abandoned buildings. The young deputy and another junior cop, Kent, a black guy a year older, were instructed to wait back at the station in case anyone called with a tip.

The hands of the aluminum-caged wall clock crawl along. The deputy is at his desk with his legs crossed, a pretzel of pale skin forming around those skimpy shorts, plugging away on paperwork a senior officer left behind. He begins whistling "Lay Down Sally" by Eric Clapton. Kent glares at him, however the deputy doesn't notice and keeps on cheeping.

Lieutenant Ramos barges through the back door. Marching toward the pot of coffee, he asks, "Anything?"

"No sir," the deputy says.

"Kent?"

"A call from Mrs. Fester on Lilly Road…" Ramos stops, gazing at him with eagerness. Kent lowers his voice as if to lower expectations when he adds, "She couldn't get her hot water to come out. I transferred her to public works."

Ramos's eyes flutter in disappointment, then he pours himself a cup of coffee. He needs some damn caffeine in his bloodstream. With these three renegades still on the loose, it's shaping up to be a late night.

"Sir?" the deputy calls out.

"What is it, Noah?" the boss asks as he tops the dark liquid with a splash of Coffee-mate creamer.

"I have a question about one of these sections." The deputy taps twice on a form on his desk.

This is the last thing Ramos feels like dealing with, however he's read enough books about leadership to know that teaching is just as essential as vision. He imagines one of his favorite gurus coming alive on a book jacket and reprimanding him about dismissing his inferior's question. So he walks over.

The deputy reaches clumsily to his side, snags the chair of an officer out combing the woods, and wheels it next to him. Ramos sits in it, much less comfortable than his own. The deputy launches into a longwinded comment on the form that's not really a question, more a laundry list of statements about it, each stated in a tone denoting a general sense of confusion.

Ramos can't help drifting, his eyes out the window on the darkening pine trees under the falling sun which stand in the municipal complex between the police office and the shed for parks and recreation (its purpose isn't to house sports equipment, but people, inside it the two desks of the two-person department's director and assistant).

"So what do you think?" the deputy asks at the completion of his speech.

Ramos, who missed the whole second half, debates offering up a bullshit answer, then remembers the jowly mug of the guru from the book jacket. What was that one quote from his last release? *Teaching is at the core of a leader's success. And at the core of teaching is listening.* Something like that. It was one of the so-called "rules." Ramos likes rules. His dad, a dirt-poor Mexican immigrant, always told him America is a structured place and if you follow rules long enough, one day you'll have a decent life here. So far the advice has been pretty accurate.

"Sorry," Ramos says. "I...I didn't catch a couple of those last things you said. I've been preoccupied. With...well..." He signals to the near-vacant office, trying to get across the concept, *This place is empty because all our people are out on assignment, and they're out on assignment because of the manhunt, and I can't focus on your form because I'm thinking about the manhunt.*

The deputy nods. He gets it. He may be goofy but he's not an idiot.

"This is a big opportunity," Ramos says, "these escapees landing in our corner of the county. Hawkins said the story is already getting play on CNN. It has a national profile because of the one guy. Zorn—"

"Professor Predator."

For an instant Ramos doesn't know what he's talking about, then figures Professor Predator is a label the media gave Dr. Philip Zorn, the rapist, twelve years ago, the name dusted off for the current news cycle.

Ramos says, "Imagine if our department, in a little nine-thousand-pop town, was the one to bring him in. All three of them. A nationally featured case. Solved by the Rene PD. Think about *that*."

The deputy glances upward, his big Adam's apple on full display. A nod. A grin.

"Where do you see yourself in five years, Noah?" Ramos asks.

"Five years...hmmm." He adjusts positions in his seat, keeping his legs crossed but swapping the role of each. "Hopefully I'd be married then. Maybe even a little tyke around...or on the way. Of course I'd need a girlfriend first." Now with a cathartic quality to his words, "To get a girlfriend I'd have to go on multiple dates with the *same* person. Getting that first date ain't too tough. But for some reason they all have some kind of appointment when I call them up and ask them on a second. My mom says I'm too nice. But that right there never made a whole lot of sense to me. Doesn't a nice lady want a nice man?"

Ramos eyeballs him over the rim of his Styrofoam cup as he sips. "I'm not talking about your personal life in five years. Your professional one."

"Oh." He scratches his chin. "Oh." A moment. "Well, a cop, of course." He shoots his boss a crinkled-face look as if puzzled he'd even ask.

"But not still a deputy then, I'm sure. Whether you stay in Rene your whole career or wind up transferring to another department, you'd rise up the ranks a lot faster if your name were attached to a case like this. That gets cracked."

The deputy offers him a slow nod in return, expressing agreement but without the excitement level commensurate with the vroom in Ramos's voice.

Likely the deputy is just thinking about catching the bad guys tonight, not his career five years down the line. Possibly that's what the rest of the force, scattered about the streets and forests of Rene, are thinking about too.

But not Ramos.

He peers at his desk across the station, at the framed photo of his wife and daughters, a bit blurry from back here, but he can still make out the three faces. An image of the three escaped convicts shines in his mind. The results of this manhunt can change his family for the better. Forever.

Unlike the deputy, in five years Ramos doesn't envision himself wearing a badge anymore (though he'd never tell it to anyone in the department). By then he'd already have his twenty-three years logged, long enough to lock in a sixty-percent-salaried pension. Then he could move on to bigger things. Sure his life has been okay as a first-generation American, but it could be better.

When he was in third grade, a teacher told him he had a "way with words, maybe a future in politics." The remark from the past resonated, sticking with him through elementary, middle, and high school, the year after graduation he worked at a Dairy Queen, all through the police academy and his career on the force, and still with him today, a year or so shy of his fortieth birthday.

In the early Nineties, a few years after the teacher, Mrs. Dumont, made the comment, a few months into John Ramos's dawn as a citizen old enough to care about the political system, he realized the encouraging words were no more than that, words. A Latino earning office in an American election was a long shot, especially one without money or connections.

However, as the years of his youth passed, and the demographics of Texas changed, the encouraging words, like an egg in a nest, went from something to just look at to something with life. Something with wings. By 2010 the population was nearly 40/60 Hispanic to non. And the growth in the open-mindedness of the non was just as staggering a change. John Ramos, the son of a valet runner and house cleaner, could actually see himself fulfilling the life goal Mrs. Dumont unintentionally cemented for him in third grade.

His career on the front lines of crime fighting would anchor his political brand. A law-and-order Latino Republican in a red state that craves law and order and contains a large Latino citizenship. Not to mention, he was good with words.

John Ramos, mayor. John Ramos, state senator. John Ramos…US senator. Politics is just as structured as anything else in America. It has its own rules. If he followed them long enough, who knew how far he could go?

He'd be doing it for himself, but more importantly, his family. All three living generations of it. Though his parents are proud of him, a seat in public office would catapult them to exultation. All those assholes his father parked cars and his mother scrubbed toilets for would become worth it, merely obstacles they needed to get over to raise their boy, their boy who'd be a big shot making big decisions for this country.

Ramos's wife, also a first-generation American of Mexican-immigrant parents, would of course love talking policy with him in bed on their pillows. As opposed to listening to him vent about perps.

And then his daughters. All the connections a politician could line up for them. The right schools. The right social circles. The right everything.

All of this goodness goes into motion the moment Ramos catches the Crick escapees. If he does, his photo would be all over America's news. The governor, a Republican, might even call him with congratulations. Maybe Ramos can plant the seed for his political pivot during that chat. Tell him he's interested in getting in that game when he's done with this one, only four years left.

Ramos has a sip of coffee. He stops daydreaming, his focus returning to his underling. While they converse, the front door opens. A man in a suit, with an uneasy expression, takes slow steps toward the counter.

"I'd like to report a robbery," he declares to the station.

Kent, the third cop, says, "Why don't you have a seat, sir?" He shifts some folders around on his desk, clearing some room for a guest.

As the man paces through the station, Ramos examines him with his detective eye, not that there's anything criminal about him, just that it's second nature after nineteen years on the job to venture into physical details when you cross someone new. The details make the detective.

His suit and shoes don't appear cheap or expensive. Standard pickups at either shop on Dixie Street selling dress clothes. Like his outfit, his looks are neither on the high end nor low, a typical, wrinkling middle-aged face atop a typical, slackening middle-aged body. His hands are a bit odd, faint dabs of paint near his cuticles, weakened after a washing yet not fully gone. The oily sheen in his hair suggests he's been sweating.

The visitor sits in a chair across Kent. With an uncapped pen propped above a fresh police-report form, Kent asks, "Name?"

"Lenny. Lenny Gant."

Ramos listens. Though he's still determined to assist the deputy, he can't help but divide some attention to this.

"When did the robbery take place, Mr. Gant?" Kent asks.

"Sometime late last night, possibly early this morning."

"Were you assaulted at all during it?"

"No, no. Nothing like that. I wasn't mugged."

"A break-in?"

The man snaps his eye contact off the officer, fixating on his lap for a moment. He points at the police report. "Is that confidential?"

"People...uh...others in the department do have access to—"

"I don't mean other cops. I mean the public." He holds up his left hand, a wedding band on it, a spot of red paint an inch above. "I care about my wife. I'd rather...what I'm about to tell you...I'd rather it not be public record, with my name attached, something she might come across in the police blotter of the local paper."

"Perpetrators don't have privacy when it comes to the public record. But reporters of crimes do. As part of this statement, you're not planning on divulging anything illegal *you* did, are you Mr. Gant?"

"I didn't do a thing wrong," he says, his tone a tad too defensive. "I'm a victim."

"Understood." Kent grins, awkwardly trying to appear disarming. "So…what was the estimated value of the stolen property?"

He folds his arms and blows out a long breath. "Five grand, I'd guess."

Kent's eyebrow rises a bit, as if the size of the number is a surprise. "Did they break into your home, office…vehicle?"

"They didn't break into anything." He keeps his right arm tucked to his chest, while unfolding the left, its hand cradling his cheek. "The…thief was…I let them into my house."

"Someone posing to be the cable guy, that sort of thing?"

"Not quite." The man's voice gets softer, as if embarrassed, when he adds, "And it wasn't a guy. It was a girl."

That same eyebrow spikes up again on Kent. "This female. This was someone you knew?"

The man's hands lower to the knees of his pleated suit pants. The overhead light hitting his head's dark, greasy hair gives it the air of the black ice that overtakes roads in colder states of the nation each winter. "I'm a painter," he says. "Landscapes mostly. I take photos around the county, paint them, then sell them. A lot online. Flea markets. Every now and then to a motel for the rooms. I don't make much. But I've always wanted to be a painter. So to me it's heaven."

Kent writes all this down.

"My wife," the man continues, "God bless her, allows me the luxury to immerse myself in my passion. She's a stewardess for Delta. I'm not ashamed to admit that job covers most of our expenses. As you can imagine, she travels a lot. I'm home alone a lot. Yesterday was no exception." He pauses, waiting for Kent and his pen to catch up. "I like painting outside on the deck. When the sun goes down, naturally, I call it a day. At night, when she's flying, I usually watch a movie or two before going to bed." He scratches a spot outside his right eye. "But she's been working a lot. And I've been watching a lot of movies. So last night I decided to change things up. I figured I'd get out of the house for a little."

"So you weren't home when the robbery took place?"

"I'll get to that."

A moment. "Go on."

"So I drive down to that sports bar on Berillt Ave."

"Ike's," Kent says with a grin of recognition.

"Ike's. Right. So I walk into Ike's. I order a Lone Star. I check the place out. Typical crowd you'd assume would be inside from the looks of the outside. Mostly men my age drinking beer and eating nachos. One group of college-aged guys. Then..." He scrapes at his right hand with the nail of his left thumb. "There was this girl." A pause. "I think I already told you I love my wife...if I didn't, know I do. I love her. And I didn't do a thing wrong. Not last night. Not ever. Not a thing. You understand?"

Kent nods.

"Now that that's clear," the man says. "There was this girl. She caught my attention. She looked...she had the sort of look that would catch any man's attention. Just a biological fact right there. Married or not doesn't have anything to do with that. She stood out. Let's just put it at that."

"Stood out," Kent says, reading aloud what he's writing.

"She's at the other end of the bar. A few of the men are talking to her. When they're done, she sort of looks around, and her eyes meet mine. She...eh...she caught me glancing in her direction you could say. She smiled. I smiled back. I waved. She said hi. I said hi. Being a gentleman, I offered to buy her a drink. She said sure. So she came and sat by me."

"Did you get her name?"

"She mentioned it. Just once. When she first sat. It was a really plain name. Nothing distinctive about it. I'd just be guessing if I told you."

"Understood."

"Her story though...*that* was distinctive. She wasn't from here. Tells me she's hitchhiking across the country. To California. Some truck driver got her this far from the last place she was at. Dropped her off before heading on a route north. So she was kinda stranded. Until she could hitch a lift out of Rene, back on her way to California. Sweet girl. She really was. I told her I had a car, but couldn't give her a ride west, not with my wife due home the next day. Also told her Rene is pretty dull at night. She probably wouldn't have much luck hitching at that hour. We had another beer. Being a gentleman, I offered her a couch for the evening. I told her she could get some sleep, then I'd drive her to a busy intersection first thing in the morning where she could try to find another trucker. She agreed."

Kent's eyebrow goes up its highest yet.

The man continues, "So I brought down a blanket and pillow. Set her up on the couch in the den. We had a few more drinks. Nothing crazy. Just some beers. Then I headed up to my room, took off the watch I'd been wearing all night, put it on my dresser, got into bed, and went to sleep. The next morning, *this* morning, I go downstairs to give her that ride to the intersection. And she's gone. It was a little sad to see her go, after no goodbye and all, but I didn't think much about it. I eat breakfast. Do my painting. Then I decide to tidy up the house some. In preparation for my wife coming home. While I'm cleaning up the bedroom, I notice my watch, just like the girl, is gone."

"I realize you don't have a name for her. But what about a description? Anything unique about the way she looked?"

"Yes, in fact. A lot. Very attractive. Like I said. Tattoo on her arm. Her hair...in her hair she had this dyed part. A purple stripe. Height was about—"

"Did you say purple stripe?" Ramos asks from across the room.

Kent and the man turn to him, both with startled expressions as if neither had any idea he was paying any attention.

"Yes," the man says. "Purple. In her hair."

"And the rest of it was black?"

He nods.

"And her eyes...blue?"

He nods.

"And the tattoo...also blue...a flower?"

He nods. The startled in his and Ken's expressions changes to amazed as Ramos makes calls like some clairvoyant cop on a sci-fi crime show.

Ramos stands. Treading toward them, he blurts, "I saw this girl. Today."

She looked nervous when he talked to her. Now he knows why. She lifted this guy's five-thousand-dollar watch.

"Where did you see her?" the man asks.

"You said she was hitchhiking?"

"To California."

Ramos stops at the corner of Kent's desk. "Did she have a problem with her Buick?"

"What Buick?"

"The big black one she drives."

No sign of recognition in the stay-at-home husband's face. Something isn't fitting here. "Hitchhiking?" Ramos mumbles to himself. Then asks the man, "You didn't notice her with a car at all?"

"The only thing she had was a suitcase."

"Huh. When I saw her, she had a car...but not a suitcase." Over nineteen years Ramos has gotten good at sniffing out little inconsistencies with cases, things other cops would miss. The details. And he's proud of himself for sharpening the ability. But this right here, a Buick and a suitcase trading places, is no little inconsistency. This is an enormity a child could see. Yet, ironically, the sheer blatantness of it makes it harder to wrap his head around than those subtleties he's faced on other cases.

Either way, something is buried in this. And he's going to dig it out.

"Noah?" he calls across the station. The deputy looks up. "Stop what you're doing. I need you to pull a vehicle-ownership report across East Texas, model years from 2005 up. Four-door, black Buick sedans."

Nineteen

Green and yellow triangular flags flap high on a string stretched between two posts along a local El Paso highway, the sinking sun behind them. Perched atop one of the posts is an arrowed sign that says "Customer Parking," atop the second a much larger sign reading "Rourke Tractors and Equipment."

The Ford King Ranch pickup truck Danny's dad owns moves along the highway fifteen miles an hour above the speed limit. It cuts into the right lane, exits at the tractor dealership, passes a promotional arrangement of six shiny John Deere models shaped into an "R" (for Rourke), then settles into a slot in the customer parking lot.

Ben and Hannah Marsh step out. A thought springs into Ben's mind of Danny as a small child. After a hard day of work in the field, Ben's back would get tight and he'd lie down in the family living room and have Danny walk on it. Little Danny used to love it. He'd laugh and tell his dad he felt like a giant on top of him.

Danny's parents enter the dealership. The receptionist, red blouse, hair of the same color but a lighter shade, clicks her mouse a couple times, then looks up. Recognition glints in her eyes. "Mr. Marsh," she says with a grin.

Ben doesn't grin back. "Is he in?"

Stroking a red hair strand, she turns around and faces the showroom, where three unoccupied salespeople wait like vultures. She rotates back to Ben and says, "He's probably still finishing up paperwork in his office. He should be out soon." She gestures toward two cheap leather sofas, a Keurig coffee machine, and a TV, all tight together. "Y'all can make yourself comfortable in the lounge in the meantime."

"I need him. Now."

"Like I said, he should only—"

"Now."

A pause. She reads his expression. Her own turns meek. "One moment Mr. Marsh." The girl stands. Head down, the freckled white of her neck exposed, she paces across the showroom. One of the on-the-prowl salespeople gazes at her with expectant eyes, as if she's looking to introduce the two up front. The eyes lose their glimmer when she walks by, continuing to a row of doors along the back wall.

She knocks on the corner office. A few seconds. She cracks the door. She peeks her head in and points toward the Marsh couple. She's talking but Ben can't make out what she's saying. Her head resurfaces. With it comes another figure, a larger figure. Male. Mid-forties. Tan suit topped with a ten-gallon hat. He's more than just chubby, less than plain fat.

"I'll be, Ben Marsh in June," he says, a white smile widening across his face toward a rosy cheek at each end. He crosses the showroom and clasps Ben's right palm with his own, then lays an enthusiastic left over Ben's knuckles. "You're a fall and winter man. I haven't sold you a darn thing in the summer-time. Delightful surprise. Really. Really."

"Caleb, my wife Hannah."

Caleb extends his thick-fingered hand and bright-toothed smile to Hannah. She offers him only a limp wave. Maintaining his grin, he slowly closes his marooned grip and tucks it into his pants pocket.

"Let's talk in your office," Ben says.

Caleb's head dips back, the wide brim of his cowboy hat circling his sloped face. "Certainly. Certainly."

He leads them through the door labeled "President/Owner," and settles in behind his desk, the Marsh couple beside each other across. Next to them is a window, a rectangle of dying daylight from it on the floor, in its center the silhouette of a cactus cast by the potted plant on the sill.

"Would you say I'm a man of my word?" Ben asks Caleb.

"Sure. Sure."

"And in the eighteen years we've been doing business together, have I ever had any trouble financially?"

"Not for a second."

Ben looks out the window for a moment. Then at his wife. Then straight ahead. "I need to ask you a favor."

Caleb, his fingers interlocked on his leather desk mat, leans forward a pinch, a hint of curiosity in his face. "Are you looking for a discount on one of the new models? I know that eight series is expensive, but—"

"I don't need a tractor."

"Better terms on a service contract for one you got?"

"What I came here for has nothing to do with tractors." Ben reaches into his back pocket and unearths a checkbook. He sets it on the desktop, then plucks a pen from a gold holder on the leather mat. "I'm here to write you a check."

Caleb analyzes Ben's face, Hannah's, then Ben's again. "You came here to write me a check...without fixing on buying anything from me?"

"That's right."

"Well." Chuckling, he glances at the checkbook, as if calling out the humor in the idea of a salesman making money without a sale.

Ben gets the joke, but his face doesn't reveal so, showing only the expression of determination it has since his arrival. "Consider this a swap of two equals. Something came up. And I need cash. Cash I'm good for, but can't access right now, not with the bank closed on the weekend. I write you a check, you give me the equivalent from your safe. If you don't have the full amount I need on hand, I'll still take whatever you got. Anything can help right now. My wife and I fell into a bind. And I'm coming to you as a friend. A friend in need of a favor."

Caleb's arms fold as his eyes roll upward in contemplation. "Huh," he says to himself. A moment passes. Another "Huh." Another moment. "How much you need?"

"A hundred eighty-two thousand dollars."

Caleb's rosy cheeks lose their hue. "That's some bind, Mr. Marsh."

"I reckon it is."

"I don't see a church-going family man like you ending up in the sort of position where he needs money of that caliber on such short notice."

"I never did either."

"Everything…" His voice hushes. "All right?"

"Hard to say at this point."

Caleb's eyes lift again in contemplation. "Huh," to himself. The fingers of his right hand tap the right arm of his armchair. "Huh." His gaze drops from the ceiling to Ben's. "As a business owner in El Paso, I have a responsibility to stay current on all the news in this great city. Same is true, to a lesser extent, across Texas. To a lesser extent across this country of ours. Economics, cultural trends, political climate. Actual climate. All of that, in one way or another, affects how I sell tractors. And parts."

Through the closed door, from somewhere in the showroom, flows a chipper hello from a saleswoman greeting a customer.

Caleb goes on, "El Paso may have a population of six hundred seventy-four thousand people, but the portion in the agricultural community, the portion you and I find ourselves in Mr. Marsh, ain't as big as some would think. Word travels fast. Though you and I never discussed it, I'm sure you were aware I was aware about the DUI business with your boy. Daniel. A shame. Though I never met him, he's made an appearance in my prayers multiple times. Being keen to this situation with your son, I was of course intrigued when I went over to the coffee machine for my after-lunch cup today, flipped to the news on the television set, and saw the name Daniel Marsh all over the screen. I can't say I wasn't equally as intrigued when I saw you walk through my front door on the very same day. You see where I'm going with this?"

"Not sure yet," Ben replies.

"This bind you got yourself into. I can't help but imagine it has something to do with what I saw on the television set today. As you know, I have three kids myself. And if they were in a situation where they were scared, alone, and needed help... financial help...I'd do exactly what I presume you two good people are doing now. I'd do whatever the hell it took to make sure they were safe. To get them what they needed. The law would take a backseat to that."

Ben squints.

"But now," Caleb says, "as much as I'd want to help, I'm not looking at this through the eyes of a parent. I'm looking at it through the eyes of a business associate. And friend." He holds up his finger. "Of course, of course...and friend." He lowers the finger. "In a situation like this a friend doesn't have the same...what's that doggone term..." A moment. "Tunnel vision. The same tunnel vision as a parent, where you're blinded to everything except the end goal, blinded to any byproducts of it."

"What do you mean...byproducts?"

"I'm sure the Texas authorities are looking into your son's whereabouts with the diligence they're known for. I'd bet some of that diligence will find its way into financial records. When the police want someone, they follow the money. You must know, one way or another, they'll monitor your accounts. As the boy's parents. Parents with means. You must?"

Ben's squint narrows.

"If the police, whether now or in the future," Caleb says, "see I cashed a six-figure check from the fugitive's father, dated the day of his escape, they're going to drag me into this. I'm no lawyer by any stretch, but I'm sure some nosey prosecutor could hit me with aiding and abetting. Let's say we make up a story. And say you gave me the money for a tractor. Maybe they wouldn't be able to prove otherwise. And maybe a criminal charge on me would never stick." Caleb exhales with force. He leans back in his chair. His fingers drum its right arm. "But like I said, word travels fast. Even a peep or two about possible money laundering would ruin my reputation. And in a good Christian community like ours, reputation is everything." A pause. "I really hope you understand."

The stares of the two men remain tethered to each other for a while. Then Ben looks away, toward the cactus on the windowsill. The initial reaction in his gut tells him to protest, commands his body not to leave the office until he has what he needs. But Ben, unfortunately, does, as Caleb hoped, understand.

He figured the exchange would be clean. A swap of equals, check money for cash money. But what he's asking for isn't equal. The other person would be made whole financially, but would also inherit a whole bag of legal woes, composed of materials from a recycled paper trail.

Ben realizes he didn't think this through, see the full picture. He was thrilled to hear his son's voice for the first time in two years and jumped at his first idea to help.

He stands. Caleb watches him, his face braced for some kind of rebuttal. But all Ben does is stick out his right hand. "Thanks for taking the time to hear me out."

A pause. Caleb's shoulders relax and he shakes the offered palm.

Ben glances at Hannah. Her lips are pressed so tight they're hidden. Her eyes, rimmed raccoonish by black circles of streaky makeup, howl an angry look at her husband, as if to ask, *You're giving up?*

After eighteen years of small talk, Ben knows Caleb is just as much a family man as him. And he knows he'd never do anything to jeopardize his reputation, and his wife's and kids' by extension. "We don't have time to waste," Ben tells Hannah, checking his watch. "Let's go back to the house. We need to reevaluate some things."

The impossible task of corralling a quarter million dollars in cash for their son by sunrise has just gotten a little more impossible.

Twenty

Danny, still in the sauna that's become the Buick's trunk, is stuck in the crouched position he's been in the last two hours. All because Phil wanted to wait for nightfall to pull over and let him out. The cramped muscles in his neck and back experience no therapeutic relief from the sauna's heat.

He feels the car coast to a stop. He hears the distant whoosh of passing vehicles. Then the nearby clinking of a driver-side door opening. Footsteps. The trunk's hatch rises, fresh air lowering to Danny. He gulps a couple mouthfuls.

Above him is a sky that's blackened since he's last seen it, extending across it shards of light from a lamppost that blend with the view of the constellations, seeming, in Danny's still-adjusting vision, like beams blasted from the stars themselves.

Amid this image is Phil's grinning face. "A job well done by our hitchhiker," he says.

Rubbing his eyes, Danny sits up. He scans his surroundings. They're at a rest stop off the highway, tucked behind a one-story brick structure for bathrooms, not visible from the road. He smells the rancid stank of a dumpster stuffed with bags of trash. Beyond it is a row of eighteen-wheelers parked along the edge of the property where the asphalt meets the woods. Two girls smoke cigarettes by a vending machine, one in fishnets, the other a pleather skirt, prostitutes he'd assume (this specific kind known as "lot lizards" he's heard).

He gets out of the trunk, leaving behind the magazine-ad sketch he set down earlier. He cracks his neck, then raises his arms to stretch his back. Phil slams the hatch, exposing a view of the Buick's rear window. Danny sees Jane. Her head, trapped behind the glass, reminds him of a fish in an aquarium, an exotic thing taken out of the wild and imprisoned in a small space.

"How is she holding up?" he asks.

"As you can imagine," Phil says with a sigh.

Danny watches her, barely visible through the tinted window. She's fidgeting in the driver's seat, rubbing her bare shoulder, peering out the window, brushing her hair back. He thinks about pieces of her life he missed these last two hours in the trunk. If they got this far, Phil must have draped himself in a heap of her personal belongings, held a loaded gun on her, and told her it wasn't yet over. A lot to digest.

His first reaction as he looks at her is emotional. His second is rational. Jane is an unknown quantity in their equation, a necessary complexity they needed to bring on in order to pass the police checkpoint. And now she's fettered to them until they let her go in El Paso. Over the drive ahead, she has the potential to demolish this entire operation. If she snags the attention of a cop, or even the wrong civilian, Mexico goes out the window and Danny goes back to prison.

"Open the trunk," he tells Phil.

"You want to go back in?"

"Just open it."

A moment. Phil does.

Danny reaches inside, pulls out Jane's suitcase, and closes the hatch. Phil gazes at him and the luggage, then paces to the driver door and knocks on the window. The simple sound startles Jane. Her back snaps into the seat, hand over her heart.

"I'm driving from here," Phil says. "Sit behind me."

She takes a second to catch her breath, then gets out. As she cracks the driver-side rear door, Danny opens the passenger-side counterpart. He climbs in, then lugs her luggage in with him. They share the backseat, the bulk of its surface, and the rug's below, overflowing with Jane's belongings.

He gives the suitcase between them a little shake and says, "I figured you'd want to put your things away." A nice gesture. She wouldn't want to keep her underwear on display for two random men for the next eight hours.

She leans forward to look at him, half her face masked by the bulky case. Even with this partial view, he can recognize resentment emanating off her. Mouth tight. The eye he can see he sees as a lidded slit, only a speck of blue at its center detectable. No appreciation in her face for his nice gesture. She's scared of him. He notices something even darker in her expression. Disgust. Come to think, why shouldn't he disgust her? From her vantage point, he's no more than an abductor.

Just as he's about to leave her with the luggage and get into the front passenger seat, he feels the car move. "Jesus," he says to himself. Phil is driving. Danny gropes for the handle of his still-open door and closes it.

They pass the brick bathrooms, the parked semi trucks, and the hookers at the vending machine, then roll onto the highway, mixing among everyday sedans and vans while carrying two of the most wanted men in the state and their hitchhiking hostage.

As the Buick distances from the rest-stop lampposts, their shine subsides. Soon the amorphous tree line beside the highway eclipses the last of the dimming, trailing rays, rendering the car reliant on only its headlights to navigate the road. The pavement on this stretch is especially smooth and the worn automobile seems to negotiate it with especial ease. It cruises up to eighty, overtaking a couple other vehicles, leaving none observable ahead of it.

The flat Texas terrain tapers toward the horizon, where the dark road seems to merge with the dark sky, giving Danny the impression they're driving off the edge of the earth. The clear air gives way to the radiance of the stars, millions of them, which appear to be waiting in embrace, ready for them to cross over the planet's cliff into their realm and encounter some promise Danny feels was made to him at one time, though he doesn't know by whom or about what.

Jane slouches in the seat, her profile hidden from Danny behind the stood-up suitcase, yet he can see her reflection in her window and notices she's staring at the stars also. He wonders if she too is thinking about some promise she can't place.

Danny bends forward, picks up a pair of her jeans, and folds them on his lap. He lays the case on its back, her face now unshielded by it, opens it, and sets the jeans in the corner. She doesn't watch him, her attention still out the window. He retrieves a blouse beneath his legs and stacks it on the denim pants. Next a cable-knit sweater, then two tank tops with one scoop of his hand.

A red Converse sneaker. Three scrunchies. The other sneaker. A Minnie Mouse tee shirt. Two interlocked sterling silver bracelets. The jewelry jingles a bit when he packs it in. She glances at the noise, then at him.

Back in Rene he didn't have the time to view her as a human being. It all happened too quickly. The police checkpoint. The second checkpoint. Phil's idea to use the hitchhiker. Something in the car about California. About a tattoo. He was too anxious to pay much attention. Then the Sig Sauer at the schoolyard. Or possibly time had nothing to do with it. Maybe he just didn't *want* to view her as a human being. It would humanize her as the victim of this inhumane undertaking he consented to.

But now, in the quiet of the night, alone in the backseat with her and all her belongings, all the scattered fragments of her, he can't help but look at her as a person. And for the first time he sees her face, actually sees it, the eyes and nose and cheeks and lips, all belonging to a life, a life which at some point saw a purpose for a Minnie Mouse tee shirt, red Converse sneakers, and the rest of this stuff, and foresaw enough future use to pack them for California. As he takes in this face for the first time, he thinks how beautiful it is.

He reminds himself he hasn't seen a girl in a year and a half. His bar for beauty might be unnaturally low right now. Then he watches her for another second. And makes up his mind. No, no it's not because of jail. No.

She asks neither of them in particular, "So what were you guys in prison for anyway?" The tone of her voice surprises

Danny. It's not panicky like he'd assume. Yet, it's still far from cheerful. Reserved, he'd say. Guarded.

"I was framed, my dear," Phil answers. "You have nothing to be afraid of. I'm not a criminal. Like I mentioned earlier, I'm a scientist."

"What sort of scientist?"

The right corner of Phil's mouth curls to a half-grin, as if delighted at the opportunity to answer. "Have you ever heard of the mind-body problem?"

"Is that like mind over matter? Like if you're hurt, you pretend you're not and it feels better?"

A chuckle. "Not quite. The body is of course considered a physical entity. We can see it, touch it, measure it. But what about the mind? What's that made of?"

"Brain tissue you mean?"

"Not the brain. That is an organ. It's part of the body. I'm referring to the *mind*, the phenomenon that *results* from the brain. Take the seat you're in for instance. It's leather. It feels a certain way on your skin. Different than cloth. The cells on your legs react to the leather as they touch it, translate their response into an electrical impulse, and send it to your brain. Once there, the electricity is directed to certain neurons. As it runs through them, a thought blossoms in your mind. In this case the thought is the *feel* of the leather seat. You perceive the sensation in your legs, though that is merely an illusion. The sensation is born inside your head. It's generated in your mind. So again, I ask, what is this thing, the mind, made of?"

Jane peeks down at her thighs, tight together in her denim skirt, the skin of her hamstrings on the beige leather.

Danny watches her wiggle her right leg across the surface for a moment.

"I'm stumped," she says.

Danny finds her curiosity in this moment oddly attractive. If any of the suburban girls he knew in high school or college were coerced at gunpoint like she was, with so much to digest, they'd be bawling and banging their head into the seats, not discussing psychology with their captor. She has a cool grace this Jane chick, one beyond her years. He wonders where it came from.

She must have been through stuff. Who knows what? But something. Maybe a few things. And developed a high threshold for suffering. Happy girls with easy lives don't pack all their possessions in a shitty suitcase and trust strangers to drive them as far from home as the bounds of the continental United States allow.

"Don't feel ashamed for being stumped," Phil tells her. "The problem has perplexed some of the world's greatest thinkers for the last four hundred years, since it's been formally debated. Nobody has been able to definitively define the mind. Some contend that mind and body are inherently different. That a thought is something magical. Immaterial, spiritual even. Can you imagine? In 2016, many acclaimed neuropsychologists still adhere to this. People who actually call themselves scientists."

"What do you believe it is then?"

"A thought is material and objective. It has *mass*. It can theoretically be measured by anyone, regardless of the head it originated in. Before my unfortunate set of circumstances led me to prison, I was making progress toward proving this.

I was on my way to resolving the mind-body argument, the greatest enigma in psychology."

She scratches her knee, slowly, the nail of her index finger gliding on and off. "How can you measure the thoughts in *my* head? How can I measure the ones in *yours*? It's impossible."

"Think of consciousness like breathing. And thoughts like air. At any given moment, as long as my respiratory system is working, I am engaged in the act of breathing. It's continuous. Air is in my lungs. And all is well. However, does that air really belong to me? Of course not. It passes through me, but it's not mine. It may look invisible, but it's made up of tiny particles, billions of which enter me in clumps when I inhale. When I complete a breath, the particles are recycled. They're constantly engaged in a complicated dance, breaking and joining each other in the atmosphere, flowing into and out of human bodies. Yet, we don't notice any of this chaos. We simply notice the steady, fluid experience of breathing. Consciousness works the same way. It feels fluid and unchanging. But it's really an erratic mishmash of particles that zip in and out of us. And these particles, just like the ones that make up air, are invisible to the eye, yet very much so physical, very much so real and measurable."

Jane is quiet for a while. Then says, "People are more than little particles bunched together. They have souls. You can't measure that."

"You'd be surprised, darling. Technology has come a long way over the last four centuries. The capacity of measuring instruments was astounding twelve years ago when I had my lab in Austin. And today's devices are far better. I'd been able to smuggle a few smaller ones into prison. The large ones, the university-grade models, are sheer marvels." He lets out a long breath. "Unfortunately, I'll never have the opportunity to work with one. No academic institution would let a well-known fugitive onto its staff, even one outside the States." His voice trails off wispily, as if expecting sympathy from her.

She doesn't give it. "I don't care how powerful some gizmo is. It still can't see a *soul*."

"Of course it can't. Nothing can. Because a soul doesn't exist." A pause. "I used machinery to study the brains of living animals, to analyze the electrical impulses in their neurons at the moment a thought was conceived. On an exponentially smaller scale than an atom. I was close to developing a quantum physics formula based on something called the double-slit experiment, which could've used my data from the animal brains to prove, beyond a doubt, that a thought isn't an emergent bit of magic. No. It's nothing more than a snapshot sum of small physical bits of nature. Mysticism has been dying a slow death since the Middle Ages. I was on the verge of hosting its funeral. The silly concept of a human soul that makes its own choices is just another illusion. Each day of our lives, we are merely acting out the physical dance nature throws our particles into."

The wind hits the windshield, the slightest trace of a whistle to it. Jane, grinning, shakes her head as if she doesn't buy Phil's hypothesis. Danny, who never heard Phil utter an opinion on psychology anything short of dazzling, is surprised to admit he doesn't buy it either.

It's probably best no university will let Phil through its doors ever again. He'd only waste his time on this fool's errand.

An anonymous life in Mexico will serve him well, force him to focus on a new undertaking, one with hopefully more promise than looking inside monkey brains for touchable thoughts, or whatever the hell he said.

Sunny Mexico. It's getting closer. Danny plans to put this whole day, and the last two years, behind him once he arrives.

He checks the burner cell phone for a message from his parents. Nothing yet. Though he understands how difficult their cash-collection task is, he has faith in them. For the first time in hours, he feels a shred of hope. Look at how far he's come. He successfully escaped a maximum-security prison, held strong through chloroform and kidnap, and dodged the police. Jane, though a bit spooked, seems relatively stable. And Monty, according to the picture messages he's been receiving, seems unscathed.

No, things today haven't played out as planned. Not even close. However, Danny believes they're finally on track to work out. Just under eight hours till El Paso. Then Mexico. Where all his problems will end. And his new life will begin.

Twenty-One

Ramos and the deputy cruise in a squad car through a neighborhood of Rene known as Golden Forest. Like the metal derricks that went up in the Thirties, Golden Forest was a product of the East Texas oil boom. Rene's population quintupled in ten years as eager workers flooded the county. Houses sprouted up in these woods to hold them, and the area was tagged "golden" as homage to the surging wages.

When the oil boom waned, the residents of Golden Forest dwindled. The ones left didn't have the money they used to. Eighty years later they still haven't caught up. Today Golden Forest is checkered with a trifecta of home types. Shitty, condemned, or for sale.

The deputy ran the vehicle report on four-door, black Buick sedans from '05 on. One entry on the list stood out. A sale three weeks ago right here in Rene.

"Don't you find it a little strange?" Ramos, at the wheel, asks.

"What?"

"This. Today. Everything."

The deputy has a sip of coffee from a blue Thermos. "It's sure been the busiest day since I've been on the force."

"Forget about the hours. Look at the *events*." Ramos comes to a stop sign, makes a full stop though no other cars are around, then picks up to his former clip. "We don't see much crime in Rene. And when we do it's spread out. A mugging here. Domestic abuse there. Shoplifting two weeks later. Now think about today. And all that's happened. We get a call from the county about three escaped prisoners this afternoon. Hear a young girl stole a five-thousand-dollar watch. Then she magically turned a suitcase into a Buick and drove it past a police checkpoint. To make it even more interesting, that Buick was last registered to a junkie Hawkins and I busted for meth possession two years ago."

Ramos is slightly out of breath after saying all that.

The deputy glances at him, then rhythmically bobs his head as if replaying the speech in it as a song. "It is pretty dang weird. You think they're all...connected somehow?"

A grin springs onto Ramos's face. A hopeful one. "I wouldn't go ahead and say that. We have no links, no common thread." He pauses for a second. Then in a gruff yet airy voice, "But you can't tell me *something* strange isn't going on."

The deputy takes a swig from the Thermos. He tucks it between his thighs, folds his arms, and stares at the glove compartment. "I don't fix to, sir."

In a minute they pull into a gravel driveway. A dozen or so feet ahead is a barn-shaped aluminum structure, "Ness Automotive" painted on its face, beneath the lettering a square opening giving view to a mechanic workstation. Nobody is inside, the cement floor covered in a black shadow, the scattered spots of grease on it even blacker.

The deputy checks his watch. "A little after nine thirty. On a weekend. I guess I'm not surprised."

"I knew the garage would be closed. Ness lives on the property. Out back." Ramos opens his door and steps out. "Come on."

The deputy follows his boss along the gravel, the crunch of their soles on the little rocks contending with the chirp of the crickets in nearby nooks of Golden Forest. They pass the large shed of a shop and see the lot behind it, a fenced-in pen of vehicles, about a dozen, a handful with prices scribbled on their windshields, the rest prepped to become scrap metal, their tires gone, front hoods and trunk hatches bent open like tabs on soda cans.

A house on a little hill sits a bit back. It's of the shitty variety. The blinds on the front window are closed. Yet the thin-barred pattern of vertical light between them ascertains someone is home. As the officers near, Ramos hears the punchy guitar and angry vocals of heavy metal.

He knocks.

A few moments. A hand grabs the blinds and peels a few slats back. An eyeball scopes them from the window for a second. The hand lets go, the blinds popping back together, a slow sway to them now.

The music cuts.

Ramos hears voices and footsteps inside. Both nervous.

A half-minute.

The door opens. Elrod Ness. Early forties. A hundred thirty pounds at nearly six feet tall. A slick of blond hair tucked under a souvenir cap from a professional motocross race.

"Evening," Ramos says.

Elrod eyes him with both recognition and suspicion. "What *you* want?"

The moment he opens his mouth, Ramos knows he's using again. The teeth.

"Throwing a little party?" the detective asks, peeking inside, noticing four men and three women, all fitting members of Elrod's social circle off appearance. One of the females holds a baby boy in her arms. She seems more anxious than the rest.

"It's Saturday night," Elrod tells Ramos. "It's a free country. And I'm a free man. So what if I'm having some fun?"

Ramos points at the coffee table, dense with empty Busch Light cans, a purple bong rising above them. "Rehab didn't take, huh?"

"I know my rights. You can't just—" Elrod coughs, pounds his chest, and continues, "You can't bust me for having that in my private home. You got no cause to waltz in here like this."

"I didn't come here to bust you."

Elrod's glassy eyes study him. Then the deputy. They pendulum between both men in a confused trance.

"I want to ask you a question," Ramos says. "Just one. Then I'll leave."

"'Bout?"

"The used-car business you run out of the garage."

"What's going on?" another voice, higher-pitched, asks. Ramos notices the lady with the baby in the doorway. She wears jeans with a bedazzled rear and a tank top with a be-dazzled front, "Miami Beach" written on it, nothing else.

Her skin is a deep red and reeks of booze, but her teeth seem fine. Alcoholic, Ramos thinks, not a junkie. A band wraps her left ring finger. Must be the wife.

She peers up at Elrod, waiting for him to answer her. When he doesn't, she turns to the policemen. "What he do wrong?" she asks, in a tone that's so genuinely disappointed it gives Ramos a tickle of delight in his stomach. He likes when crimi-nals make mistakes. Likes when they face the consequences at home. It helps keep society in order. Elrod though, at least this time, hasn't actually made a mistake.

"He didn't do anything wrong, ma'am. We came here to ask Mr. Ness a question, that's all." Ramos turns to the deputy with an outstretched hand. "You have it?"

The deputy unbuttons a shirt pocket, pulls out a folded piece of paper, and hands it to his boss. Ramos unfolds it, shows it to Elrod, and says, "We're here about a Buick like this you bought three weeks ago."

Elrod and his wife study the stock photo of a black 2009 Buick Lucerne printed out from the internet. He coughs a cou-ple times, his collarbone protruding under his thin, unhealthy skin. "I don't really remember it. I get a lot of cars coming through there."

"Mr. Ness," Ramos says in long, sarcastic syllables. "You don't remember a large Buick? From just three weeks ago?"

"Sorry."

"Well, the DMV records remember it. They said it was purchased by your lot."

Elrod looks him in the eyes. He lobs him a little fuck-you grin. "Sorry, officer."

Ramos gives him a fuck-you grin right back. This prick is lying and Ramos can't wait to painfully force the truth out of him. He has his tactics.

"What's he talking about, El?" the wife asks. She adjusts her grip on the baby, hitching it upward on her shoulder.

Ramos tells Elrod, "Seems like you started a family since the last time we crossed paths. Do the right thing for them." He folds the printout of the Buick and hands it to the deputy. "Like I said, I didn't come here to bust you. But if you keep lying to me, I'll leave here *wanting* to bust you."

Elrod glares at him.

"I know you're using," Ramos says. "And I know whenever you run out of whatever stash you got in here, you're going to buy more. And when you do, we'll jump on you. Last time you got off with rehab and a little fine. For a second offense? You're going to jail." Ramos points at the mother and child. "That's not fair to them, is it? Abandoning them like that?"

The top of the wife's red face begins sweating.

"The choice is simple," Ramos tells him. "Answer one question for me. And I get out of here. Or don't. And I have a couple of my guys follow you around until they catch you buying. I'll have another couple waiting around on your street. No sane dealer will come here for a house call with a black and white out front."

The baby starts to cry. "Shhh," the mother tells it. "Shhh." Clutching the child with one arm, she dabs the perspiration on her forehead with her free hand.

Elrod glimpses his family members, then asks Ramos, "What's this question of yours?"

"What's the name of the person you sold the Buick to?"

Elrod looks at his wife again. Then son. Then the floor. He adjusts his cap. He coughs. "I don't know if I can do that."

He seems scared. Which interests Ramos. If he sold the car to that cute little girl with the purple hair, what would he be frightened about? Why not just give up the name? No, he sold it to someone else. Someone he's afraid of.

"Sure you can tell me," Ramos says, stepping closer. He strips all attitude from his voice and addresses him almost like a friend, "This is just between us. Nobody will know you told me a thing. Nobody will know I was even here. This can never be traced back to you. I just need a name, Elrod." Of course someone can eventually trace it back to him with enough effort. If it's the wrong kind of person, Elrod may even get hurt over it. But Ramos doesn't care about that. Not if it happens to a sleazy substance abuser like this.

The baby's wailing loudens. Twenty seconds go by as Elrod sways his head in contemplation. "I don't know," is all he comes up with.

"Think about your choices. You tell me the name, nobody knows about it, and the police department becomes your friend. Or you don't tell me the name, the police department becomes your worst enemy, and you wind up in prison in under a month. I don't want it to have to go the second way, Elrod. But a crime was committed, and it's connected to that car. And I need to know who you sold it to."

His wife hits him with a stare that has the potential to break into wrath. Ramos has him cornered. The wife must know he's back on meth. She knows he'll trip up if the cops hawk over him long enough.

Elrod glances at her, then settles his eyes on the detective. "You guaranteeing me nobody will know I was the one who gave the name?"

"You have my word."

The child stops sobbing. Quiet cuts through the house, punctured only by the faint chirrups of the crickets in the surrounding forest.

Elrod takes a deep breath, then says, "Wade Lorendinski."

Twenty-Two

Danny gazes out the car window at Austin's skyline, a brightly lit geometry of steel and glass, shadow shapes of the buildings reflected as wavering hazes on Lady Bird Lake, a downtown body of water over four hundred acres in area. It's Saturday night in a party town, an army of young people buzzing around, their heads bopping in the distance.

This is Danny's first time in his state's capital. The cityscape reminds him a bit of El Paso's at home, only grander. He's next to Jane in the back, her suitcase, now packed and sealed with all her clothes, sits amid them.

"Isn't this place known for food trucks?" Jane asks Phil, who's driving. "I'm starving. Can we stop to grab something?"

"Absolutely not," Phil snaps. His voice is testy, almost like an upset kid's, a tone Danny's never heard on him before.

"I'll run out, then in," she says. "It'll take a minute. You can watch me from the street. I'll even get something for you two."

"We have a bag of food in the trunk. I'll pull over soon for it. But not in Austin. Once we're past it. We can't risk stopping in Austin, not even for a second."

"What's so dangerous about Austin?" Danny asks.

"Statistically, the likelihood someone recognizes me here is higher than anywhere in the state."

Then Danny remembers. This is where Phil taught. This is where he was prosecuted.

The annoyance in Phil's voice inches upward as he says, "When the allegations, the *false* allegations, came out against me a dozen years ago, I was turned into a figure of infamy. On a daily basis, my photo was on the local papers and local news. The media even came up with a despicable nickname. People in this city know my face. Even if it's for all the wrong reasons."

Now Danny understands why he's testy. He doesn't like it here. Not anymore, anyway. Too many memories. Danny glimpses Phil's face in the rearview mirror. His entire demeanor bears a defensive aura, an isosceles triangle of stress lines peaking upward toward the peak of his dyed hairline.

Phil has always been a model of composure. Every day in jail. Even this morning when they were escaping he hardly seemed anxious. That façade for the first time is fading. And Danny sees a person he's never met before. An insecure one.

"What was the nickname they called you?" Jane asks Phil.

No answer. The shadows of his stress lines deepen and darken.

"It was twelve years ago," Jane says, leaning forward. "Who cares? Just tell me. I'm curious. What did they—"

"You're a nosey little runaway, aren't you?" he fires.

A moment. She sinks back into her seat. "Christ. I was just curious. If you're going to make me sit here and starve at least you can tell me—"

"Would you just shut up already?" he yells, a fleck of spit launching from his mouth, landing on the steering wheel.

"Hey, don't talk to her like that," Danny says.

Phil spins his head over his right shoulder. The tide of tension dammed up in his forehead has broken through whatever barriers he'd been using to mentally keep it at bay. His face is now a storm of pure anger, accompanied by veins bulging on his neck.

He holds an accusatory stare on his former cellmate for a couple seconds, then turns back to the road. "I see what's going on here..."

"Think about all we asked *her* to do today," Danny says. "And she can't even ask you a question without you screaming at her to shut up?"

"I know *exactly* what's going on here. You've grown tender on our hitchhiker here, haven't you?"

Danny feels the warmth of embarrassment reddening his face. "I just think she's done a lot for us, and we should appreciate that a little."

"I think you wanted to prove something to her," Phil says with a hiss. He seems like he needs an outlet for the stress this city is causing him, and he's setting his sights on making it Danny. "You wanted to show her your masculine side. Let her know you're not afraid to stand up to something. Did you feel your pathetic gimmick would work? Berating me in front of her? She can see through your tricks. They don't sexually excite her. So stop with the gimmicks before you make a fool of yourself."

"It wasn't...it wasn't a calculated thought. You were being an asshole, and I called you out. Just show her some respect, okay?"

"So it's about respect then? Ah. How do you expect me to believe you fret over the level of respect I show this girl you hardly know, while you don't even respect your own flesh and blood?"

"What the hell does that mean?" Danny asks, genuinely dumfounded.

"Why don't you tell our little runaway what you told me in our cell that one Thursday evening in August of 2015 when we were discussing your childhood? Tell her."

"Relax," Danny says, hoping Phil doesn't say what he predicts he will.

"When he was four, Daniel's mother had a miscarriage. Another when he was six. She was able to have a child before him, his older sister Kayla, but not after. He told me he had more nightmares about it than anything else growing up. While inside his healthy, young mother, he made her barren. He—"

"Be quiet," Danny shouts.

Phil keeps going, "You created the conditions that killed those helpless babies four and six years later. Your siblings. Your own flesh and blood. Was it a coincidence? Or was there something inside your fetus brain that made you do it on *purpose*? To assure no children could come after you, to selfishly hog up as much of mother's attention as you could." Phil turns from the road, facing Danny face to face, no mirror-glass intermediary. "Isn't that right, Daniel? You—"

Thrupppt. A loud noise bangs its way into the car, which swerves left. Phil clamps the steering wheel and refocuses on the road.

Jane shrieks as the Buick dips over the dividing line into oncoming traffic.

Phil whips the wheel right, straightening out the vehicle just before a horn-blaring Mack truck whacks into it.

Danny, his heart slamming, looks out the front and side windows. They're back in their lane, out of harm's way. He takes a few deep breaths. He lets the moment settle. Holy shit. What just happened? There was a noise. They must've run something over, knocking the car off course. First the undeserved lashing from Phil, then a near crash with a semi. Danny has a headache from processing so much negative stimulation in such a short time. A few more deep breaths.

His heartbeat finally mellows. However, his temples are on fire. How could Phil drag such a private piece of information into a bickering match? Danny told him so many personal things in jail. He spoke to him like a patient on a therapist's couch. And now he's using them against him for spite? Just because he needs an outlet for his stress about Austin? This isn't the Phil he knows.

Danny tries not to let Phil's psychoanalytical rant get to him. He doesn't believe what Phil said, anyway. He'd never kill a sibling.

Or would he?

He was so young. He of course doesn't remember his time in the womb. He can't recall *not* doing what Phil said. Could it be possible he was made with something in his "fetus brain," as Phil put it, that could make him do such a horrible thing? Does he have evil in him? No, Danny thinks. No.

But how could he be certain?

Dammit, he's letting it get to him. This is what Phil want-ed. Stop, Danny. Just stop. Think about something else. So he does. He pictures a beach in Mexico. He pictures the sand around his feet. He pictures a place where all his problems will be gone.

The car rolls along. However, something seems wrong. They're going slower than they were. And no longer moving smoothly, the Buick's trajectory buckled, its left side jerking up and down with a clanking sound.

On the farm, Danny used to see this sort of lopsided wob-bling on the tractors every now and then. When they got a flat tire. Which is what he's positive this is.

"Pull over," he urges.

Ignoring him, Phil hits the accelerator. The increase in speed doesn't correct the car's motion, only makes its flaws more pronounced.

"We have a flat," Danny states.

Phil keeps going. "We can't stop. Not here. Not *Austin*."

Danny grips the headrest of the empty passenger seat for support and pulls himself forward, his mouth inches from Phil's ear. "You keep driving on metal like this, you're going to grind the wheel to a nub, then we'll be *stuck* in Austin. You want that?"

Phil presses on, yet his expression tells Danny he indeed does not want that.

"I'm sure there's a spare and a kit in the back," Danny says. "I know how to change a tire."

Danny assumes Phil's big brain is crunching a bunch of options and outcomes. In five seconds Phil arrives at the same conclusion as him, veering off the main road and parking on a side street, where Danny can have space to work. Phil's eyes anxiously scan the drove of nightlife pedestrians, closer now than they were before.

"Nobody can see me," he tells Danny. "Nobody. Do this quickly."

"Unlock the trunk," Danny says, his voice lit with urgency. He opens his door and dashes toward the back of the car. A few people around his age walk by with Saturday-night smiles, the patter of their footsteps and chatter of their voices melting into the sound of live country music thumping from a rooftop bar a block behind.

Danny throws open the trunk. He searches for the spare tire well, soon locating it. Sure enough, a tire, jack, and wrench are waiting for him. Their sight sends an optimistic flicker through his flittering heart.

Just to confirm his presumption, he glimpses the wheels on the vehicle's left side. As expected, a flat, in the front, specks of glass fleck the sack of deflated rubber wrapping the wheel, a slight shimmer to them in the shine of the overhead streetlamp. Danny guesses when Phil took his eyes off the road during their argument he hit a beer bottle that'd rolled into the street, which the Lucerne's aging tire couldn't best.

"Okay, okay," Danny says to himself, wiggling his fingers at his sides. He's done this before. On the farm with his dad. But never on a consumer automobile.

His nerves high, his thoughts don't fluidly move through his head, but flash on and off, like movie sub-titles at a cranked-up pace.

What first, what first? Raise it. The jack. He clasps the contraption. As he turns toward the flat, a splash of blue light spins across the metal interior of the overhead trunk hatch, hooding Danny in its glow for a split-second till it disappears. Before his mind can fully process the image, it duplicates, red swapped for blue this time. Now blue. Red again. Now blue. Red again. Now he understands.

The flanks of muscle from his armpits to his waist constrict, sending cords of pain down both hamstrings, while his grip loosens, the jack toppling from his hand and plopping into the trunk.

Police.

He remains hunched in the trunk, his heavy breath just as audible in this cocoon as the squad-car lights are visible. He doesn't want to look back.

"Excuse me," a voice behind him says.

The sub-titles now move through his mind at super speed. Should he run? They'd catch him if he did. Austin probably has over a thousand cops, each only a radio call away from each other. Jump back in the car and tell Phil to floor it? No, the flat, they couldn't beat anyone in a chase.

"Excuse me," the voice behind him says again, with more force.

Danny reasons his only valid option is to face this. Whatever it is. And play it from there. He slowly rotates his shoulders.

A muscular man in an Austin PD uniform stands beside his cruiser about a dozen feet from Danny. His whirling red-and-blue rays behind his head overpower it with so much light they swallow it, the man appearing decapitated.

Squinting, Danny waits for this headless body to address him.

Nothing for ten seconds.

Then the cop asks, "A flat?"

"Yes sir." The sub-titles in his brain slow, the words clearer now. This isn't one of the manhunters on their trail. If it were, he wouldn't ask about a flat tire. Danny would be pressed to the pavement in cuffs by now. This is just a local cop who noticed a broken-down vehicle in his jurisdiction. This guy doesn't know who Danny is.

"Going to a bar?" the officer asks.

Though the cop didn't yet pick Danny out as a fugitive, it doesn't mean he won't make the connection soon. Austin is a bit far from Crick, so it's unlikely the authorities would surmise they're here and have officers on close watch like they were in Rene. However, Danny knows his face was on the local news in the Piney Woods this afternoon, and is sure the story spread through the state by now. Even if this cop wasn't explicitly told to patrol Austin for people of Danny's description, there's still a chance he could've seen his photo on TV.

The policeman takes slow strides forward, his head distancing from the cruiser lights, its details emerging. He has soft facial features, contradictions to his iron-muscled body. A rectangle of a moustache rests between his nose and lip. He gets a close look at Danny, who maintains an external coolness, though his insides are thrashing.

"I asked you about a bar," the cop says.

A puff of tension releases from Danny's neck. This is good. The officer saw him up close and hasn't cuffed him. Possibly it's the shaved head. Possibly this guy didn't catch the TV news today. Who knows? Who cares? He got a good look at him and doesn't recognize him.

"Actually on our way to San Antonio," Danny says, the first city that comes to mind.

The officer takes a step to his left and checks out the silhouettes of the other two passengers in the vehicle, both their backs to him. Danny's sense of calm shatters when he remembers what Phil said. People in this city may not know Danny's face, but they damn well know Phil's.

Word of Phil's escape is surely frothing through town. About forty-five years old, this cop was more than likely on the force twelve years ago when Phil was Austin's top public enemy. Potentially even worked the case. He'd notice Phil the second he got a partial look at his face. He'd be a local hero recapturing Professor Predator. And Danny would go down with him.

Trying to divert the cop's attention away from the passengers and back to him, Danny says, "Yeah, family reunion in San Antonio. Heading down with my dad and my girlfriend. Ran over a beer bottle I think."

The officer's gaze returns to Danny. "You been drinking tonight, young man?"

"No sir, not a sip."

The cop chews gum as he peers at Danny, the left edge of his moustache lifting every second or so. "My wife actually used to have a LaCrosse."

"Huh?"

"You have a Lucerne. She used to drive a LaCrosse. Buicks."

"Oh," Danny says, forcing a fake chuckle. "Of course, yes. My dad considered the LaCrosse before going with his La... Lu...Lucerne."

"I used to do some work on it for her. I know these things pretty well. Let me have a look at your flat." The officer takes a step forward.

Danny's hands shoot up in protest and his voice shoots out, "No," in a tone a tad antsier than he intended. He tells himself to cool down, before adding, "I can attach the spare myself. I appreciate the gesture though, sir."

The busted tire is on the front of the driver side. Right next to Phil. Even with the window tints, you could make a face out if you're close. Danny has to keep him back.

"It's more than just a gesture," the cop says, any friendliness now out of his voice, which has taken on an official, man-of-the-law quality. "I don't know what you ran over. Maybe it was a beer bottle. Maybe it was something bigger. You can have debris trapped under your car. A spare won't fix that. The debris could cause all kinds of erratic behavior with the vehicle. It'd be a safety hazard letting it back on my streets like that. Let me have a look."

This man is determined. No use in trying to stop his inspection. However, there may be use in trying to block his view.

"No problem, sir," Danny says, then cuts toward the front of the car. He leans against Phil's window, covering as much of the surface he can, then points at the problem tire. "It's this one right here."

The officer paces over. He reaches to his belt, unclips a Maglite, and drops to his knees by the head of the car. He flips the flashlight on, the edges of its white gleam mixing with his still-spinning blues and reds.

Danny can feel his heart beating through his back, its pumps punching the window glass he leans on.

The cop examines the tire. With his thumb and index finger, he unsnarls a jagged triangle of glass lodged in the rubber. He analyzes it. "Yup. Looks like a beer bottle."

Danny's knotted face ekes out a grin.

The cop flicks the glass to the asphalt, then bends lower, angling his head under the vehicle. He floods the undercarriage with his Maglite beam.

Two seconds. Five seconds. Danny's heart hiccups. Seven seconds.

The officer's head reappears from beneath the Buick. His voice is friendly again as he says, "Looks clean, you should be good to go."

"Great. Thanks for checking."

The cop turns off the flashlight and, with a light groan, stands. "Enjoy the reunion in San Antonio. If you can't get that spare on, give us a call at the station and we'll send out a tow service."

"Definitely. Will do."

The officer smiles a departing smile and Danny thinks he's going to go, thinks that this is over. However, something nabs the man's attention. Over Danny's shoulder. The driver's window. His body isn't covering all of it. Some of Phil is visible.

Danny's heart starts sputtering again. The cop points the Maglite to the right of Danny's throat. He turns it back on, a laser of brightness shooting into the Buick.

Numbness all over Danny's face. He watches the policeman, waiting for him to drop the flashlight and pull his gun. All the sounds of the city seem to hush, the passing cars and pounding music and promenading bar hoppers. Danny's world goes quiet other than a soft ringing in his ears.

"Now that's what I call a smart man," the cop says. He's peeking into the window.

Danny turns around and looks through the glass. Phil has the driver's seat reclined all the way. His blazer is off, draped over his head and chest like a blanket. He looks like he's taking a nap.

The cop waves goodbye and begins walking back to his car. He chuckles and says over his shoulder, "Fella gets a flat tire while he's driving, makes his son do all the work to change it, and takes a snooze during the whole thing to boot. Your old man is a wily one."

A moment. "I think you might be right about that."

Twenty-Three

The glow from Lieutenant Ramos's computer screen lights up his near and eager face and flows onto the deputy and Kent, stooped over the boss's shoulders.

They all gaze at an online police-records library, a program that only runs on Internet Explorer, its graphics from a late-Nineties clipart gallery. Ramos, who's filtered the site's geographic reach to a three-county cluster, types "Wade Lorendinski" into the search box and clicks a green button marked "GO."

Loading...

One result. "Lorendinski, Wade III – DOB February 09, 1973."

Ramos selects it.

Loading...

It says he lives in Rene. It also says he has a criminal record dating back to 1992. Ramos licks his lips. He opens the crime history.

Loading...

A mug shot of Wade stares back at the three officers. He has a fat lip and black eye, as if the photo was taken after he was arrested for a dust-up. His expression is cocky versus conquered, his eyes suggesting, *You should see the other guy.*

To the right of the picture are listed his imposing physical proportions and identifying physical marks. Beneath them his arrest record.

Ramos recites tidbits to the other two as he reads. "Ninety-two. Possession of a controlled substance with intent to sell." A moment. "Ninety-six. Armed robbery. Did five years." He scrolls down the page. "Impersonation of a police officer in 2003. Coupled with assault." He scans an accompanying blurb in the "Description" column. "Says here he did this in connection with the Lost Circle biker club. A gang he's allegedly the leader of, known to draw members mostly from the Aryan Brotherhood. Main business, smuggling drugs into the US from Mexican cartels, and distributing them through East Texas."

"Jesus Christ," Kent says, his voice slow and soft, yet deep. "This is a bad dude."

This is the sort of dude Ramos despises. The sort responsible for all that's ugly in this beautiful country. A lifelong rule breaker. A disease. His file shows he's not married, no kids, no known family. Nothing to balance him out and keep him in check. Pure id. These dudes not only evoke hatred in Ramos, but fright.

Ramos lets go of the mouse. He winces. The younger officers watch their boss situate his fist on his cheek and angle his eyes toward the heavens, a sort of Socratic pose. Thinking aloud, Ramos says, "Elrod Ness told us he sold Lorendinski the Buick two days ago. So, the leader of a drug-smuggling gang buys a car on Thursday, then on Saturday a pretty little girl with a stolen watch is in it driving to Houston." Then, almost but not actually rhetorically, "How do you see that fit?"

Over ten seconds go by.

"Don't forget about the disappearing suitcase," the deputy adds.

"You think she stole the car from this Lorendinski fellow?" Kent asks.

"Why wouldn't he report it?" Ramos asks back.

Kent gestures at the screen. "Guys like that don't like going through the cops. Street-justice types."

True. Ramos gives him a nod of agreement.

"We know she clipped the watch," Kent adds. "She's obviously capable of theft. Who's to say she wouldn't boost a car?"

Nobody is saying that. But still, this doesn't *feel* right to Ramos. Pawing a little watch off a dresser while that stay-at-home husband was sleeping is one thing...but a Buick? Either she needed to hotwire it somehow or swipe the keys off Lorendinski, the big and grizzly gangbanger. By her appearance and demeanor, she didn't seem capable of either.

"I got a good look at her," Ramos says. "Young, more anxious than hardened. Didn't come off like a seasoned criminal. A troubled girl maybe. But not a professional thief. I don't think she stole the car."

A moment.

"Maybe he's screwing her," Kent suggests. "Gave it to her as a gift. If he's running drugs for the cartels, I bet he's got plenty of extra cash."

"Wouldn't rule that out," Ramos says, his voice gaining some buoyancy. He stands and paces, his mind racing. The slap of his shoes echoes through the quiet station. Still, it doesn't *feel* right.

His tone sinks as he adds, "If he's screwing her, why didn't she take him with her, though? She said she was driving to Houston to visit some friends. It was a social trip. If she's close enough to him that he bought her a frigging car, wouldn't you think she'd bring him on the trip? Especially if it was just two days after he gave it to her? Also, the stay-at-home husband said she was just passing through town, right? Not like she was a local Lorendinski had gotten to know and struck up a relationship with." He stops pacing. "Besides, she was out of his league."

Kent lets out a convoluted noise, a groan with a sigh mixed in. Then silence.

Ramos says, "We can stand around debating it all night. At this point I'm more concerned with where she is in that car *now*, than how she got it in the first place. Hopefully we hear word from Houston on that APB you put out on the Buick."

"I'm on standby, boss."

The boys in Houston would arrest her. But Ramos would get credit for the catch. More importantly, he'd get a chance to question the girl. She likely knows things he'd want to know. Something strange has been going on in this typically un-eventful community today. Is it just a coincidence it's the same day three escaped convicts are on the lam in the area? Possibly. But Ramos's detective instincts tell him otherwise.

Does this out-own-town girl know the fugitives? Was she here because of them? Did she steal the watch for them so they could sell it for food, supplies, fake IDs, whatever else? When they catch her in Houston he'll get it out of her if it's there. He has his tactics.

Then a stick of dynamite goes off in his mind that explodes his chain of thought. How could he be so fucking stupid?

"If she just stole a five-thousand-dollar watch," he says, "she would've given me a phony destination. Son of a bitch. She's not in Houston."

Kent huffs.

Ramos goes on, "She can be almost anywhere in Texas by now. Put out an APB for a 2009 black Buick Lucerne across the whole state."

"Don't you think that's a little aggressive, sir? It's not like she murdered someone."

"I have a feeling something bigger is going on here than a stolen watch."

"The car is a generic model in a generic color. And with a net as wide as the state, I don't know how much urgency other departments will have. Especially for a watch. *But...*I'll of course call it in. Maybe we'll get lucky."

"The car might be generic, but a girl with purple hair and a blue rose tattooed on her arm isn't. Make sure they look out for someone with that description inside."

"I'm on it." Kent scurries off.

Ramos, hands on his hips, takes a deep breath. A little garden snake of nerves and excitement wriggles in his stomach.

"Hey lieutenant," the deputy says, in that annoying voice he uses when he needs something.

Not now, Ramos thinks. Then he envisions the face of the guru from the book jacket. *A good leader has patience.* Ramos turns to his underling.

The deputy is seated at Ramos's desk, at his computer. He's scrolled down to the bottom of Wade Lorendinski's criminal-record page. "You might want to see this, sir."

Ramos walks over.

"Check out his most recent arrest," the deputy says, point-ing at the screen. "Larceny. He did two years in prison for it. 2006 to 2008. Look where he served them."

Ramos inches closer to the computer. Above the deputy's fingertip, in blue text, he sees it. The Thurgood L. Crick Unit.

"That's where the three men escaped from this morn-ing," the deputy says, as if Ramos didn't already make the connection.

He made the connection. And now that garden snake of nerves and excitement in his stomach is a boa constrictor.

The deputy goes on, "Marsh and Montgomery, the younger ones, they didn't get to Crick until a few years af-ter this Lorendinski character was gone. But Zorn...Professor Predator...he was there before. Lorendinski's sentence crossed over with his. You think they knew each other?"

Ramos is still for a bit. "I'm not sure, Noah." He snags his squad-car keys off his desk. "But we're going to find out."

Twenty-Four

Monty sits in darkness. Wade doesn't have the decency to keep the cellar lights on for him.

A stack of horizontal moonlight stripes from the blinds provides the only visibility. A thin beam crosses over the metal shackles on Monty's ankles, another his shins, another his pulled-back and cuffed arms, another the dry blood spots on his tee shirt, and a final the lump by his eyebrow the blood spilt from.

Without air conditioning or a fan in the basement, the heat eats at his skin, balls of moisture nearly marble-sized seeping from his shaved scalp.

Brightness. His tired eyes blink. Footsteps.

Wade descends the staircase, a burner cell phone in one hand, a ring of padlock keys the other. He unlocks the chains around Monty's wrists, the length of metal links limply dropping to a motionless mass on the concrete like a snake suddenly killed in the wild.

"Eleven," Wade says.

Monty displays five fingers on his left hand, five his right, and closes one eye, indicating eleven PM. Wade snaps a photo with his phone. He takes a few seconds to send it to Danny's.

"I gotta piss," Monty says, the gag removed from his mouth a few hours ago once permitted to eat.

Wade studies him, suspicion in his gaze.

"I'm serious, man," Monty adds. "I haven't took a leak since Crick last night."

A moment. Wade pushes his leather vest to the side, revealing a pistol holstered beneath his left armpit. "Fine. But don't get any ideas."

Monty chuckles and shakes his head. "Hell, I don't think I could take you even if you didn't have the gun. I ain't gonna do nothing but piss and come back down here."

Wade huffs, the puff of air pushed through his nose with the gravelly quality of a smoker's voice. He goes to a knee and undoes the ankle restraints, then nods toward the cellar door, gesturing Monty to go first.

Following him up the steps, Wade keeps his right hand over his sternum, close to the gun. Monty doesn't move with his typical energetic gait. The barbed-wire gash behind his knee pushes back on him.

After a pained climb he emerges in the kitchen, the first time in hours he's seen anything but the darkness of unconsciousness or the baseness in the basement. His gaze sweeps over the night-swept trees framed in the window above the sink, the unrefrigerated condiments on the counter, and the faux-wood cabinetry.

"Left," Wade says.

Monty turns into the den, toward a half-closed door along its back wall. Wade shifts his attention to the TV, on it a top-ten segment of moments gone wrong at monster-truck rallies. They're up to #6. He reaches down to the leather couch, the upholstery ripped in a few places, the foamy yellow guts poking out, and digs the remote control up between two cushions. He clicks the channel-down button a few times, stopping on the local news. "Crick Prison Escape: The Latest" is across the screen's bottom in beveled blue letters.

Monty goes through the bathroom doorway. Soon a furious stream of urine strikes the toilet, the sound gurgling through to the den. He hears Wade turn up the TV volume. When Monty is done, he washes his hands and slurps water from the faucet.

He steps out, greeted by his own face on the television, Danny's and Phil's beside it. He wipes water from his chin with the back of his hand, then takes a couple steps forward. He and Wade, side by side, watch the report.

The newscaster, a blonde in her forties who looks ten years younger, explains how the police have some theories, though nothing is firm quite yet. She goes on to urge all citizens in the county to lock their doors and keep household firearms at arm's length.

Smirking, Wade points at Monty's name, written under his photo on the screen. "Is that really your name? Monty Montgomery?"

"It's what's on all my documents, official ones, like the ones I had when I was in court, so yeah, I guess it's my real name, in the eyes of the state, if that's what you mean."

"I mean, is that what your mother named you?"

"I think she wanted to call me Jerome when I was born. I don't know if it ever went on anything. I never seen my birth certificate. Probably don't even exist at this point. But see my dad, his last name was Montgomery. I never knew him, but supposedly everyone on the block would call him Monty. So when I was born, way I heard it, when my moms took me back home from the hospital, everyone in the neighborhood just called me Little Monty. When I got older, with my dad out of town, ain't no more 'Little.' I was just Monty. So that just kinda became my first name."

Wade presses a derisive stare on him for a few seconds, chuckles with even more derision, then turns back to the TV.

The newswoman segues into a spotlight on Phil. A picture pops onto the screen of him in prisoner attire in a courtroom, sitting beside three defense attorneys in bespoke suits. In the 2004 photo Phil sports a thick head of blond hair without any gray, circular specs as opposed to today's rectangular variety, and a vitality to the complexion of his chipmunk cheeks, as if prior to jail food he ate very nutritiously.

"Phil Zorn," the reporter says, "made national headlines in 2004 when he, a world-renowned professor, was tied to rape allegations in Austin. The case received notoriety not just because of Zorn's high profile in the academic community, but because of the sheer oddness of it. Unlike most victims of sexual assault, who are often left tattered and discarded in the wake of their attacker, this young lady reported waking up in a park one morning in November 2003, nestled into a brand-new sleeping bag she never saw before, her head propped up on a pillow. No signs of physical trauma were found on her face or limbs. Though her memory of the night, which she spent at a Sixth Street bar, was nearly all absent, she recalled bits and pieces of a face, and bits and pieces of an attack. Watching surveillance footage from the bar with investigators, she pointed out a patron she felt was a match. That man was Zorn, then thirty-five. A subsequent DNA test officially linked him to fluids uncovered on the victim."

Monty's lips tighten. He takes a step closer to the television.

The newswoman goes on, "Stranger, after the incident was reported, five other Austin-area females independently came forward, recounting similar experiences of waking up in a park in a sleeping bag with a pillow. Unlike the initial victim, the other five had no memory at all of the night before. No *memory* of an attack. Yet, when they woke up, they sensed they'd been violated. As for the five who came forward later on, due to time lapse, genetic tests weren't feasible. Though Zorn was never officially linked to any of these other accusers, the similarities of their stories to the initial victim's are eerily apparent. According to authorities, all women were of similar age and physical description. All were devout Christians. Their memory loss was symptomatic of the chemicals found in the system of the initial victim, chloroform and diazepam…"

Monty's eyes bulge. "What?" he screams, throwing up his hands. "Ohhhh, whaaaaat?" He lowers his palms to the back of his head.

Wade gives him a glance.

"Chloroform and diazepam," Monty says. "That's the shit you and that other biker used on Danny and me at the water park. Phil said it in the basement before. I'm sure he was the one who told you what chemicals to mix. I ain't never forget no weird word like diazepam."

"Enough TV for you." Wade grasps Monty's bicep. "Back downstairs. Come on."

Monty doesn't even notice the hand, his eyes stuck to the television. "I knew it," he mutters to himself. "I knew his story was bullshit." He looks at Wade. "Framed my ass. He really did rape those girls."

Wade clicks the power button on the remote, the screen flashing then blackening. "Downstairs." Wade marches into the kitchen pulling the smaller, though not small, man with him.

"I knew it, yo," Monty says under his breath. "That motherfucker."

Wade stuffs him through the cellar doorway.

Twenty-Five

Danny cranks the jack, the Buick ascending as his hand spins. After the encounter with the Austin officer, Phil forced the busted car a few more blocks into a quieter nook of the city, out of view from pesky pedestrians and poking policemen. They're parked in an alley behind a closed arts and crafts store, enclosed in the foliage of one of Austin's many parks.

The punctured tire rises a bit more, now about an inch of space between it and the asphalt. Should be enough, Danny deems. He sits cross-legged in front of the wheel well, where his wrench waits for him, the small floodlight bolted to the rear of the craft store illuminating the tool and the rest of his workspace.

The other two riders cleared out of the car before he lifted it. Phil, paranoid about standing outdoors in Austin in any sort of light, is a short distance away in the canopying shadows of the park, completely out of sight to passersby. Jane leans against the brick wall of the store's backside, drinking a can of Coke and munching on a bag of Doritos from the stash in the trunk.

Though Phil is removed from the other two, he watches them, especially Jane. Not much of him is visible in the dark park, yet the metal temples of his eyeglasses sporadically glint in the headlights of passing cars.

Danny fits the wrench around one of the wheel's five lug nuts and begins turning. He thinks about all those young people he saw on the street before. Most looked a few years out of college. He imagines a typical life of theirs. Living in a cool city, working weekdays on a progressing career, catching Longhorn football games on weekend afternoons, partying on weekend nights with friends, dating, striking a claim in the adult world, carving out a slice of the American dream.

That could've been him. Austin has the most booming technology sector in the state. He may have ended up at a graphic-design job in one of those office buildings overlooking Lady Bird Lake.

But no. Not now. Not ever.

He loosens the first lug nut, then spins it free with his fingers and sets it aside the jack. As he attaches the wrench to the second, he ponders what in fact will become of his future. The last nine months he's been so hell-bent on simply getting to Mexico he hasn't thought much about life once he gets there.

If the tech scene south of the border isn't great, maybe he can freelance online. He can create a profile on a graphic-design job board (under a fake name of course) and bid for contracts. It sure wouldn't be like working at Amogo Studios or one of those majestic Austin complexes on the water. But what other options does he have? Staying in America means staying in prison. And he can't take any more of that tapeworm inside him.

He removes the second lug nut. Starting on the third, he notices Jane walking past him. She tosses her crumpled Doritos bag in a garbage can at the edge of the park. Then approaches the Buick. She stares down at him. Sips her Coke. He glances up at her, then back at the tire and tools and task at hand.

"How's it going with that?" she asks.

"Getting there."

A few moments.

"Thanks," she says. He chucks her a confused look. "For before. In the car. Standing up for me."

He places the third fastener on the pavement. "Oh." Now to the fourth.

She peeks over her shoulder, gauging the position of Phil, who's out of ear range. "You seem...different...than the other guy. He gives me the fucking creeps. Hard to explain. Feminine intuition I guess."

"We are different."

She shakes the soda in her can, the bubbles emitting a light fizz. "Can you believe all that crazy shit he said in the car about the thoughts in your head having weight?"

"Didn't make much sense to me either."

"Don't you find it a little...off-putting? I've seen people like him on Netflix documentaries. They think science can explain everything in the universe. It freaks me out. I don't know. When people feel they have the right to play God."

He groups the fourth lug nut with the others. "What do you mean, play God?"

She leans her thin body against the front of the car, grace-fully, making sure not to knock loose the jack. Her blue eyes narrow in thought. "People like him, real science freaks, they love making fun of the religious for following the Bible. They say it's ridiculous to believe in the God from those stories, you know, because he's never shown himself, never came down from above to actually validate any of it. But the science freaks do the same sort of thing, just in a different way." She holds up a palm. "Now, don't get me wrong. I'm no believer in the Bible myself. Obviously all of it's made up. By human beings. But if a human being like him..." She nods toward the woods, toward Phil. "If he can sit here and declare the world works like this, and the mind works like this, and he has no facts from above, just the so-called *facts* from his own human world, doesn't that make him no better than the ones who wrote the Bible, or the ones who believe its stories? In either case, nothing superior came down to let us know if someone was right or wrong. It's just...people down here. It's always been that way. Just people."

He sits still, his wrist resting on his right knee, wrench dangling from his grip. He thinks about this for a while.

"Thirsty?" she asks.

"Umm," he says, snapping from his contemplative daze. "Sure."

She goes to the popped trunk and grabs him a Coke. He cracks it and has a sip. As it streams down his throat he realizes it's the first drink he's had since they've been on the road. That tastes good. Damn good. It's warm, but all the sweetness is still there, all the little bubbles tickling the center of his tongue. The Coke brings him back to his days as a kid going to the movies in El Paso with his older sister Kayla when she first got her driver's license. She'd let him order the extra-large soda-popcorn combo, something his mom never permitted.

"He was different, you know," Danny says. "In prison. Never snapped at me. Never snapped at anyone. Generous. Modest. In our bunk he was only ever concerned with my problems. Never had the urge to talk much about his own past. Who knows what he really thinks of himself, if he thinks he's a God? Frankly I don't care. Once I get on my feet in Mexico, I'm sure I'll never see him again."

Jane sits next to him, her back against the driver door, bare legs stretched from her skirt across the gravelly pavement. She catches his gaze as he sips his Coke. She brushes her purple-streaked hair from her face and grins.

He hasn't seen that look on the face of a girl in a year and a half. But its type is unmistakable. A warm shudder scuttles through his heart. She must feel a little something around him.

Not a full-on crush. He's not saying that. Not in the extreme conditions she met him. He scared and disgusted her most of the car ride. He supposes a crush can't bloom in that environment, just like certain crops on his dad's farm can't grow in the winter. Besides, she hardly knows him. But something. That look says something. And he's sure his face has been giving her a similar one back.

"You don't come off like a criminal," she says.

He wipes some sweat from his brow with Wade's billowy tee shirt. "I don't really know what I am. Technically, I *am* a criminal. I committed my crime. I wasn't framed or falsely accused." He stares at the pavement. "But am I a bad guy? I don't know. I've thought about that a lot. I don't know. I made a bad decision one night. I was neglectful. It was nobody's fault but mine. So…maybe…I'm not sure."

She studies what traces of his down-angled face she can see. The muscles around his left eye twitch. "You don't need to tell me what you did to end up in jail," she says. "But whatever it is, I gotta say…it doesn't seem like you're over it."

He looks up. "I just want to get to Mexico and put it all behind me."

She tilts her chin and bats her eyes, a look that's affectionate and judgmental at the same time. "If you're not over something that happened here, do you really think changing your location will make it just…disappear?"

He holds his attention on her for a few moments, then grasps the wrench and goes to work on the last lug nut. It comes off, then he tries to detach the old tire from the Buick. He yanks on it a few times without luck, specks of beer-bottle glass flaking off. Finally, with a grunt, he frees it. He walks to the garbage can where Jane threw her Doritos bag, drops the ripped ring of rubber inside, then grasps the spare from its compartment in the trunk. He kneels with it at the wheel well.

Jane asks, "You ever have to deal with family issues?"

"*That* I'm not talking about."

"Fair enough." A moment. "Well, I have too. And I'm finally able to talk about it. It fits. With your situation…about Mexico. Hear me out." Another moment. "My dad died when I was seven. Heart attack. Just like that. This drove my mom, who was never very stable to begin with, into a…a…whole different realm of instability. She drank. With determination. Every day. Picture a single parent raising two little girls in a state like that. She was miraculously able to hold a job for ten years, but the drinking got…it became too much. Then we began living off government checks. She kept getting worse. Just when I thought the booze was gonna kill her, she met a guy. At the local pub of all places. She met Don."

"Okay," he says, guiding the rim of the new tire on the hub.

"On paper he was fine. Had an okay gig as a security guard. One who walks around malls, places like that. Treated my mom great. Was nice enough to me and my younger sister, Maggie."

"Uh huh." Danny blots some sweat on his brow.

"My mom lost her driver's license. DUIs over the years. Don had a car. So one Sunday morning about a year ago she asks me if I want to go to the nail salon with her. She really was just using me for a ride, not like she wanted to spend mother-daughter time together. But anyway, I agreed. So I bring her in Don's car. We get there, and I didn't really feel like staying. I had a bad headache. So I tell my mom I'm going to go home, pop some Advil, lie down for a little, then pick her up when she was done."

Danny twists the first lug nut onto the new tire. "All right…"

"So I get back home. Keep in mind Don thinks we were both gonna be gone for an hour, maybe more. I walk in. And what do I see on the couch in the den?" She closes her eyes, a slight tremble to her upper chest. "Don…and my little sister. Maggie. Who's fourteen at the time. On the couch. And they're…"

He can guess. And he knows it's paining her to utter the words. So he cuts her off, "It's okay."

"They weren't having sex. But they were…he was making her…" Her shoulders shake with revulsion.

"You don't need to say it." He sets down the wrench and turns away from the tire. He faces her squarely. She has his full attention.

"So I keep this locked inside me for a few days. I don't mention it to Don or my sister, even though they knew I saw. But especially not my mom. I just didn't know *how* to say it. If that makes sense?"

He nods.

"So finally I decide to just come out with it. No frills. The raw, ugly truth. And I'll never forget it. This bitch pours herself a Solo cup of vodka, downs half of it in one sip, wipes her mouth with the back of her hand, then tells me she was sure it was just an innocent mistake. She'll talk to Don and tell him to knock off whatever it was." She lets out an exasperated laugh. "Her fourteen-year-old daughter. An innocent mistake. Imagine."

He can't imagine. Though he had a major falling-out with his dad, this sort of helter-skelter upbringing is alien to his own.

"I was floored," she says. "I couldn't figure it out. Why wouldn't she be furious? Throw Don out? It took me a week to come to a conclusion. The answer was simple. She was selfish. That was all. If she left Don, she'd be alone again. An unemployed alcoholic without a husband. Nobody to hold her hair back when she vomited in the middle of the night from the vodka. Nobody to pay for her trips to the nail salon. Don was the only person she cared about. Because he *gave* her things. She didn't care about her girls. Not after that, I was convinced. We were burdens. We only *took* things."

"That's terrible, Jane. I…I'm sorry."

"So I confront her about it. And I tell her if she's not going to get Don out of Maggie's life *completely*, if she's not going to leave him, then I'd have to do something about it myself. She told me if I did that I'd be ruining my own family. That she and my sister wouldn't be able to survive without Don." She takes a long breath, the top of her chest quivering again. "But I knew what had to be done. So I made the decision. I went to the cops."

Danny's eyes widen.

"They arrested him. He's in jail now. My mom got worse and Maggie moved in with one of our aunts on my dad's side, my *real* dad. My mom of course hasn't spoken to me. I've been living at my friend Sheila's house. There've been nights when I thought that maybe I could've kept Don out of jail, but away from Maggie at the same time too. Maybe my mom was right, I'd stay awake thinking. Maybe I made the wrong choice." A moment. "But I'd been stopping by our aunt's about once a week. To see Maggie. We never talked about it. All that. We talked about school, or soccer…she plays soccer…or you know, girl stuff. But never that." A hint of a tear buds at the edge of her right eye. She dabs it with the tip of her pinkie. "Just this week, on Wednesday, I'm over there. And me and Maggie are watching TV. And she turns to me. And you know what she says?"

Danny shakes his head.

"'Thanks.'" She grins. "That was it. 'Thanks.' And I knew. I knew what she meant. I told her I loved her and that I'd call her soon. That night I packed my suitcase and started hitch-hiking to California."

He muses on this as he gazes at the light-trickled brick aback the arts and crafts store.

"Now do you see what I mean about Mexico?" she asks.

He gives her an unsure look.

"I wanted to get out of there," she says. "Georgia. But the decision I made, about going to the cops, was holding me back. When my sister let me know that I *did* make the right choice, that she was better for it, I was able to quiet that voice in my head. The one telling me that maybe my mom was right. Going to California alone wouldn't have solved that. I still would've been carrying it with me. I needed proof, in my soul, I did the right thing for Maggie and she was okay without me. That I could move on." She has a sip of Coke, finishing the can. The hollow aluminum chimes when she sets it on the pavement. "Now you see?"

He realizes she's just trying to be helpful. However, as he considers her angle on Mexico, he's filled with angst. He thought Mexico would be a fresh start. And it will be. Right? Hearing otherwise seems otherworldly, out of touch with his reality.

Danny has enough concrete issues in his head right now. Like dodging the police. He doesn't need to fret over any abstract questions like the one Jane is posing.

So he decides to take the spotlight off him and make the conversation about her again. He brushes aside her question with a quick nod, then asks, "What's the first thing you're gonna do in California?"

"Can you keep a secret?"

"Try me."

She giggles, then reaches into the back pocket of her denim skirt and pulls out a watch. Danny admires the clumps of steel and gold cradled in her palm. "First thing I'm doing is selling this for cash."

His head notches back in suspicion, then a second time, in rhythm with the thoughts *That looks too expensive for a broke hitchhiker* and *That's for a man.*

"I stole it," she whispers, a mischievous sparkle in her eyes. "So I guess we're both criminals."

"Stole from who?"

"A guy who I thought was nice. Then found out was just another pig. Offered me a couch to sleep on last night. When we got to his place he wound up getting really drunk and wouldn't give up on getting in my pants. Married too. I warded him off for an hour. Then he finally passed out. It left a bad taste in my mouth. Him trying to take advantage. Especially after everything with my sister. So screw him. I stole his watch. I spent the day trying to get out of Rene." She smiles, sarcastically. "Finally, you guys offered me a ride. And now…I'm in Austin with two fugitives, one holding me hostage at gunpoint. Some day, huh?"

Danny can't help but smile too. A day just like his, one problem after another. It's time for this Goddamn day to end.

He secures all the lug nuts, lowers the Buick on the jack, and stows the tools in the trunk. Jane climbs into the backseat.

Danny searches for Phil's outline in the woods. He notices a glowing light in front of it. A cell-phone screen, of the second burner Wade gave them. Phil's texting. Danny wonders whom he's possibly texting right now, then whistles, getting his attention, and signals him over to the car.

Danny looks at both passenger-side doors. And chooses the one in the rear, getting in next to Jane. Her packed suitcase now in the trunk, nothing sits between them but a thin column of warm Texas air.

He enjoys a moment of relaxation. He solved the problem. He got the spare on. However, the relaxation begins disintegrating when he thinks of the dinky, thin-treaded replacement tire, much littler than the three others. He heard you shouldn't drive more than seventy miles on a spare.

They have to go over five hundred.

He also knows you're not supposed to ride fast on one. Phil will have to significantly drop his pace, lengthening their journey, increasing the time they'll linger in America, increasing the likelihood the manhunt will hammer down on them. If they run over another sharp object and the frail spare busts, they'll have no chance at all. They'll be stranded.

The scent of Crick prison springs into Danny's nasal cavity. His subconscious is readying itself for his return to jail. His conscious mind represses the thought. He tells himself it'll be fine.

But this is likely a lie.

Twenty-Six

A gate arm lifts and a Rene Police Department squad car creeps down a windy pathway toward Thurgood L. Crick prison. Ramos drives, the deputy riding shotgun. Ahead of them the blocky silhouettes of the penitentiary's buildings cut into a backdrop of nighttime-gray clouds, the black forms intermingled with tangles of barbed wire spiraling across the sky, which sporadically cross the stems of guard towers that rise toward the higher-perched moon like chalices, each topped with the shadowed outline of a weaponed man.

Ramos parks. He and the deputy enter a facility. A white-walled corridor leads to a taupe-rugged lobby.

"Hi," a pretty Asian woman in a smart blouse says from behind the reception desk.

"Evening," Ramos replies. "We're from the department in Rene. I called earlier."

"Yes. Sergeant Caffery should be able to help." She grins. "I'll notify him you're here." She picks up her phone.

In about a minute a buzzer sounds and a steel door loosens on its hinges. A man in a gray uniform with blue trim traverses the doorway into the lobby. He's in his early sixties, with a wing-shaped sunglass tan and a skinny/fat body, thin in the arms and legs, thick in the trunk and back.

"Hudson Caffery," the corrections officer says, extending his hand.

Ramos grips it. "John Ramos."

"Noah Gleep," the deputy says, shaking it next.

Caffery scopes the height of the deputy's shorts and lets out an uncomfortable chuckle. A moment.

Ramos says, "Just to confirm, I asked for a guard who's worked here at least ten years. Back to '06. When exactly—"

"Ninety-eight," Caffery spits out, as if the confirmation request insulted him.

Ramos spins his shoulders to the deputy and snaps his fingers. On cue, the underling unbuttons a front pocket of his shirt, unveils a folded piece of computer paper, and passes it to his boss. Ramos butterflies open the sheet, revealing to the guard the mug-shot image of Wade Lorendinski. "You recognize him? Former inmate. '06 to '08."

Caffery's hazel eyes, encased by a white patch of sunglass-shaped skin, flinch as they absorb the photo. "He was one of the men with the nuclear codes."

"What do you mean?"

"A max-security prison is its own…globe you can say. With its own nations. You got the Hispanics. Got your blacks, of course. Your whites. A few types of whites. Like the Mexicans and blacks, you get a fair amount of 'em in gangs. Each of these groups, these little countries, got their own governments in here. Leadership. And these countries don't like each other.

We as guards got to be up on sensing if a war is about to break out. Because if it does, that's when we lose guys. That's when riots happen...we can get our guns snatched, or we can get shanked. We want to squash these wars before they even start. But at the very top of these governments, there's maybe one or two inmates who can start a war with just a nod. No matter how much the guards try to keep the tensions down. If they make the call, everyone in their group listens. And we got hell on our hands. We call them the ones with the nuclear codes. For the Aryans, Wade Lorendinski was one of those men."

Ramos takes a moment to absorb this, then says, "Philip Zorn. One of the escapees. Lorendinski and him were at Crick at the same time. They know each other at all?"

"Zorn used to buy things. Contraband. I swept his cell a couple times. Not drugs. Science shit you'd see in a classroom. The Aryan Brotherhood runs the smuggling operation at Crick. Has since well before I was here. Zorn must have been a customer."

"What about Lorendinski in particular? Did you ever see the two interacting directly?"

"This is going back years, but now that I'm thinking... maybe. I can recall seeing them chatting in the dining hall. But I'm only about seventy percent. Couldn't tell you for certain. Lorendinski talked to a lot of people when he was here. What's this all about? You think he had something to do with Zorn escaping?"

"I can't prove anything. But I've been doing this for nineteen years and...I, well...just have a hunch is all. Lorendinski lives in our jurisdiction. We have his address. But we didn't want to talk to him until we had a concrete starting point we could question him from, something to scare him, to let him know we're connecting the dots. What I need is a rationale. Why would Zorn specifically seek out Lorendinski for help?"

Caffery sniffles and rubs his nose. "So you need to get in Zorn's head?"

"You can say that."

Caffery laughs. "Nobody can fully know what's going on in that rat's nest of a mind." A moment. "But someone here knew the sick fuck pretty well. If you want to learn more about how Zorn thinks, you'd want to talk to her."

"Any information can help at this point."

Caffery taps his foot. "She usually doesn't work night shifts. But with all the madness this afternoon, a lot of the employee schedules got bumped up. She might be here. Hold on." He strolls to the pretty Asian receptionist. They chat for a few seconds, then she picks up her phone and talks for a few more.

Caffery turns back to the policemen and says, "You're in luck. Come on."

The buzzer sounds and the steel door opens. Ramos and the deputy follow him through an unadorned hall. When they reach the end, the ceiling jumps up.

They're in Crick's B Block, three levels of metallic-barred compartments bordering them on the left, each dark at this post-curfew hour. Ramos glances inside the cells, which are scarcely lit by traces of moonlight pouring down through a glass atrium, the soft rays passing through the spinning blades of two industrial-sized fans before touching the faces of scattered in-bed inmates below. Ramos sees a few of these men are not sleeping, the whites of their eyes studying the uniformed trio making its way through their space.

Ramos has been inside prisons during the day, when they're active and noisy. This is his first time in the dead of the night. The whirling fans generate the only sound. The human beings are quiet, most unconscious, the awake ones looking, waiting, not much else. B Block right now reminds Ramos more of the cancer ward at Rebus Memorial, where his grandmother died, than a jail.

Caffery unlocks a passage to an administrative wing and leads the cops to an office, "Ruth Feckstein" etched outside on a glass pane, "Director of Psychotherapy" beneath. Behind the open doorway is a small-boned woman about fifty, her head hidden in a heap of curly black hair.

"These are the fellas from Rene we just phoned you 'bout," Caffery tells her. "I'll leave y'all to it." He walks away without saying goodbye.

Feckstein looks at Ramos and the deputy. Bags almost as dark as her hair hug the undersides of her eyes. She points at a pair of chairs across her desk.

Sitting, Ramos asks, "You were Philip Zorn's shrink?"

"He refused to participate in therapy sessions. So his 'shrink' would be a misnomer. I did conduct research on him, though. Which is why I presume the sergeant suggested you see me."

"What sort of research?"

She lifts a cigarette out of a pack of Camels stashed among her paperwork, lights it, and leans back into a coquettish pose reminiscent of a mid-century screen starlet, though watered down by her weathered, half-a-century-old face. She sucks and blows. An S-shaped ribbon of smoke rises from her mouth. This makes Ramos antsy, since he supposes smoking isn't allowed in the penitentiary.

"Prisoners are wonderful test subjects," she says. "It's legal to monitor everything they do. A basic carrot, say an extended hour of recreation for a month, is enough to get them to consent to most any exam. And there's nowhere for them to go if they get cold feet." She takes another drag. "Phil Zorn was a much savvier negotiator than the everyday inmate. He wanted access to a microscope, a specialty Swiss model they have at the local university. For some experiment he apparently wanted to conduct. I arranged for them to bring it in, for forty-eight hours, and allow him supervised use. In exchange he was to participate in a battery of assessments for Clear Horizons, a federally funded program I'm on the board of. Acquiring the microscope was a bit of an inconvenience, but Zorn was such a fitting candidate for the program it was worth it."

"Clear Horizons? Never heard of it."

She pulls a plastic ashtray from her top drawer and pats off into it the end of her cigarette. "A plethora of psychological data already exists in the field of criminology. We understand, in depth, the motives behind most crimes. Money, jealousy, revenge…in one degree or another are the typical culprits. Clear Horizons is directed at the gray areas. The unusual crimes where the motive isn't straightforward. Zorn drugging and raping devout Christians and wrapping them in sleeping bags is one of those crimes."

The deputy closes his eyes and, with his index finger, traces a quick sign of the cross over his heart, a show of respect for the victims.

Feckstein goes on, "The first part of the Clear Horizons evaluation is an intelligence test. Simply, are these perpetrators smart enough to have crafted a broader motive at all? The hypothesis is that some motives may be uncertain to us because they never really existed, not in the traditional sense anyway. Take a feeble-minded individual, acting upon the pleasure principle, who does something spontaneous as a joke, say pushing his best friend out of the bed of a moving pickup truck. This in fact did happen last year in Tyler, with two nineteen-year-old boys. The one never intended to kill the other, figured he'd just bruise him some. He said he'd seen his friend fall from similar heights before and be fine, his mind unable to grasp the idea that speed, not simply height, impacts the severity of a fall."

"So it's a moron test, basically?" Ramos asks.

"Yes and no. Yes in that its main intention is to chalk certain crimes up to sheer ignorance. However, that's not its only scientific tell. The subjects who test at the high end of the exam's bell curve provide richer depths to probe than the ones at the low. Because we can assume they knew exactly what they were doing when their crimes were committed. This adds much more complexity to a case."

"Zorn tested at the high end?"

"No." She puffs her cigarette. "He broke the ceiling. His score wasn't technically valid since it was, literally, off the chart. When I contacted the feds at Clear Horizons about this, they mailed me a special exam. The sort they give candidates applying for senior positions at the NSA. Like the normal test, it consisted of a verbal and quantitative component, yet with much more complicated question types. The verbal focused on multi-token anagrams and the quantitative on prime factorization of four-digit numbers."

Ramos has no idea what either of these things is. His expression must show so, because Feckstein elaborates, "An anagram is a word with its letters scrambled. The subject must look at the jumbled letters and say the word. This test was particularly difficult because phrases were used, up to *five* words, with no indication where the spaces fell."

"You have an example?"

She clamps the cigarette between her teeth and uses both hands to comb through a desk drawer. She extracts a seafoam-green folder, opens it, and peruses some pages inside. "W. R. L. O. E. V. N. M. T. N. O. H. E. G. F. T. T. E. E. A. N. O. E."

Ramos stares at her, then glimpses the deputy, then returns to her. "You got me."

"*The Two Gentlemen of Verona.* An early Shakespeare play."

Ramos's lower lip lowers a bit. "Zorn was able to answer that…from *that*?"

"He didn't just answer it correctly. But quickly." She reads something else in the folder. "Eight seconds."

Ramos rubs his brow.

"The math portion was just as difficult," she says. "With prime factorization, the subject must break a number into the prime numbers multiplied together to produce it. For instance, the prime factors of six would be three and two. Three, a prime, times two, another prime, gets—"

"Six," Ramos says with a dash of sarcasm. Which she doesn't appear to appreciate.

"In the exam, numbers in the thousands were used." She scans the contents in her folder. "For instance, he was given forty-five hundred sixty. To which, without much of a delay, he accurately answered two times two times two times two times three times five times nineteen."

Ramos slouches in the bucket chair and steeples his fingers. This isn't good. He's considered the smartest detective in Rene. Figures he'd be in the running for that distinction at the county level too. But this is a whole different game. Ramos can't compete with Zorn intellect for intellect. Wherever he is now, he's likely two steps ahead of the law. This is going to be even tougher than he thought.

Feckstein continues, "Following the intelligence appraisal, Zorn was given a completely different Clear Horizons test. This one was for criminals, like him, who were cognizant of what they did. The question here was, did they lack something at the emotional level that enabled them to carry their acts out?" She breathes in the Camel, its tip glowing red, then exhales gray fumes through her nostrils, which waft toward the cops. "The test we administered was similar to what a clinician might use to diagnose a sociopath. We showed the subjects illustrations of people in various situations. And had them free-associate. Blurt words that came to mind. Some images were rather blunt, for instance, a woman in a burning building. Though there were no objectively *correct* or *incorrect* answers, we of course paid attention to abnormalities. Say, if an inmate described the lady and the fire as 'funny.'"

"That's how Zorn answered?"

"No." She stubs the top of the cigarette into the ember bed of the ashtray and grinds, snuffing the life from it. "For each illustration, he responded just as a healthy, empathetic individual would. Even for the more nuanced depictions. For example, some sketches were close-ups of a face with the slightest indication of emotion on it. Say flared nostrils. Some were even intentionally misleading, like a man smiling without crease lines by his eyes, a typical, though very subtle, indicator of a phony grin. Zorn, I remember, responded to this one with 'apocryphal.' Based on the assessment, he didn't suffer from an inkling of sociopathic tendencies."

Ramos muses on this for about ten seconds. "So, with the girls...the victims...he was fully aware of what he was doing *and* felt their pain as he was doing it?"

"Whether or not he feels pain we'll never know. A test can't verify that." A moment. "Would you like my personal opinion?"

He nods.

"Zorn, in my view, responded appropriately to the images not because of underlying emotional health. Not because of heart. No, I feel he was relying instead on his brain. His replies, though appropriate, seemed studied. Too academic. As if he spent time in his past analyzing the human condition from the outside in. I became nearly certain of this when I saw his results on the final portion of the evaluation. Which involved colors. It was very similar to the part with the illustrations of people. Except these were abstract. Colors, in shapes and patterns. Nothing representative of anything in the real world. These were images Zorn had never seen before. He wasn't capable of studying them in any capacity." She adjusts the collar of her discount-outlet business suit. "Detective, if I were to show you a drawing of a yellow square with purple circles on it, how would you say it made you *feel?*"

"Cheery, I guess."

"Precisely. Ninety-nine percent of respondents answer in a similar way. Conversely, if I showed you a nebulous gray blob with bits of red checkering it, you'd likely say it made you feel 'unsure,' 'worried,' even 'scared.'" Chin angled down, she holds her gaze on him as if to ask, *Am I right?*

"Yeah," he says.

She shifts her expression to the deputy. "Scared," he states.

"We showed Zorn twenty of these. Not only did his answers veer from the norms of common respondents, but they were all over the place even among themselves. There was no connective logic to them. No rhyme or reason. It was as if he was just randomly reading adjectives from the dictionary."

Silence.

"I appreciate the psych profile on Zorn," Ramos says. "It helps us know what we're up against. Which never hurts." He straightens his posture in the seat. "But what I'd really like to get is some insight around his decision-making process specifically for the escape. Would you have any idea where he might be fleeing? What his plans would be on the lam? What he'd need on the outside, what he couldn't live without? I have a hunch about a possible accomplice, but I need more context to tie the two men together."

She picks up the pack of Camels, yet doesn't remove one, instead just taps a corner of the paperboard box against her desk. "One thing struck me as interesting earlier."

"Yes, what?" Ramos removes a small spiral notepad from his pocket, a mini pencil embedded in its spine.

"I wasn't surprised to see Zorn attempt a breakout. After what he did to those girls in Austin, it's evident his tolerance for criminal risk is quite high. His cellmate however, Daniel Marsh, was quite the opposite. I spoke to Danny a couple times over the last few years. He's not a lawbreaker by nature. I was shocked to learn he was part of the escape. I'm assuming he was prodded into agreement somehow."

"You're saying Zorn manipulated him into escaping?"

"Based on Zorn's high intelligence and expertise of the human emotional spectrum, he'd theoretically make a formidable manipulator. However, like you detective, all I have is a hunch." A pause. "One memory came to mind earlier that was rather intriguing, though. About a year ago, Zorn filed a mental-health complaint about his former cellmate. I'm required to conduct one-on-ones with the submitters of these reports. He told me this man constantly threatened to kill him, and once even held a filed toothbrush handle to his jugular as a scare tactic. Was any of this true? Anyone's guess. Zorn begged for a new cellmate. Said he couldn't deal with the duress of his current environment. In the event he was telling the truth, I recommended a transfer. This was right around the time Danny

Marsh's cellmate was being released. Zorn and Marsh each needed a new prisoner to bunk with. So they were paired up."

Ramos falls into that Socratic pose he does when deep thought sets in. "So you're saying the death threats could've been bullshit? That Zorn somehow timed his cell-transfer request right before Marsh needed a new cellmate?"

"It seems beyond coincidental. Was Zorn intentionally looking to bunk with Marsh for some reason? This didn't occur to me of course until earlier, when I saw they were both involved in the breakout. What Zorn's reason might be is unclear. I'm afraid that's all the insight I can provide on decision making around the escape. I wish I had more for you, detective."

Ramos closes his notepad without writing anything in it. This information doesn't bring him any closer to Wade Lorendinski. He has a lot of puzzle pieces, but still can't fit any together.

"Thanks for your time," he says, rising, extending his hand. Feckstein shakes it. Then the deputy's. The cops walk toward the door.

"Gentlemen," she says. They turn. "One more thing about Zorn." A moment. "Please catch the cocksucker." She picks up a pen, looks down at her desk, and returns to work.

Without any real evidence or even leads, catching the cocksucker seems undoable. However, John Ramos is no quitter. He never read a rule in a leadership book about giving up. He's going to have to get creative now.

Twenty-Seven

A paper plate of Wonder Bread shrouded in shadows rests beside Monty's chair, the "dinner" his keeper carried down a bit back. Monty didn't want it. He's lost his appetite. From thinking.

For the last hour he's been thinking about just two things. Chloroform and diazepam.

That's what Phil used on those girls in Austin. That's what the bikers used on Danny and him. That's why Monty is certain Phil committed the crime he claimed was a frame. Monty of course had his suspicions before today. Inmates at Crick chattered about Phil's rape rampage. On the face of it, he seemed guilty through and through. The news report simply doused any doubt. Chloroform and diazepam.

Phil's story had holes. Set up by rival professors? Monty knew that sounded like a bunch of dog shit when he heard it in the pickup truck on the way to the water park.

If some academic enemy wanted him out of commission to that extent, it would be much simpler to just have him killed.

Monty's heard about transactions like that on the streets where he grew up. They're just as straightforward as hiring someone to mow your lawn. You find a guy who's done it before. Agree on a price. He does the job. You pay him in cash. Problem solved.

Much cleaner than orchestrating a slate of college chicks to voice phony sexual-assault accusations, not to mention obtaining Phil's DNA and planting it on one.

Monty knew something wasn't right with Phil. Living in a rough area, you need to develop an airtight sense of intuition about people. In the ghetto anyone could be gunning for you. If you can't decide who's good and who's bad, you're dead. Monty's intuition told him Phil was off from the moment he met him. Not dangerous necessarily. Just off. He could never quite categorize it. Yet sensed it.

Not Danny. Phil got through to him somehow. Danny trusted him, looked up to him even. Monty never understood it. Danny's no idiot. It was like Phil brainwashed him.

Monty had no clue Phil was as demented as he really is though. Deceiving Danny and him about the debt to Wade was one thing. But what he did to those poor girls? Six of them. Maybe there're more the media doesn't even know about. And the way Phil did it was the sickest part. Drugged them, fucked them, then tucked them into sleeping bags in a park.

For the last hour he's been trying to assess what Phil's goal was. You disrespect someone's body enough to rape it, then suddenly respect it enough to stick around, upping your risk of getting caught, just to move it to a comfortable place and wrap it all snug? What logic is in that?

Monty's been mystified. Then he recollects Phil often mentioning Charles Darwin. He did it a bunch at Crick when they were planning the escape, warning Danny and him that a mistake means death, only the strong survive, the weak wither away before they can pass down their genes. Phil even cited Darwin in the pickup truck earlier. Monty is no dope. He knows what Darwinism is. Was Phil trying to get these girls pregnant…spread his seed?

Possibly that's why he left them in comfortable conditions, in the sleeping bags. They were potentially carrying his kids. Possibly that's why he targeted devout Christians. They were unlikely to opt for abortion.

It gives Monty the chills. But makes the most sense. He figures no girls would want to sleep with dorky Phil on their own volition, so to spread his seed he resorted to this abomination.

But now the idea of a sperm bank pops into his mind. If Phil's purpose was simply to scatter his DNA among the female population, why not make a deposit at a fertility clinic? Why not make a lot of deposits? They're quick, safe for all parties involved, and legal. This knocks Monty's line of reasoning crooked.

So he decides to give up on reason. He'd never been able to figure out Phil. And he doesn't feel he can now. Did Phil enjoy raping those girls? Was there a pleasure motive in it for him, some weird thrill of domination? Monty doesn't think so. Was Phil abused himself as a child, like many other sex offenders, and stalked those innocent girls to nurse his own wounds? Monty doesn't think so either.

He used to believe Phil was like a computer. Intelligent, yet cold. But that's not it. Computers are too artificial. Phil is certainly a child of nature. He breathes, he eats, he sleeps. And he wants things. A liberation from the manhunt. A legacy.

Yet, he isn't quite human.

Monty considers him a complex organic entity, just like a human, yet lacking something that brings it all together. Something all people possess. Monty isn't positive what this something is. But he knows Phil doesn't have it.

And since Phil isn't quite the same species as him, it's impossible to get into his head. Monty will never know his real motive for those rapes. Nobody will.

The basement is bleached with light. Monty blinks a few times, his tingling eyes adjusting. Wade walks down the steps with the phone and the shackle keys. He unlocks Monty's hands and says, "Twelve."

Monty holds up all ten fingers and closes both eyes. He feels ridiculous making these idiotic poses every half hour, but he's aware they're the only way Danny will know he's safe. Danny is a solid dude. One of the few in prison. Monty cooked up a conversation with him on the slop line one day and they became instant buddies. It was no coincidence Phil suggested Monty as the third member of the escape trio. Phil knew Danny cared about Monty. Phil knew he'd make the perfect insurance policy.

Wade snaps the photo.

Curious for an outside opinion, Monty asks, "You really don't believe the professor is innocent for that shit in Austin, do you?"

No response. Wade sends the picture and slides the phone in his pocket.

"You don't find the whole story kinda disturbing?" Monty asks.

Wade leers at him from high above, then circles behind him and tightens the chains back around his hands. "Not much disturbs me anymore."

"You're his partner though, aren't you? I mean, I'm assuming you expect him to hand you over the dough he's bagging off Danny's folks. You trust a guy like that, a rapist, as a partner?"

Wade snidely chuckles, a hint of his pumpkin-hued teeth exposed. "You were his partner, weren't you?"

Damn. Good point. No, Monty never felt comfortable around Phil, but the thought of escape was too alluring. If Phil knew a way to get him out of Crick and into Mexico, Monty would be happy to keep his mouth shut about disliking him.

"Yeah, I was his partner," Monty says, "and look where it got me." He mockingly nods at his manacled ankles. "You're getting scammed the same way I did. I dug a hole in a wall with screws for that son of a bitch for nine months. With *screws*. This is how he thanks me. You really think he's gonna meet you in Mexico and give you all that money?"

Wade strolls across the concrete, leaning against the cinderblock wall. "How the hell did you make it as a gangbanger knowing so little about criminal enterprises?"

"I never was no gangbanger. I borrowed a car one day. That was it."

"Apparently. Two hundred fifty grand for some phony IDs, a car ride to Mexico, and a power saw? If the thugs in whatever shithole you're from sold black-market stuff at those prices they'd have a better chance knowing who their fathers were than staying in business."

"I get it's a shitload of money. You knew you'd have Danny by the balls once he was on the outside, so you're extorting him, jacking him for as much as you can."

Wade folds his arms, the two slabs of blue-inked skin meeting like bodies of water. "I'm not the one doing the extorting."

What the fuck is he talking about? Monty deliberates for a few moments, but can't make sense of the comment.

Wade goes on, "You're right about Zorn. He's far from an innocent schoolteacher. He's planning on setting up some private underground laboratory in Mexico. To continue his old research. That high-tech equipment is expensive. Some of my guys are stealing the shit for him from a nearby college. And my cartel connections are moving it to him in Mexico. He'll pay me through them. With Danny's money. He tries to stiff me, he doesn't get his lab. My ass is covered. After my men get their cuts, I figure I'll personally walk away with about fifty Gs. Money my cartel guys will bring to me right here in Texas. I ain't going to Mexico tonight. Or any time soon." He smirks. "And neither are you."

Monty's neck stiffens like a taxidermied animal's. A half-minute passes. "If we're not going to Mexico...what're you doing with me?"

Wade's gaze slants to the floor.

Silence.

Monty heaves at his chains. "What're you doing with me?" he screams. The chair legs rumble, a rickety din resonating through the basement. "Tell me, yo."

"Just calm down."

"No. No." The seat tips. Monty's shoulder smashes onto the concrete, then his head. He doesn't even feel the pain. He's on his side, unable to move his limbs, like a quadriplegic who fell in a wheelchair.

Once Phil has that money, he'll no longer need an insurance policy. The cartel will act as a middleman, Phil on one end, Wade the other end. And Monty becomes just a loose end.

He suspects how guys like Wade deal with loose ends.

"Nooooo," Monty shouts, his right cheek grinding on the floor.

Soon his words fade. Weeping replaces them. Tears flow from his face onto the gray surface it's pressed against. Wade studies him for a few seconds. Then pushes himself off the wall and climbs the steps.

He leaves the lights on for him.

Twenty-Eight

The rubber of the spare tire slowly wears as the Buick rips west across the Edwards Plateau. It's held up for a couple hours, but Danny doesn't know how much life it has left. Over that time the view out his window changed from the glowing glass of glossy Austin high-rises to the karst topography of Texas Hill Country. No other people or vehicles are within sight on this stretch of interstate at this late hour.

Moonlight cascades onto the green leaves of sparse patches of Ashe juniper trees, which appear navy blue under the awning of the night, and spreads across the sloping formations of granite overtaking the bulk of the landscape, metamorphosed relics from the Mesoproterozoic Era, pre-dating man by over a billion years.

Peering out the window, Danny thinks how big the world is. So much of it is still a mystery to him. He recalls what Phil said before about the girl on the cancer-fundraiser billboard. Nature isn't fair or unfair. There's truth in this. Danny has always personified the world too much. Especially in bad times.

He'd imagine it was playing cruel games with him. But now he feels he was wrong about this. Jane had a hard past too. Nature hasn't singled him out. It's not out to get him, or anyone else. As Phil says, it is what it is.

However, Phil's thoughts on nature are too extreme. The world shouldn't be personified, as Danny used to believe, but by Phil's logic, *people* aren't even personified. He mentioned earlier they're just collections of little particles being pushed into predetermined fates by nature. No. This is wrong too.

Maybe, like Jane said, we'll never know the universal truths about our world. In this case, all we can rely on are ourselves and what's inside us. Nature certainly plays a key role in building us. We can't control physical things like our eye color, and even mental things like our behavioral tendencies. However, Jane, unlike Phil, believes in a soul. Danny feels a soul is something that sits outside nature, an opening in the world that we *can* control. A distinctly human thing where free will resides. What personifies us.

Where it comes from he doesn't know. But like Jane, he thinks he has one.

Danny's mind drifts from the big world around him to the journey he has ahead of him. That was a close call with the cop in Austin. And they still have a lot of road to cover before El Paso. Pride is at the heart of law enforcement in Texas. Danny's sure the cops are pissed they haven't caught them yet. Insulted, even. He knows they're closing in by now, foaming at the mouth, ready to bite into him, spit him out in prison, and increase his sentence exponentially as punishment for the escape.

He checks his phone. Still no texts from his parents. Nothing all night. He puts it back in his pocket and peeks over his left shoulder at Jane, who's taking in the portion of the landscape south of the road.

"We need gas," Phil says, nodding at an illuminated "Food 'N Fuel" sign in the distance. "If either of you has to use the lavatory, now would be the time. We won't be stopping again."

"I'm fine," Danny answers.

"Fine too," Jane adds.

Phil exits the interstate in a town Danny doesn't know the name of, a half a dozen houses dispersed through the hills above, all their windows dark. They take a dirt road toward the filling station, passing a decaying, thirty-foot-tall decorative windmill with no markings on it that doesn't seem to belong to the business or one of the residences. As it spins a creak seeps from its old bolts and echoes across the black sky.

Spires of dust rise from both sides of the Buick as it travels the unpaved path. Phil leans into the brake in preparation for a left into the lot. Danny stares at the station, which looks like an artifact from the Fifties, white wood, a pair of fire-engine-red pumps out front with analog gallon counters. Through a window, a thin, thirtyish man in headphones and an apron, oblivious to their presence, mops the floor of a boxy space containing a drink cooler and a wall of junk food.

Phil turns in and pulls toward one of the red pumps. Jane bends forward to tie her shoe, the crown of her head touching the rear of his seat. He kills the engine, the hush of its thrum accentuating the squeaky pulse of the windmill in the distance. *Shrseept. Shrseept. Shrseept.*

Among the noise, Danny hears a soft moan from Jane. He looks left. Her head is still butted into the back of Phil's seat, yet she's not tying her shoe. Her left arm is hidden. Her teeth are clenched.

"What are—" Phil mutters.

Jane's left arm reappears, recoiling at high speed from the front of the car. Danny sees the flash of something shiny. For a split-second he doesn't know what it is. When his mind computes the fast-moving image, his heart freezes.

Phil's gun.

She pushes open her door, dives out the vehicle, skins both knees on the asphalt, and with freshly struck lines of blood oozing down each shin, runs into the night.

Young and in shape, she's fast. Middle-aged and unathletic, Phil bumbles unbuckling his seatbelt and lumbers out the car after her. She darts toward the white structure with the attendant inside. Phil's Italian-leather loafers don't get much traction, yet hold up just enough to keep him on her tail. Danny climbs out of the car and watches.

Clutching the Sig Sauer in her left hand, she bangs on the station window with her right, the vibrating thuds a bass balancing out the high-pitched *shrseept* of the windmill, the marriage of the sounds almost melodic.

"Help," she screams. "Help me." The attendant, his head swaddled in headphones, his back to her, doesn't notice. More slamming on the glass. "Hey." More mopping.

Phil makes it over, placing his body between Jane and the station door. "Just take a breath," he tells her in a friendly voice. "Be smart. And hand over the gun." She stares him down, the bright lights inside washing out the right side of her face. "Think Jane."

She glimpses the still-unaware attendant with her anxious blue eyes. Then the door handle behind Phil. The strip of blood on her right leg dribbles down to her ankle, its red tainting the white lace of her sneaker.

Phil takes a step closer. "Just give me the gun and I'll forget all about this." Then smiles. "Come on, Jane." He inches closer, now no more than a yard from her.

She takes a step back. Her nervous breath is audible. He takes a step forward. His smile widens. His eyes lock on the gun. He gets a touch nearer.

She spins around and sprints toward the hill aback the station. He takes off after her, his dress shoes slipping under him. She races past a propane refill rig onto a craggy incline, at its summit one of the houses Danny saw from the road.

Danny feels his pulse pounding on his temples. On the left end of his vision the aloof employee continues cleaning the snack shop, and on the right end Jane's abuzz body negotiates upward around yucca shrubs, Phil chasing about a dozen feet behind.

Danny's emotions are mixed. A part of him wants Jane to make it to that house on the hill and get away. She'd be home free, removed from the Buick's journey and the dominion of Phil.

However, another part of him knows how calamitous that could be. If she banged on the door and screamed "help," when the startled homeowners opened up, they'd see Jane, along with Phil right behind. If he were recognized as an escaped convict from TV, the police would instantly be called. Even if he were not identified as a fugitive, the police would likely still receive a call, simply from the chaos of the scene, a bleeding girl with a gun crying for help in the middle of the night.

Of course Danny and Phil could get back in the Buick and race away. However, they wouldn't last long. The local police would track them. Danny is positive this isn't Jane's intention. She didn't think that far ahead. She doesn't want Danny to go back to prison, just wants to get herself out of the prison Phil created for her.

Danny runs after them. He needs to get to Jane and talk some sense into her, convince her to ride out the last few hours of this car ride. He climbs the arid earth. Craning his neck, he sees her ahead. Phil lags her but not by much, about eight feet. Above them all, set against the three-quarter moon, is the two-story house.

The hill's surface steepens toward the peak. Gravity bearing down, Jane's pace slows. But she keeps pushing. For support, she grips a bush and thrusts herself up some. With a grunt, she does it with another. The ground's angle intensifies. She slips the gun into the waist of her skirt and drops to all fours, heaving herself toward the safe haven from rooted plant to rooted plant.

The *shrseept* of the windmill loudens as they ascend closer to the source of the sound thirty feet in the sky. Jane squirms upward, nearing the apex, her grated kneecaps leaving red dabs on the clay-colored ground. Phil, slithering on his stomach from bush to bush, has a longer wingspan than her and achieves longer gains with each reach.

She's less than ten feet from the top of the hill. Her left arm swings through the air, her hand latching onto a prickly bush, unflinching from the needles. She tugs herself forward, the gun jiggling within the denim band engirdling it, almost jumping loose. As she brings her right arm around, Phil's hand clasps her left ankle.

She screams.

He yanks on her hundred-five-pound body, dragging it toward him over yuccas. She kicks him in the face, shattering his glasses. He lets go of her, feeling at his ruined frames. He discards them in the brush and glares at her with naked eyes that show nothing but animosity.

Jane, gripping a branch for balance, points the Sig Sauer between those dark eyes. "Go back down the hill or I pull the trigger," she says.

Danny, a few yards below, gripping tree bark for balance, observes with heavy nerves.

Phil slowly raises his hands. He studies her skittish expression. "You won't pull that trigger."

"Watch me."

He snickers. "Give me the gun."

"Go back to the fucking car. I'm serious." She stabs the weapon forward.

"You're causing yourself more problems than solutions."

"Go. Or you're dead."

"Jane. I already know you won't shoot me. You're not a killer. You're scared. Which is understandable. But I'm not here to hurt you. Drive with me for a few more hours, then you're free in El Paso. All you need to do is sit in the car. Or you can shoot me now and saddle yourself with blame for the rest of your life. You'd be a murderer. Every day you woke up you'd be leading the life of a murderer. From tomorrow until forever. So just give me the gun, come back to the car, and sit down. Soon it'll all be over. That's the answer. You're not a murderer Jane."

"You don't know what I'm capable of. You don't know *me*."

"Let's see. Your complexion is too good for you to be malnourished, so I'm assuming you don't come from poverty. But you are poor. The cheap stitching on that skirt says as much. Your other clothing, that I hid under in the car, was generic enough in design not to look dated, yet a lot of the brands on the tags were old, very old, discontinued, leading me to believe it came from thrift stores and as hand-me-downs from a relative." A pause. "Not an older sister. You're too bold to be a youngest child and too self-confident to be a middle. You're a firstborn. The clothes came from your mother then." A pause. "She raised you alone. If you had a father at home, you wouldn't have gotten into a car with two strange men in Rene. He either left your mother or he's dead. And all alone she didn't do much of a job with you, did she Jane? If she did, why would you run away? She probably supported you off handouts or some shitty job in whatever shitty town you come from in the backwoods of Georgia. She never made it to college. And that boat is sailing past for you too. You're about the age of a coed, but wouldn't be off to California if you were enrolled anywhere. You're turning into her, aren't you Jane? Too trusting of men, too dumb or too distracted to get an education. Shall I keep going?"

Her hand holding the gun quivers. Her eyes water. "Fuck you," she says in a faint voice.

He climbs a few feet closer to her. "Give me the pistol, Jane."

She steadies her shaky aim. "Back up. I'll shoot."

He smirks.

Shrseept. Shrseept. Shrseept.

He charges at her.

Danny watches the back of his dusty blazer close in on her little body, bracing himself for the sound of a gunshot. Yet it never comes. Phil tackles her to the ground. Danny hears a clunking noise, but nothing from the Sig Sauer. Phil was right. Jane isn't a killer.

As Phil rolls off her, the weapon wrestled out of her hands into his, Danny sees a look of unconsciousness on her face, which hangs beside a rock. He assumes that clunking sound was her skull crashing into it.

"Jane," he shouts, scrambling uphill. He fights the slope to her, kneeling at her side. He brushes some hair from her face. Her eyes are closed, expression unresponsive. He shakes her shoulder. Nothing. "Oh shit," he murmurs to himself. He glances at the dark home towering above them, then at Phil.

Tucking the gun back in his slacks, Phil stares at Jane. Her passed-out state doesn't seem to faze him. He says, "Some people just don't know how to listen to what's best for them."

Rage heats Danny's skin. He springs from his crouch into a sprint and smashes his shoulder into Phil's breastbone. The two men tumble down the slope, a juniper tree choking their descent as their bodies slam into the trunk. Danny climbs on top of the smaller man and raises a right, ready to plow it into his face.

"Monty," Phil utters.

Danny at first doesn't know what he means by this. Then in a few seconds he gets it. Panting, he lowers his hand, forfeiting the blow. Monty, as in the insurance policy. Saying the name was supposed to stress that Wade is only a phone call away, that Phil can easily inform him if Danny gets out of line, that Wade can easily enact retribution on the body of helpless, chained Monty.

Catching his breath, Danny climbs off his old bunkmate and peers at him, the moonlight igniting the patchiness of his dyed eyebrows. Danny doesn't recognize this man at all anymore. It's more than the new hair color. The tender professor inside jail has morphed into a monster on the outside in a matter of hours. First he tears into Danny in Austin about a childhood trauma out of pure spite, now he knocks an innocent girl's skull into a rock and doesn't bother checking on her, then offers up innocent Monty's body on the altar of a threat.

Danny stands, holding a dirty look on Phil. Then hurries back to Jane. Who's still not moving.

Twenty-Nine

"Here you are, dear," a waitress says, setting a plate of Belgian waffles topped with vanilla ice cream in front of the deputy. "And the number eight for you," she tells Ramos, placing an order of steak and eggs on the booth's table.

"Yum," the deputy says, unwrapping his fork and knife from the paper napkin they're rolled up in. "Thank you ma'am."

"Anything else?"

"A little more coffee," Ramos says, nodding at his empty mug.

"Sure," she replies with a smile, then walks off along the chessboard floor, passing the diner's only other patron, a brawny man in his seventies wearing Carhartt coveralls, and disappears into the kitchen.

"I'd get some more caffeine in me if I were you," Ramos tells the deputy. "We need to be sharp when we talk to Lorendinski. Questioning someone for the first time, when they're unprepared, is your best chance to get them to slip. We only get one shot at it."

"Too much coffee gives me the jitters." The deputy drizzles syrup all over his mountainous late-night breakfast, slices off a pancake corner with his fork, swoops it through his scoop of ice cream, and sticks it in his mouth. Chewing, he says, "I've actually been thinking about our approach, sir…" He keeps chomping, his large Adam's apple flexing, then swallows. "And feel it's a little late to visit him tonight." He points at a silver-rimmed clock on the wall, showing twenty-one past one.

"He's a criminal. I don't care about interrupting his beauty sleep."

The waitress returns, insulated coffee pitcher in hand. She tops off Ramos's cup. "How is everything, officers?"

"Just delicious," Ramos says, though he hasn't taken a bite yet. She leaves with a grin.

The deputy drags a forked chunk of waffle in a puddle of syrup and melted ice cream. "It's not his beauty sleep I'm settin' on." He puts the pillowy morsel into his mouth. "Say we knock on his front door. He won't just open it. Not at one something in the morning. He'll look out the little peephole. And see a pair of big ole badges shining. Under normal circumstances, a former felon like that probably wouldn't open up." He guzzles some water. "But if he's really involved in this escape, he *definitely* won't open up. We don't have no warrant. And sure as heck can't get one at this hour. The minute we leave his porch, he'll pack a bag and hightail out of town. We'll lose him. Just like a scared fish hoppin' off a hook."

Ramos leans back in the brown booth. He crosses his arms. The kid has a point. "You keep thinking like that, Noah, and you'll be a detective before you know it."

The deputy blushes. Ramos stares out the window at the dark road, one set of headlights coasting along. He should've realized all this without his subordinate informing him. It's late. It's been a long day. His mind is weary. And occupied. With thoughts of the governor paying him that phone call, thoughts of his two little girls at a fancy private high school in a few years.

"Okay, we won't go tonight," Ramos says. "Tomorrow. The crack of dawn. We park down the street. Stake out his house. The second he steps outside...to get the Sunday paper, go for breakfast, whatever...we walk up to him and catch him off guard. Question him right there."

"I like it," the deputy says with a full mouth. "What do you reckon we say to him?"

Without any evidence linking Lorendinski to the escapees, Ramos will have to come in at an indirect angle, try to scare him another way.

"According to his file, this guy is the leader of a motorcycle gang, right?" Ramos asks.

"Right."

"How many men are in those things? At least a dozen. Sometimes way more..."

The deputy nods.

"The gang is tied to the cartels. So they're likely moving drugs through Rene. Hell, Elrod Ness probably buys his meth off them, which is how he knew Lorendinski in the first place." Ramos smirks. "What if we say we busted one of his lower-level gang members for dealing?"

"But we didn't."

"He has no way of knowing that. We'll offer it up and try to leverage it against him. Manipulate him into giving us what we *really* want, information about the prisoners."

"You mean lie?"

Ramos looks down at his still-untouched steak and eggs, the heat coming off of the plate dissipating. "I mean say what we have to in order to catch the fugitives. Whether it's true or not doesn't matter."

The deputy sets down his fork. He taps his chin with his pointer finger for a bit. "I don't know, boss. I never been comfortable lying. Gives me the jitters same as too much coffee."

"I might be wrong about you being a detective, after all. A good cop does what he needs to put criminals behind bars. The ends matter. Not the means. Sometimes you have to lie when you're questioning a suspect. There are no rules against it in the police handbook. People like Wade Lorendinski, law-breakers, don't deserve any morality."

The deputy nods in agreement, though his discomforted expression tells Ramos he doesn't really agree. "How are you gonna use the lie to get him to give up the fugitives?"

"First I tell him I'm *certain* he helped them escape. I won't tell him how, keep it open-ended, keep him guessing. By the look on his face I'll know whether or not he did. Then I'll tell him about the gang member we apparently busted. I'll say he gave up Lorendinski's name in the interrogation room." He sips his coffee. "Then I'll assure Lorendinski I can make it all go away if he lets us know where the prisoners are."

"Hmm. Think he'll fall for it?"

"Fifty-fifty. But without any real evidence, that's the best we'll get." The road outside is barren of headlights, totally black. Ramos cuts into his meal for the first time and eats a big piece of sirloin glazed in egg yolk. "But I have a good feeling about it, Noah."

Thirty

The lower half of Monty's right leg feels chopped off. It went numb, an aftershock from the spurt of pain that was recently gushing through it. At twelve thirty when Wade came down to snap his photo, Monty protested posing, declaring he'd no longer play along now that he knew Wade was killing him.

In response, Wade unbuttoned Monty's jeans, ripped them down to his ankles, unwound the bandage around his right knee, then rammed a Phillips-head screwdriver into his wound and kept it there until Monty consented. With the jeans back on, the freshly opened, bloodily flowing gash was hidden, and the photo to Danny didn't carry a hint of suspicion.

Monty is staring at the odd sight of his right leg, this part of his body he can't feel. He wonders if death will feel the same way. Is it just numbness? He doesn't know. But he will soon. He assumes Danny must be closing in on El Paso by now. Once his parents pass him the duffel bag of money, Phil will put a call into Wade and Wade will put a bullet in Monty's head.

Pondering all this the last hour or so, Monty came to the conclusion that Danny won't get out of this alive either.

When they were planning the escape, Phil always discussed their margin of error. Once Phil gets his hands on that cash, Danny himself becomes Phil's potential for error. And Phil always preferred eliminating his potential for error.

Monty knows how important Phil's science is to him. He's using the money for a lab. The last thing Phil would want is Danny's pissed-off parents, down a quarter million bucks, trying to track him down in Mexico to reclaim their stolen loot.

Wade isn't meeting Phil and Danny south of the border. Once Danny gives Phil the money, he'd become suspicious if Phil never continued on to hand it off to Wade. He'd realize Phil was keeping it. Something he could share with his parents.

Now it's clear why Phil wasn't upfront about his intentions, why he lied to Danny and Monty earlier and said the full quarter million was for Wade. During the car ride to El Paso, he didn't want Danny informing his parents it was Phil who was robbing them. His parents know what Phil looks like. His photo is all over the news. And they have the means to hire a private investigator to head down to Mexico searching for a man with that appearance.

Danny is the sole link between his parents and Phil. He's the sole reason Phil's lab may not become a reality. Once Danny produces the money, Phil needs him gone. And now that Monty is certain Phil had the potential to commit those heinous rapes, he's sure he has the potential to squeeze a trigger and squash the last of his potential for error.

Thirty-One

Jane's head rests on Danny's left shoulder, waves of her black and purple hair gently swaying across his chest from the motion of the car. After she was knocked out cold behind the gas station, Danny carried her back to the Buick. He periodically shook her in the backseat. She soon woke up. Though she's lucid, she's been slipping into slightly loopy spells.

They've covered a lot of ground since stopping for gas, now nearly at the Stockton Plateau. In that stretch of three-plus hours, Danny has predominantly been focused on keeping Jane awake. He's almost positive she has a concussion.

Phil, sitting on the gun, is hunched over the wheel, his face close to the windshield. Danny assumes to compensate for his lack of specs, which Jane busted with that kick. It's a bit frightening a man with bad vision and no glasses is operating the vehicle. Not only have their chances of running over a sharp object gone up, but those of an accident. In either case they'd be trapped out here among the hulking mesas bordering the Pecos River, prey for police.

Danny would volunteer to take the wheel, but doesn't want to leave Jane. If she falls asleep with a concussion, he knows the health risk is severe. He peeks down at her. Her eyes are still open. Good. He feels her snuggle into him. Not good. She's getting too comfortable, which means sleep could set in.

Sure enough, the blues of her eyes soon disappear beneath their lids. "Jane," he whispers, shaking her. "Hey," a little louder.

One eyelid lifts. "Hi," in a sleepy voice. Then the other. "Hi."

He reaches down to a partially drank can of Coke between his feet and guides it toward her lips. "Have some more of this. It'll keep you up."

"I don't need any of that." She giggles.

"Just a few more sips."

She sticks her finger inside, wets it, then sucks it. "That counts as a sip." Another giggle.

He takes a deep breath and says to Phil, "We need to drop her off at a hospital. This is ridiculous."

A moment.

"Four more hours," Phil replies. "She can go to a hospital then."

"She needs to go *now*."

"And *now*, we need to make sure the police don't find us. You want to go back to jail because your girlfriend has a little headache?"

"It's more than a headache."

"Don't worry about me," Jane says to Danny, patting his knee. "I'm okay."

He stares at her for a bit. Then turns to Phil and says, "We do it like they do for college kids who overdose. We pull up to the hospital, drop her off, then zoom away."

"Hospitals are crowded. Too many eyeballs. Even if we don't get out of the car, someone may spot us. Not worth the risk. We need to keep our margin of error as high as possible. You know that, Daniel. You're just distracted by our runaway here because she has a nice ass."

The way Phil says "nice ass," with a carnal gutturalness, turns Danny's stomach. This hospital debate is futile. Phil doesn't want to stop, and as long as he holds Monty as his hostage, he calls the shots.

Danny pivots to the window, vacantly watching the spikes and stalks of green sotol whip by them on the limestone-dominated expanse of landscape as he thinks.

"You gonna hang out at the beach in California?" he asks Jane, trying to get her to talk, hoping to keep her up.

"Definitely."

"Surf?"

"Nah. When I'm at the beach I like reading a book on a lounge chair. I never go in the water. It's always too cold."

"Even in California?"

"I don't know." Her eyes close for a second. He gets anxious. Then they open. "I want to go to Joshua Tree."

"I heard that place is awesome," he says in an overly enthusiastic voice, angling to nudge this nugget of interest offered by her into a conversation. "You'll camp out when you go?"

No answer. He scopes her face. Her eyes are open but already seem detached from this chat. She hums, "Doo doo, doo doo, doo doo doo…."

Has she lost it?

"Are you going to visit me in California?" she asks.

The intelligibly worded question gives him some relief. Her mind is still there. "I can't see you in California," he says. "Mexico. Remember?"

"Ahhhh. Yes. Mexico." She nuzzles a bit closer to him.

He reflects on what she told him in that alley in Austin. He planned to just brush it off, but couldn't. It's squeezed his head like a too-tight hat since they left.

Will Mexico provide the freedom he envisioned?

This question has bothered him the last few hours just as much as his worries about the replacement tire and ramping-up manhunt. To properly contemplate this, he decides to lay out a timeline in his mind of everything leading up to his choice to flee south of the border.

Two years ago he hit Robert Patrick Flynn's car with his. And he ran. From the collision scene, from what he did. He felt remorse, sure. He was sorry. But he was scared. So he ran.

Immediately after the accident, stricken with a broken collarbone and glass-slashed skin, he was thrown into the vortex of the legal process, with all those inquiries and papers and statements. Then the trial. Then prison. His mind shuddered into defense mode. All his mental energy was channeled into self-preservation and adaptation. He had no leftover capacity to deal with something as complex as the dissection of his guilt.

But the guilt was there. Though he tried to pretend it wasn't.

He never quite adapted to jail, and though he preserved his life, he always felt it was on the chopping block. The worst ass kicking came one afternoon around Easter. In the yard. Danny isn't definite what provoked it. Potentially, just because he made eye contact with the wrong man a second too long. This short but steroid-pumped Aryan kneed him in the gut. When Danny hunched over, he took another knee to the thorax, then a third to his nose. Two hands clamped his throat and strangled.

The guards broke it up before Danny was suffocated into a life of brain damage or nothingness, killed. There was a lot of laughter around the yard as he rolled around wheezing.

After they cleaned him up in the infirmary they sent in the prison shrink to talk to him, to see how he was holding up after the mauling. What was her name again? Feckstein. With the frizzy hair. He liked her. She was nice. But she couldn't fix his situation, couldn't prevent any future attacks in the yard. Her speech was nothing more than a figurative pat on the back (and if he remembers correctly, she even gave him an actual pat on the back).

Then his new cellmate Phil came along, a much better counselor than Feckstein. He warned that Danny had a psychological problem, but not guilt. Rather, weakness. Phil said Danny was depressed in prison because he came from the upper middle class and couldn't co-exist with the underbelly of society.

He advised that Danny shouldn't be ashamed of his weakness, however must acknowledge it because it would soon mean life or death. Phil cautioned that Danny wouldn't survive much longer in Crick, that the next beating could be his last, that there was nowhere to run.

Phil admitted he wasn't made for prison life either, however enjoyed protection from the Aryans because he purchased things from them. He mentioned Danny could consider that route. Or opt for something much better, something that wasn't a mere security policy but a real solution. That's when he told him about his plan to escape and the potential for a fresh start in Mexico.

Danny was hesitant. The idea of a breakout was frightening. A guard could shoot him dead. However, Phil stressed that Danny was already at a life-or-death crossroads since jail would kill him eventually, physically via an inmate attack or mentally via a deterioration of his psyche. So why not take a risk to get out alive?

But tonight Danny wonders if Phil really had his best interests in mind. Was Danny so weak that he was sure to perish in prison before his sentence was up, like Phil promised? He's not certain if he could've done his time or not. However, he is certain that Phil wanted him to *think* he couldn't. If Danny remained in prison, Phil couldn't retain him on the outside as a pawn to pay Wade.

Danny is beginning to see that Phil's deception was deeper than he first figured. And recognizes that Jane might be right. Maybe Danny isn't over the loss of Robert Patrick Flynn's leg. Maybe Phil tricked him into further repressing it. Maybe that chunk of ice that's been in his stomach the last year and a half, the one that didn't disappear when he escaped, isn't the coldness of prison, but rather, the awareness that he hasn't dealt with the guilt of his crime.

If so, the ice won't melt away in the Mexican sun.

Jane again hums, "Doo doo, doo doo, doo doo doo..." Then, off-key, sings, "And I remember she used to fall down a lot. That girl was always falling again and again. And I used to sometimes try to catch her. But never even caught her name." A pause. "Yes I sometimes even tried to catch her. But never even caught her name."

He doesn't know what song the lyrics are from.

"Doo doo, doo doo, doo doo doo..." Her eyes close. A second. Two. Three.

"Jane." He shakes her.

"Hi." She's with him again. "Hi."

And she stays with him for the next half hour. Danny glances at the console clock. 5:08 AM. The sky is dark-grayish with purple-rimmed clouds, yet Danny expects the morning to show through soon.

A vibration on his leg. The phone. Carefully balancing Jane's head on his shoulder, he reaches into his pocket and removes the burner. Two messages. He must've not felt the first, which is a check-in picture of Monty. Five fingers for five AM. The last few hours Monty has looked terrible in these photos. No injuries, rather, something in his expression. It's been devoid of that spark Monty always has. Danny assumes it's from sleep deprivation.

He closes that message and scopes the second. From his mother's number. Excitement surges through him. He guesses they finally got the money in order. He opens it and reads:

Went to 24hr pawn shop in city. Sold my diamond ear rings and some bracelets. We're still short. Tried all nite. Ppl scared to give $ with you in news. How much longr til u get to el paso?

The excited current in his body is cut off. He writes back:

Any other options?

She answers:

Dad will sell truck at lot when they open. Still wouldn't be enough tho. We have a little less than half. about 110k. when will u be in ep?

He doesn't reply. He needs to think about this. A hard-ass like Wade would never accept a penny under the demanded amount. If they get to El Paso and Danny doesn't get the full of it, Monty remains Wade's captive.

Danny could possibly convince Wade to wait until Monday, when the banks are open and the remainder of the cash can be withdrawn. Danny and Phil would have to hide out in El Paso over the weekend, with the manhunt swelling around them. It's hazardous, but could be the only option.

But no. Jane. Phil won't let her go to a hospital until they have all of the money and head out toward the border. Who knows how serious her head injury could get if Phil kept her imprisoned in El Paso without medical attention all weekend?

Danny can't draw this out. All the money must be there before they arrive. Every dollar. In four hours. How could they do it? Danny is a clever guy. He can figure this out. He thinks about his old job at Amogo Studios, how they'd instruct the team to approach new problems deductively, starting with broad categories, then drilling down into the specifics. He does this now, running subjects and scenarios through his head.

He soon comes up with something. A rush of excitement runs through him. If this works, he'll have all the money. Then he can finally take a breath of relief.

Thirty-Two

A gray van with "Southwest Electric and Power" stenciled on the side rides through Rene, the pinks and oranges of nautical twilight spanning the horizon.

Ramos mans the wheel, the deputy in the passenger seat, both in jeans and tucked-in polo shirts with chest stitching matching the lettering on the side of the vehicle. Ramos, who bagged no more than two hours of sleep, is artificially alert on caffeine, not actually rested. He woke up with the kernel of a cold in his throat, a soreness he predicts will worsen through the day.

The deputy takes a pull of coffee from his Thermos. His foot taps the mat on the floor at about a rep a second. Ramos makes a right, a loose milk crate in the back grumbling over the metal surface and clunking into the wall, the sound startling the deputy, some coffee spilling onto his denim lap.

"Dear," he mutters, looking down. "Any paper towels in here?"

"This is a stakeout van, not a food truck."

In five minutes the tips of Rene's oil derricks peek out atop the tree line, their forms still silhouettes in the not-quite-risen sun. Ramos turns left onto Hatchet Trail, Wade Lorendinski's street. He parks at the end, a few hundred feet from the house. "The brown one," he tells the deputy. "Second from last."

Leaning forward, the deputy peers through the windshield. Ramos fishes a set of hunting binoculars out of a milk crate between the driver and passenger seats. He holds them to his eyes, peeping Lorendinski's property. A Harley Davidson is parked in the driveway, beside it a utility van with tints that looks similar to theirs, but black instead of gray.

This is good, Ramos thinks. A full driveway means Lorendinski is likely home. However, the windows are all dark. He peeks at the clock, 5:31 AM, and says, "A little early for him to come out. Get comfortable. We may have to wait for a while."

"What if he's not there? Say he has an old lady and slept over her place."

Possible, Ramos reasons. If a girlfriend picked him up last night, his vehicles would be in his driveway, but he wouldn't be in the house.

Ramos pets his chin with his thumb as he says, "We'd be wasting valuable time tracking down these escapees if we staked out a vacant house all day. In our disguises, with our badges hidden, he wouldn't take us for cops. We could just ring the bell now. He'd have no reason not to open the door."

"He'd probably open it, sir. But maybe not. He's a lifelong criminal. I'm sure plainclothes policemen have approached him in the past, before he moved to Rene. If he's up to no good he may get suspicious if two fellas he don't recognize come a knockin' on his front door, regardless of what they're wearing. He'd hunker down in there all day, avoid us. Like you said last night, boss, we only have one shot at this. Would be best to catch him totally off guard, when he comes out on his own doing."

Two shifts in a row the subordinate is beating Ramos to the answers. It's the lack of sleep, he assures himself. And the cold. "Fine. But we should at least confirm if he's home then. We'll have to get up close. See if we can hear footsteps through a window. Voices. Even a TV. Anything. We've got to be careful, though. Quiet. If he notices us snooping around, his guard will *really* go up."

"Okay," the deputy says, opening the door.

"What are you doing?"

"I thought we were going to check out the house?"

"Not now. He's probably sleeping. Let's wait until he'd be up, making some noise." Ramos points at the clock. "We'll try at seven AM. If we don't hear something inside, we'll go back at nine. Then eleven. If no noise by then, we'll call it a wrap."

The deputy closes the door. "Good thinking, sir."

Ramos rubs his palms together. An excited grin forms on his face. "We're close, Noah. We get to Lorendinski, he gets us to the fugitives. These hoodlums are going down. And we're going to get all the credit."

"I just want to make sure they're off our streets."

"That too, Noah. That too."

Thirty-Three

Ben Marsh drives his Ford King Ranch pickup through the Upper Valley of El Paso, the rays of rising sun in the east sweeping across the summer sky and streaking the brown ridges of the Franklin Mountains to the west.

His wife, nervously gnawing at the cuticles of her middle and ring fingers, sits beside him. The radio is off. During the last half-day, as they drove around in this truck dropping in on business colleagues and family friends with an incessantly unsuccessful IOU pitch, they kept the radio on to keep awake. But one too many times the music faded into an advisory about the dangerous prisoners on the loose, one being their little boy. So they've stopped listening.

Within the quiet vehicle in the quiet neighborhood, Ben can hear the sound of Hannah's front tooth clamping on the frail rim of skin cupping her fingernail and clicking on the keratin.

In three minutes they pull up to a twenty-two-acre lot with a driveway lined with palm trees. Ben has the same sticky feeling in his gut he had during the hour the Marsh family waited in the lobby of a veterinarian's office ten years ago to hear about the fate of their sick pet collie. There was a chance the dog would make it, but the odds were low. That's how Ben feels about this trip.

The pickup motors up the driveway, which gives way to a stone fountain and a stone mansion behind it. Ben parks. He draws a three-second inhale, followed by a five-second exhale. He gently takes his wife's hand from her teeth and holds it in his. She starts biting her other one. They sit like this for a while.

"Okay," he says. And steps out. Though the sun gleams, the temperature is cooler than he expected, his flesh taking a moment to recalibrate to the climate. He walks toward the home, its terracotta roof breaking off in four directions, columned arches beneath it and towered chimneys above. Hannah follows him to the front entrance, eight-foot windows flanking it on each side.

He grips a mounted iron ring on the door and bangs. Twenty seconds go by. Nothing. Another bang, a bit harder. Two minutes.

Just before he knocks again, the door opens. A confused, half-asleep face in its late thirties stares out at them, the body below cloaked in a bathrobe made of an expensive material Ben couldn't title. The man holds an inquisitive look on them, as if waiting for them to clarify their presence.

"Hi," Ben says. "You don't know me." A moment. "But you know my son."

"Are you aware it's six something in the fucking morning?"

"The time is irrelevant to me. I haven't slept all night. We're desperate. And you're our last chance." Ben's voice has gravity to it. The man's face now has curiosity in it. "Like I said, you know my son. He worked for you. Two years ago."

"A lot of people worked for me two years ago."

"I'm Ben Marsh. Danny's dad."

The man looks down at the floor. He pushes his fingers through his hair. He has an exotic, mixed-raced face, more handsome than not, white and Filipino Ben guesses. "I saw the news," the man says. "Last night. Is Danny...is..." He softens his voice. "Is he okay?"

"We don't think so, Mr. Chaplin."

The man's expression is no longer half-asleep, rather ultra-awake, as if Ben's recent words were espresso shots. "Call me Buddy." He wipes some crust from his eyes. "And I'm your last chance? Last chance at what?"

"Danny told us we might be able to count on you."

"With what? Hiding him? I...I'm a software guy...I don't have experience with...that...sort of thing."

Ben nods at the interior of the home behind the doorway, a twenty-foot foyer with a black piano, modern-art canvases on the walls. "It might be best if we went inside and talked."

A half hour later Danny's parents are sitting on a sofa in the living room, Danny's former employer across from them in a wingback accent chair. Ben just filled Buddy in on everything. The odd phone call Hannah received from Danny a few hours after he escaped. The apparent trouble he's in. The need for a quarter million dollars to get out of that trouble. The hundred forty thousand they're short. The IOU proposition.

The looming deadline, two hours and change till Danny arrives in El Paso.

Buddy, who's switched out of the robe into khakis and a tee shirt, holds his head in his palm, a contemplative look on him. The wall behind him is covered with framed magazine spreads featuring him, publications like *Wired, Forbes, Fast Company,* and headings like "40 Under 40," "Amogo Goes Big," and "The New Mavericks of Virtual Reality." A decorative, though authentic, samurai sword hangs horizontally on two pegs above the display.

Ben and Hannah, holding hands, wait for him to say something. He gazes at Buddy's face, anticipating a movement of the mouth, a rise of an eyebrow, anything.

"I don't have much cash in the house or in the office," Buddy says.

And the sticky feeling in Ben's stomach turns into the feeling it turned into ten years ago when the vet finally gave them the news that the family dog, Jasper, died.

"But," Buddy adds. "That doesn't mean I'm not willing to help."

Ben hunches forward. "It has to be *cash* though. Danny was adamant about this. For whatever reason, only cash will do."

"I got that." A moment. "And I don't have cash on hand. Not the kind you need anyway."

Ben feels he's missing something. Is this guy dense? Wasn't he supposed to be some tech whiz?

"When it happened," Buddy says, "in 2014, I couldn't sleep for two months. An hour here, an hour there. No more than three in any night." He crosses his right leg over his left, the moccasin on his right foot bobbing with a wiry energy. "It was a company event, after all, that Danny was at that night. I was there. I was…in charge." The moccasin moves even quicker. "I should've checked. Harder. Much harder. Before… to make sure people were okay to drive. Danny seemed fine." He chuckles, distantly. "That's what people always say though, isn't it? 'He seemed fine.' A part of me feels responsible. For what happened."

"The past is the past," Ben says. "Since 2014, I've had to tell that to myself every day just to get out of bed. I came here today to ask you about the *future*. The immediate future. The very immediate future." Ben glimpses his watch. "You say you want to help, but if you don't have cash, on you, now, I'm afraid there's nothing you could do. Even if your heart is in the right place."

Buddy nods at a six-by-six painting on the wall above the Marsh couple. "You know who painted that?"

Ben and Hannah rotate on the couch and peek up at it. An abstract painting of glass medicine bottles on a hitching post with the tops shot off, like beer bottles in the Wild West. Ben turns back to Buddy with an *I have no fucking idea* expression.

"An artist named Scorched Earth," Buddy says. "I'm guessing you never heard of him if you don't recognize that. Anyway, he's getting popular in contemporary-art circles. I bought that in Miami a year ago for fifty grand. It's worth at least two hundred now."

Ben gives it another once-over. He doesn't see two hundred thousand dollars of value hanging up on that wall, but that's for art people to decide, not farmers.

"I'm a member at Yupatta," Buddy says. "You know, the—"

"I know what it is." The ritziest country club in West Texas.

"A guy I golf with there from time to time is very into art. Norb Morton. Manufactures horse saddles. Big bucks. What did you say Danny needed? A hundred forty thou?"

Ben nods.

"Norb would be stealing that Scorched Earth painting if I sold it to him for that."

Hannah's face perks up. She squeezes Ben's thigh.

"Wait, wait, now," Ben says, his tone sobering. "Cash. We need it in cash. Him writing you a check doesn't help."

"Norb is always running around the club talking about how the big banks are nothing but a bunch of Yankee Ponzi schemes. And he's filthy rich. I'm sure he has at least a few hundred grand locked up at home."

Ben glances at Hannah. For the first time since yesterday morning he sees her grin.

"We've got to get this thing off the wall," Buddy says. "Wrap it up, secure it to the back of that truck you pulled up in, get it over to Mission Hills where Norb lives...without a scratch or it's ruined and he won't go for it...wake him up... he's a big drinker and I'm sure he's sleeping off last night...give him the painting and get the cash." He stands. "We don't have a lot of time." And claps his hands. "Let's go."

Thirty-Four

Monty doesn't react when Wade enters his field of vision. His mind is elsewhere, far from this cellar, on the good memories from his past. He doesn't think about the future because he knows he doesn't have one. He'll be dead any moment.

Wade reaches over him, the hanging leather of his vest slapping Monty's cheek, unfastens the padlock securing his hand restraints, and says, "Seven."

Avoiding another screwdriver driven into his knee, Monty agrees to go along with it. He lifts his hands, showing five fingers on the left, two on the right. Wade snaps the photo.

Monty notices movement behind the blinds over the basement window. Bluish forms, visible only through the shreds of space between the slats. He hears something through the glass. Soft, but distinguishable. Voices. Two of them. Male. Wade spins toward the sound.

Monty doesn't know who the hell is out there. But he does know whoever it is may be his only hope to get out of here alive. He musters up any remaining morsels of might in his body, directs them to his lungs, and yells, "Help."

Wade turns to him. "Shut up."

"Help. Help. Down here. Help."

The bluish forms, which Monty sees are legs in jeans, stop. "Hold on," a voice outside shouts. Then the figures vanish, zipping toward the rear of the house.

Wade's breath gets weighty. His brow gets crinkly. "You piece of shit," he says. With the fist holding the padlock keys, he delivers a backhanded blow across Monty's face, his largest knuckle punching the right juncture where the top and bottom lip meet. Monty's head breaks to the left as his neck absorbs the shock of the wallop.

A moment. He spits, two bloody gobs of saliva muddying the gray of the concrete.

Wade scowls at him, then steps past him, cautiously creeping toward the stairwell, peeking at the ajar door atop.

A thud rattles through the first floor of the house. "Open up," the same voice that spoke before says. Another thud.

Monty guesses they're slamming on that sliding glass door he remembers seeing when he went up to take a piss. His hands are still loose from the photo Wade just took. He's able to rotate his upper body. He turns over his shoulder, spotting Wade with his back butted against the cinderblock wall, his eyes angled up to the kitchen.

Dahllrun. Dahllrun. More slams resonate downstairs. That same voice says, "Open up. Police."

Wade huffs. He says something under his breath Monty can't make out. Then raises his head and voice and says something he can make out, "You stupid nigger. Look what you did. They're gonna drag you back to prison. Now I'm fucked too. All because you had to open up your mouth." Then to the floor, "Son of a bitch."

Monty swivels his head forward. He looks down at his lap. His fingers tap his knees. He thinks. The police. Okay, the police. No, this isn't ideal. But it's better than this crazy Nazi shooting him in the head once Danny gets the money. Of course he'd take jail over that. Just sit here patiently, wait for this to play out. Then back to prison. But back alive. Yes, yes, alive.

"Open up dammit," the officer demands, his voice loudening.

Twenty seconds go by.

A gunshot roars upstairs, accompanied by the shriek of shattering glass. The police shot through the sliding door, Monty figures. He spins back around. Wade throws the keys and phone down and unholsters his pistol from his shoulder harness. Clutching it with both hands in front of his face, he peers at the wedge of space at the top of the steps.

Noises flow through into the cellar. First a click, which Monty assumes is a hand unlocking the slider from outside. Then the glide of a door slab on tracks. Then the crunch of shoes on broken glass. Monty notices something on Wade's face he never thought he'd see. Panic. At Wade's feet he notices something he also never thought he'd see.

The shackle keys, unguarded.

A sword of nervous excitement cuts through him. His hands are free. What if he tried to grab the keys? He runs the possibility through his head. They're about nine feet away, way more than a reach. He'd have to get himself across the floor. Which wouldn't be easy with the metal chair still chained to his ankles. He could tip it, he supposes. Then crawl. Wade would certainly notice. Aluminum banging on concrete isn't faint. Wade would pick up the keys, putting an end to it. Probably boot him in the teeth to boot, just for trying.

The creak of footsteps on old floorboards circles above Monty. "Lorendinski, come out now, hands up," the cop hollers.

The range of the creaking widens. They're going room to room.

"Nobody needs to get hurt," a second voice, higher-pitched than the first, says upstairs.

The sound of the footsteps gravitates toward the stairwell door. Pellets of sweat fall from Wade's bushy hairline. The squeak of hinges. The cellar door is opening.

Wade pulls his trigger.

A bullet pumps through the door, shards of plywood spraying into the basement.

Calmness for three seconds.

Puchoon. Puchoon. Two return shots from the cops.

One nearly hits Wade's left rib. He drops his big body to the floor, trying to make it scarce, a difficult task at six four, two forty.

Monty, his heart clapping, watches the action from his chair, just removed from the police's line of fire. *Puchoon.*

He needs to cross into the danger zone, though. For the keys. With Wade belly-down on the floor, distracted by gunfire, now is his best chance.

"Drop the weapon," the cop with the deeper voice screams. "And come up the stairs, showing your hands."

Wade blasts another round at the cops. They blast one back. He rolls, arm wrapped over his skull, protecting his brain.

Go. Monty thrusts his weight to the side, the attached chair plummeting to the surface with him. On hands and knees, he bounces toward the keys, his back at an unnatural, upturned angle, like a scorpion's tail. The rear support of the seat bobs over him like the stinger.

Seven feet away. Six. Four.

Two.

One.

As Wade shoots at the cops, he notices Monty snatch the key ring. Wade leans toward him, however a bullet careens down the steps, causing him to hop back.

Monty flips his body the other direction and flops toward the rear wall. Along the way, he spots Wade's burner cell phone on the concrete and nabs it.

Puchoon.

Reaching the window, Monty stops crawling. He pushes the wall, propping the seat back up, repossessing footing. Then leaps. The chair weighs him down some, but he gets enough loft to land his forearms on the sill. The blinds convulse from contact with his elbows.

Behind him, he hears Wade's weapon send another shot up the stairwell.

Monty sticks the key ring between his teeth, rips the blinds over his head, and glimpses the base of the window in search of a lock. He sees it and turns it with his free hand. He pushes on the glass, the bottom half of the pane kicking out along its horizontal pivot. A gust of fresh air touches his face.

Puchoon.

He throws the phone outside, then latches onto handfuls of grass. He pulls himself forward. The green blades in his right palm tear, his momentum deadening.

His left fingers force their way into the earth, dirt now to his knuckles. He squeezes his bicep, his body slowly squirming through the window. A grunt from deep in his lungs. A groping of more grass in his right hand. All the muscles in his upper body strain. The fingernail on his left index finger snaps, pain consuming his arm to the elbow.

He heaves himself outside up to his knees. One more lunge and he'll be fully out of the basement. He pushes forward.

Dlink. He's stopped. Stuck.

He jerks his legs toward his stomach. *Dlink. Dlink.* The aluminum chair is slamming into something. Looking back, he sees it's too wide to fit through the window.

Fuck.

He's got to get the ankle chains off.

Now.

He slackens his jaw, the key ring plopping to the grass. Two keys on it, one for the already-off hand restraints, one for the currently-a-problem ankle ones. He doesn't know which is which. So guesses. Curling his torso, he grips the padlock by his feet and guides the grooved metal nub of one key into it.

Not a fit.

He retries. Nope.

"Shit," he spits out. His trembling fingers feel for the second key. Just as they grab it, his body begins hurtling back through the window. He drops the key ring and clamps the sideways windowpane for support. Glancing down his legs, through the slivered spaces among the disarray of blinds, he sees the Nazi emblem emblazoned on Wade's shoulder. He's tugging on the chair, trying to suck him back into the basement.

Monty's empty stomach burns with nerves. He fixes his left hand to the exterior wall of the house, blood streaming out his index finger where its nail used to be. He feels his spine stretch. A muscle audibly pops in his back.

A police gunshot booms through the basement and echoes through the wooded area surrounding the house. Wade, firing one back, eases up on the chair for a moment. Monty picks up the key, the *other* one, the correct one. With the same hand, he steadies the silver padlock, keeping his left hand on the house wall as a defense against Wade pulling again.

Monty tries to insert the key into the hole, using just one hand. However, a trace of a wobble to the lock makes this impossible.

"Come on," he says to himself, trying again.

The lock's body does a three-sixty on its shank as Wade tugs the chair again. Monty's left elbow buckles. Wade yanks. Monty's left fingers loosen from the house.

Another yank. Monty loses his grip from the wall. His knees slide back through the window. He can't tread this riptide much longer. He grips the glass pane. Wade pulls even harder. The screws of the window pivot quiver.

"Get back here," Wade growls.

"Suck my big black dick, hillbilly," Monty says, holding on with everything he has. His joints cry with pain as the beast tries to drag him under. Monty's body inches into the basement. He's losing this fight.

"Hands up, Lorendinski," the lower-voiced cop shouts. His words sound louder than before. Closer. Peeking through the blinds, Monty sees two other bodies in the basement with Wade. Both holding weapons on him.

The pulling on the seat stops. Monty doesn't know for how much longer. He removes his left hand from the glass and seizes the padlock. Steadying it against his palm, he slips the key with his right hand into the hole. He turns.

The clink of the detaching bolt catches Wade's attention. Despite the police orders, he throws his hand on the chair and jerks. Monty removes the lock just before the force of Wade's arm can act on it. The chains rush around Monty's ankles, loosening as the chair charges inside.

Monty jumps backward, backing the full of his feet from the basement. He glimpses his ankles, resting on a bed of green grass.

No chains.

He picks up the cell phone with his bloody hand and sprints toward the woods.

Thirty-Five

Danny tells himself how beautiful Jane's eyes are, and how dry they look at the same time. He imagines they're just as dry as the Chihuahuan Desert surrounding the Buick. As if they want to cry but are unable. At least they're open though. At least he's kept her awake.

But he doesn't know for how much longer. Fighting a night's sleep is hard enough under normal conditions. He can only picture the added difficulty when a concussion trapped in your head is trying to conk you out.

"Getting close," he tells her, trying to sound upbeat.

She doesn't answer. He's not sure if she's too tired to hear him, or heard him and is too tired to reply. It doesn't matter. Just stay awake, Jane. Not much longer to go.

In his periphery the Sunday sun rises over a steep-bodied butte, bringing to the desert the promise of a new day, its whitish-gold glisten fanning out over seemingly infinite acreage of sandy soil, stirring the colorful splendor of the flora, from the reds of the fire-belly cacti to the lime of the gypsum grama grass to the purple pads of long-spine prickly pear.

Yes, a new day, the day this will all be over.

A buzz on Danny's leg. The burner. His mom he assumes, hopefully with the news he anticipates. He removes the phone from his pocket, but doesn't flip it open. He's too damn nervous. He knows Buddy Chaplin was his last chance to get the cash on time.

Danny's heart dances. His palms dampen. He lifts the screen. And closes his eyes. A few moments.

He opens one eye. Then the other. The message, from his mother as he expected, reads:

> *We got all of it!!! Meet us at Buddy's. big n secluded property. No police around. U'll be ok there.*

He feels as if the rays of sun outside the car have come in and entered his body, invigorating him like some mythological sky tonic. He's so grateful for his great mother.

And father.

After a two-year grudge, his dad came through for him. Danny was wrong about him. His dad doesn't hate him. You don't blindly hand a quarter million dollars of hard-earned money over to someone you hate. Danny and Ben have their differences, but hate isn't a similarity.

Today, Danny is ready to give this father-son relationship another try. And end his relationship with his false father figure, Phil.

"My parents," Danny declares to the car, "got the money."

Hunched over the wheel, his bare, non-bespectacled stare attached to the road, Phil smiles so wide his mouth seems to break past his eyes. Soon it tightens into a tidy pucker and out it hums the overture from *The Marriage of Figaro*, the same tune Danny remembers him singing moments before they embarked in Rene.

Ten minutes pass. Calmness. The blue sky shimmers. Yes, a new day indeed.

Another buzz on Danny's leg. He takes out the phone. His nerves now allayed, he flips it open with a cool hand.

The message hits his unsuspecting pupils like a tossed cup of hot coffee:

> *It's me, Monty. I got out. Phil really did rape those girls. He's a maniac. He's using the money to buy shit for a lab. & he's gonna KILL YOU as soon as he gets it.*

Danny gapes at it for a half-minute. His body loses feeling, but his head continues to work. In moments of extreme stress his thoughts are usually quick and jumbled. But now they're just the opposite. Slow, painfully slow, and clear, painfully clear.

First, he asks himself if this is a hoax. He checks the number the text came from. The same one Wade has been sending him photos from since yesterday. Danny rereads the message. *I got out.* So Monty is loose? And he got his hands on Wade's phone? Danny can't imagine how. Yet, Monty and Wade have been the only ones near that burner. This message came from one of them. Why the hell would Wade send something like this? It had to be Monty. He's out. And he's looking out for Danny.

This is no hoax.

Phil really did rape those girls. Is it possible? Phil's story always felt a bit implausible, that whole DNA-planting thing. But Danny still believed it. In jail, Phil came off as such a good guy. Never capable of committing those crimes. But after seeing a new side of Phil this last day, Danny realizes his old cellmate has savagery in his heart. He very well could be capable of doing what they said he did. And Monty, somehow, must have proof he did.

So Phil is really a rapist. And if he were capable of raping, wouldn't he be capable of murdering? Both acts require the same conscious abandon for another life. If he had one deed in him, there's a good chance he'd have the other.

He's using the money to buy shit for a lab. Danny doesn't know how Monty gleaned this. Regardless, it makes complete sense. With a faculty position out of the question at any university, a rogue laboratory is a fitting solution. Phil cares about nothing more than his research, which he thought was robbed from him. And he'd rob Danny and his family to get it back. Killing Danny kills all ties back to Phil. He'd be able to research in Mexico without the threat of revenge from the Marsh family reeling over him.

Danny's mind churns even slower than it's been, producing things even clearer than it's been.

He could simply refuse to hand Phil the duffel bag of money. However, Phil, due to Danny's announcement moments ago, knows his parents have the cash in their possession.

Phil also knows the name of the Marsh family farm, where they live. If Danny balks at going along with the plan, Phil could kill him, look up the address of the farm, ambush his parents there, snatch the money, and snuff them out too. It would be messy, and risky, however, with a laboratory at stake, Phil may attempt it.

No, Danny can't do that. He can't put his family in jeopardy. He must stick with the plan, never letting on that he's on to Phil. And he can't foresee that ending any other way than with a bullet in his brain from Phil's Sig Sauer.

Thirty-Six

Wade sits in an aluminum chair similar to the one he'd chained Monty to. This one belongs to the Rene Police Department. It's across an identical, empty version, between the seats a table made of some cheap composite material, above it an onion-shaped lamp.

Peering into the reflective side of what he presumes to be a one-way mirror, Wade imagines a bunch of small-time cops on the other end, amped-up because they dragged him into the station. Fucking idiots, he thinks. They have nothing on him.

He smirks at the glass, letting these losers know they can't ruffle him, reminding them that the bad guy always wins, that the good guy and his shitty municipal salary can't quell the tide of human greed that God infused into us when he created us, and the inevitable wave of crime that perpetually pairs with it.

Did they target him for dealing drugs or abducting the nigger? He doesn't know. He's out for a profit in both cases, and the cops are out of their minds if they think they can stop that.

He hopes that spic who arrested him is behind the mirror seeing him smirk. Wade didn't like him. Too proud. Smug even. What does a spic have to be proud about in a white man's country? He pictures that smug spic gloating to his boss on the other side of the glass, exaggerating the details of the shootout in Wade's basement, trying to make himself seem like a brave cowboy. A smirk isn't much, but at least it might help put that brown cop in his place.

The pigs think they're icing him out in this room. Like keeping him seated by himself for a while is going to break him, finesse him into a confession. He laughs, a subtle though audible chuckle.

He's been in and out of police stations and interrogation rooms all over East Texas for thirty years. He knows the drill, knows all the cops' dumb tricks and gimmicks, and is actually looking forward to seeing what the spic comes up with when he questions him.

Wade recalls the first time a cop confronted him. It was a Sunday, just like today. He was thirteen. He and his friend had a fun hobby, sneaking into houses in nice neighborhoods when people were at church and painting a black "X" over each face on the family portrait in the den. The mysterious, ominous events made the local news. All those rich folks with their pretty homes and pretty lives were terrified. They thought a serial killer was sending a message. They thought each time a family member left the house, there was a chance of no return.

He loved it.

An officer spotted young Wade with black dabs of paint on his hands. He was nervous for a second, but talked his way out of it. He's never been antsy around a pig since. He's been pinched for a few things, sure, but talked his way out of ten times more. Unless they have hard evidence he did something wrong, which he can't foresee, he'll walk today without a problem.

However, he does have a different problem. The nigger. He's loose. With a phone. Wade was anticipating killing him. Waiting for Phil to confirm the money was in hand, then going to work on that black body. He'd been debating ways to do it. He decided on a fireplace poker. And to make sure not to hit anything vital for a while. Too bad.

Just as bad as the thought of not killing him is the thought of not getting the money. Fifty large. That's a good take for Wade. The cops can't stop it. But can the nigger? Does he have the wits to text the white kid, tell him he escaped, and somehow tie together a plan with him to shut down the extortion?

Wade's tension eases a bit when he remembers Phil saying he had the white kid figured out. He'd gotten into his head over the last year, duped him into opening up about his deepest thoughts, and now knows his buttons, knows how and when to press them to control him. Besides, Phil said the kid was weak, an upper-middle-class softie. Phil could create a ploy to coax the money out of him, even if the kid receives a text from blackie. However, Wade would need to give Phil some notice, give him enough time to decide what buttons to press.

He spins around and glimpses the clock on the back wall. Phil should be in El Paso soon. Wade doesn't have a lot of time to contact him. He needs to get to a phone. The police owe him one call.

Now if this wetback would only hurry up, get in here, and get this over with.

Thirty-Seven

The skyline of El Paso bulges in perspective as the Buick pursues it. Danny hasn't said a word in an hour. They're almost at Buddy Chaplin's house. And Danny is almost at the end of his life.

He catches his reflection in the rearview mirror. His skin is pale, eyes hollow, head shaved. An image stares back at him reminiscent of a disillusioned soldier on the first day of boot camp. This is a war Danny might not be returning from.

A new thought recently slithered to the front of his mind. It came from the very back, from that darkest of his soul's dark recesses, where he's buried the repressed guilt about Robert Patrick Flynn.

Hell.

Danny is not certain if hell exists. But it very well may. If free will exists, which he believes, hell's reality is more likely, a punishment for those souls who abused their free will on Earth. Danny permanently disfigured a man due to negligence. Does this make him evil, a candidate for hell? He's not sure. But it very well may. In either case, there's a possibility that when Danny dies he ends up there.

He doesn't envision hell how religious people like his dad do, red dungeons with flames, hoards of evildoers huddled in groups, tridents poking them. No. This wouldn't be it. It'd be much simpler, but infinitely worse.

Hell is a small gray room with no windows and no doors and no objects and no other people and four walls as thick as infinity. You're inside. And your physical functions are shut off. No need, or even capability, for air, sleep, food, drink, or sex. But your mind remains on. Forever. Nothing ever changes. Nothing ever ends.

Before the end of the morning Danny may not be in this world anymore, not in America his home, not in Mexico his hiding place, not anywhere else on Earth. There's a good chance he could be in a tiny gray room. And won't ever leave.

When Danny first read Monty's text he figured he was hopeless. However, once he got over the initial shock of the news, *he's gonna KILL YOU*, his thoughts broadened. He *might* have some options.

Now that Monty is free, Phil lost his only bargaining chip. And because Danny hasn't seen Phil check his phone since Austin, he assumes Phil doesn't yet know this chip has been clipped. This puts Danny in a new position to take action.

Danny considered jumping into the front seat and slugging Phil. He'd pry the gun away from the weaker man, throw the creep out of the car onto the desert floor, and deliver a cluster of cathartic blows to his face until he was just as unconscious as he left Jane back in Hill Country.

Then Danny would drive the car to the hospital to drop off Jane. On the way he'd call his parents and tell them to get out of town with the cash. Check into a motel under a fake name. Hide. He'd then take the Buick into Mexico.

It was a sweet thought. However, as Danny chewed on it, he tasted bitterness. There'd be aftermath. Danny isn't a murderer, so wouldn't kill Phil, just beat the shit out of him. Phil would be battered, but still carry breath and a pulse.

Possibly the police would find him on the side of the road and arrest him. But possibly not. Phil is crafty, conniving, and cunning. If not spotted by the cops, he could design a way out of the desert. Maybe stop an oncoming motorist, a female, anyone feebler, attack her and abscond with her car.

Fearing the manhunt, Phil wouldn't stick around in the States for long. Danny's parents would be safe at the motel. Phil, like Danny, would likely drive to Mexico. Phil, like Danny, would then be a free man. And knowing what Danny does now, this is a horrifying concept.

Unlike Danny, Phil brings danger with his freedom. He's apparently a confirmed rapist and conspiring killer. Imagine someone like that running amok in the world. Imagine all the innocent lives he can undo.

Danny wants to dive into that front seat and deck the prick in his opera-humming mouth. But he holds back. If he beats him up and flees to Mexico, sure, he'd thwart Phil's plan to murder him. Danny would not die today. However, he'd still die someday. And if he leaves Phil behind in the desert, essentially unleashing him with free reign on the human population, Danny is certain he'd end up in hell if it exists.

When Danny maimed Robert Patrick Flynn it was unintentional. But if he left Phil on the side of the road, he'd commit a conscious sin. He couldn't selfishly save himself while sensible of the wickedness Phil could inflict on the world.

He won't run.

So where does this leave him?

He's still in a unique position for action. Can he duck Phil's scheme to kill him, while still ensuring Phil won't go free?

Glancing out the window at the familiar hometown scenery, Danny gauges their location and guesses they're no more than twenty minutes from Buddy Chaplin's Upper Valley neighborhood. If Danny is going to do something, he needs to decide what fast.

He applies his trusted deductive method of thought. He analyzes options for the next ten minutes.

An answer comes to him. However, it's an answer he doesn't like. He knows how he could keep himself alive, and keep Phil away from all those innocent lives out there. Danny wouldn't be able to stop the decision once in motion. It'd be permanent. No going back. And he'd be losing something very dear to him in the process.

But he knows he has to do it.

He removes the phone from his pocket. This idea of his he can't do alone. It requires a single phone call to be made. However, he can't make it himself, not with Phil a couple feet away overhearing. He needs someone to place it on his behalf.

Two numbers are stored in his burner. His mother's. And Wade's, which is now technically Monty's. He could text his mom and tell her to make the call. But no. She'd get startled. Ask too many questions. Monty would be the better bet.

So he flips open the screen. And stares at it. Then at El Paso through the window. Then at Phil in the driver's seat. Then at Jane. He takes a deep breath. And types the message. Another deep breath. He hits "send."

Thirty-Eight

The door of the Rene Police Department's sole interrogation room opens. Ramos steps in. He eyes the burly figure in the cut-off leather vest inside the pyramid of light from the lamp. The criminal holds a conceited grin on the cop, the same one he'd been flashing the one-way mirror the last hour or so while they were icing him out. Ramos didn't like the smirk then. Face to face, he likes it less now.

"Let me make my phone call," Lorendinski says.

Ramos closes the door. He walks to the table, setting two open palms on it, and hunches forward, taking on an athletic, ready stance. He has this cretin by the balls. Now it's time to squeeze and make him squeal, find the prisoners, reap the rewards. God, he loves this country.

"Where's Philip Zorn?" Ramos asks.

"Philip who? I have no idea what you're talking about."

Ramos chuckles. "The rapist you helped escape from Crick."

Lorendinski, affecting naiveté, says, "That's right. Zorn. I do remember him. Friendly for a rapist." A moment. "He escaped? Good for him. I always knew he was an enterprising fellow."

Ramos removes his palms from the table, moving them to his hips, his back erect. He points at the patch on Lorendinski's vest, the pair of stitched-shut eyes with "Lost Circle MC" accompanying. Affecting some naiveté of his own, he says, "I believe I've heard of the Lost Circle before. What exactly is it you guys do?"

"My friends and I take long, scenic motorcycle trips through the countryside. When we're done, we gather for tea and discuss the most exciting pieces of foliage we passed that day."

Ramos grins. He begins pacing, his body entering, leaving, and reentering the pyramid of lamplight. "Come to think of it, someone told me Lost Circle functioned a little differently than that. He would know. He's a member. Was just in here. No more than a week ago."

Lorendinski glares at him.

Ramos, still pacing, glares back. The detective continues, "This chap didn't come off like a tea-sipping nature lover. He was a little rough around the edges. But not a hard guy. He *looked* hard. But when we got him in here, in that very chair you're sitting in now, we found out he was pretty…flexible. 'Bendable' would probably be the better word. See, when we found him he was making a mistake. He was selling little bags of a dangerous substance called methamphetamine. Guessing you may have heard of it. He got very apologetic about it. Felt bad and wanted to help us make things right. He had a good suggestion. You know what he said?"

Lorendinski, his glare unbroken, shakes his head.

Ramos goes on, "He said if we really wanted to curb the methamphetamine trade in Rene, we should cut it off at the head. Take out the leader. We let him go because he was nice enough to give us a name. You know whose it was?"

Glare. Head shake.

"Yours." Ramos stops, centering his body in the lamp shine. His palms return to the table. "This sounds like a whole bunch of bad luck for you. I know. But in fact, you have some good luck too. See, I'm aware you're aware of the whereabouts of the three prisoners. And right now, catching dangerous fugitives in the area happens to take priority over cracking down on meth usage in Rene. So I'll make a deal with you. One that'll expire in an hour. I might lose some sleep over it, but I'm willing to do it. You tell me where the escaped prisoners are, and I forget about your gang buddy giving me your name. I won't have my team look into you for meth trafficking. You walk out of here and we forget any of it happened. I know you've got priors, and I know you're going in for a long time if you get nailed for anything else. Help me out with the prisoners, I forget about the drugs."

Ramos keeps his gaze locked on Lorendinski's. He waits for his eyes to turn down in submission. Or at least flinch. Five seconds go by. The eyes don't veer from their leer.

Lorendinski's inked arms rise. His thick hands wrap together in a clap. Then another. And another.

What the hell?

"Were you in Menudo when you were a kid?" Lorendinski asks. "Because you're a hell of a performer. I especially liked that part about losing sleep."

A tightness vices around Ramos's rib cage. "Tell me where the fugitives are, or I have your ass thrown back in prison."

"Thrown in prison for *what*? For what crime? You really think I believe one of my guys came in here and said all that shit to you? They're not rats. They're my brothers. You've got nothing on me."

"I was at Crick last night. I know Phil Zorn used to buy things from you there. And I know he cut through the ventilation duct yesterday with a power saw, which I'm assuming your people smuggled in for him. Then he steals a pickup truck yesterday afternoon, found at that water park in Kanton, which is no more than a ten-minute drive from your house. You helped him break out. I know it. And that's a crime."

"A lot of people do a lot of business in jail. And a lot of people live within ten minutes of that water park. You can't attach me to anything."

Ramos decides to try another angle. "So you've got nothing to hide then, huh?"

"Not a thing."

"Then who were you hiding in your cellar this morning? Who was shouting for help? Who were you trying to grab through that window?"

"I don't remember a person in my cellar."

"Lying won't work. I was there."

"What I remember is you finding me in the basement with an empty chair. If someone else was down there, and I was hurting them like you implied, I'm sure one of your men assisted them, brought them into the station, took a statement from them, and had them agree to be a witness against me. If you didn't do any of this, then detective, all you've got is an empty chair. Maybe you didn't hear a *real* voice. A lot of people hear voices in their heads. It's common after a while in professions like yours with high stress and low pay."

Ramos digs his canine tooth into his lower lip. This piece of shit really knows his way around an interrogation. One of the benefits of being a career criminal, he supposes.

Of course Ramos heard that voice in the cellar. He even saw a body when he and the deputy got downstairs. Outside, through the blinds, barely discernible, but definitely there, was a body. It looked like a black guy. Who was it? One of the fugitives, Montgomery, is black. But if Lorendinski was helping the trio escape, why would one of them scream for help? No, it probably wasn't Montgomery. Ramos, once again, has nothing. So abandons this line of questioning.

Where to now? This bastard opened fire on two officers. Yes. He can use that to scare him.

"If you had nothing to hide in that cellar," Ramos says, "why were you overprotective to the point that you shot at two cops trying to go down there? The judicial system doesn't take that lightly in the great state of Texas. The law is respected here. Shooting at law officers usually comes with a long sentence. Tell me where the prisoners are, and maybe I forgive you for trying to shoot me."

Lorendinski clears his throat, a raspy grunt. "In the great state of Texas, last I checked, a man is allowed to defend himself with a sidearm if another man breaks into his home. I feared for my life this morning. There I was, doing some light reading in my cellar, when I hear a gunshot upstairs. Hear my whole glass door shatter. In come two men with weapons. Neither of them dressed as a police officer. Neither with a visible badge. So of course I exercised my right to defend myself in my own home."

That tightness around Ramos's rib cage grows spikes, like some medieval torture device.

Lorendinski ratchets its grip even tighter, "I've got a destroyed glass door in my house as proof. And I'm sure a ballistics team could check out the impact points on my walls and show it's likely that you fired the first shot, which we both know you did. You've got *nothing* on me. In fact, I have something on *you*. Blasting your way into a private residence in non-uniformed clothes, without evidence to support an entry, doesn't sound like proper police procedure to me. So how about I make a deal with *you*? Let me out of here, now, or I get my lawyer into the station...who happens to know much more about police rules than me, and probably even you...and we see just how much trouble he can get you into with your boss."

Ramos doesn't reply. He doesn't know how. Somehow Lorendinski has *him* by the balls. And he just squeezed.

"Get the fuck out of here," Ramos says.

Lorendinski, a gladiator's grin of victory on his face, extends his six-four frame up from the seat. "Where's the phone? I get my one call."

Ramos opens the door. Lorendinski cut him open during this interrogation. Ramos can at least prick him on the way out. "The phones here are only for police and prisoners. You're not on the payroll and we're not keeping you in custody, so you're neither. There are some businesses about a half mile down the road. Maybe one of them will let you use their phone."

Lorendinski pauses. And glowers. Then walks out of the room, bumping his shoulder into the cop's. Ramos, those spikes still rung around his ribs, watches him cross the station floor, exit the building, and turn toward the businesses down the road to make his call.

Thirty-Nine

The Buick cruises along Buddy Chaplin's long street, occasionally passing mailboxes of the spread-apart residences, each sitting on at least ten acres.

"That one," Danny says, pointing at Buddy's distinct terracotta roof, which he remembers from two previous trips here, the start of summer 2013 and then 2014, at the annual Amogo company barbeque Buddy hosts in the backyard.

Phil stops near the driveway. He leaves the engine running. "Here's how this will work," he says, turning to Danny in the back. "You go in, collect the duffel bag, and bring it out to me. Make it quick. No chitchat with your parents. You're going to get back in the car, then I'm going to drive to a parking lot in El Paso with you and the girl. An associate of Wade's from the cartel is waiting for us there. You and I will get in a van with him, and he'll take us to meet Wade in Mexico. Before we leave, I'll give the girl her phone back and she can call an ambulance to take her to the hospital."

So that's where Phil plans to kill him. A parking lot. Probably for one of the warehouses on the edge of the city that's closed for work Sundays. Phil will pop a round in his head, then likely one into Jane's. This is the first time Danny realizes Phil never intended for her to survive this day either. The thought kicks his anxiety into an even higher gear.

"Got it," is all Danny says, with an aloof grin, trying hard not to indicate he's wise to Phil's machinations. He gets out of the car and closes the door. Through its window, he makes eye contact with Jane. Her face is rife with fatigue. She needs to get to a hospital. He gives her a compact, though confident nod as if to say, *Everything will be okay.* Then he turns around and paces up the driveway.

But will everything be okay?

He checks his burner phone. Nothing from Monty, no confirmation that the call was placed. His elevated anxiety saddles him with something that seems like altitude sickness. He's not only lightheaded, but light-bodied. He feels like a floating spirit.

Like a ghost.

The overhanging fronds of the driveway's palm trees are perfectly still, as if no wind is in the air. The surrounding twenty-two acres are just as calm. No movement, not a person or animal. The only noise is the hum of Phil's engine, which distances as Danny approaches the house.

He steps up to the door, grasps the iron ring, and knocks. The heavy slab opens immediately. His mom is on the other side. Her image, not behind a plexiglass barricade in a prison visiting area, seems oddly alive, as if she is the embodiment of life itself. She wraps her arms around her son. He squeezes back. Harder than he ever has.

"Danny," she says into his shoulder. They stay embraced for half a minute.

He lets go. And smiles at her. Then closes the door behind him and bolts it shut.

"Hi son," Ben says.

Danny glances in the direction of the voice. Next to the foyer's black piano is his father. When Danny sees him, he's filled with the warmth of forgiveness. Ben didn't turn him in because he hated him. He turned him in because he did something wrong and, as his father, he couldn't let him run away from the consequences. Danny strides to him and gives him a hug just as tight as the one he gave his mom.

"I love you, dad."

They part. Ben takes a deep breath and has a look at his boy. A tear is in his eye, something Danny's never seen before. Ben wipes it. "I love you, too."

The pride Danny lost yesterday when he asked for the money returns, ballooning in his chest. He didn't expect this to happen. He takes a few seconds to let it settle in.

Then his gaze meets Buddy Chaplin's. His former boss stands in the corner, arms crossed. "Danny," he says, sticking out his hand.

Danny shakes it. "Thanks. For…everything."

"It's the least I can do."

Danny hears footsteps on the rustic-stone flooring. He notices his mother walking to the piano seat, where a gray duffel bag rests. She picks it up, offers it to Danny, and says, "It's all in here."

He glimpses it. And thinks about what everyone in this room went through to fill it up. Then tells her, "I'll never forget this. What the three of you did for me. But I don't need this anymore. This bag, this money, is now dangerous." Danny peeks out one of the eight-foot rectangular windows next to the door, down at the Buick idling in the street. Then focuses back on his mom. "I need you to hide it. Now."

"I don't understand, you said—"

"I know what I said. But things changed. Everything changed. There's a very bad man in a car in front of the house. He wants that money. And him not getting it is the only thing preventing him from doing some very bad things."

"Which man?" she asks, looking out the window.

"I can't explain it all now." He gently grips her shoulders. He locks eyes with her. "Mom, just trust me. I can't take a risk of him coming up here and seeing that bag. Go into another room and hide it. Hide it well. Please."

A few moments go by. She gradually pulls the gray bag away from him, into her chest. Her expression is infected with worry. She treads the stone floor under an archway and disappears with the money into another room.

Danny lets out a long sigh.

"Is this fella outside threatening you?" Ben asks. "You want me to go down there and have a word with him?"

"No," Danny shouts, throwing up his hands. "Do not leave this house. Just stay in here. I have it handled. It'll all be over soon."

Ben gives him a look Danny remembers from his teenage years, one of a father who can sense his child is stressing about something more than he's letting on. "You sure you're all right?"

Danny isn't. He still hasn't felt a vibration on his leg from Monty with confirmation. While Ben holds his concerned-father look on him, Danny removes the phone from his pocket and texts Monty:

Did you get through? How much longer till it's done?

He slips the phone back in his jeans, then glances out the window at the black car in the road. He takes a deep breath. He waits.

Forty

Jane Pilgrim feels like she has a little critter in her head. The sporadic sharpness is like the scrape of its nails, and the sporadic ringing in her ears is like the squeak of its voice. When the ringing happens, it starts soft, then spikes in volume, so loud she stops hearing the thrum of the Buick engine, then fades. It's quiet for a little, at varying intervals, then returns. Danny's right. She needs to get to a hospital.

She looks at the mansion they're parked in front of. The front door, visible in part from the street among an obscuring pattern of palm-tree leaves, remains closed. She thought this would be fast. In and out. She peeks at the console clock. Danny's been up there for over five minutes.

The driver, the wicked one (she forgot his name), is on edge, his fingers tapping the steering wheel, his eyeline transferring from the house to the clock on a loop. She hears a noise. It sounds like the engine, but tinier, and closer, something inside the vehicle. She recognizes it, but her head can't seem to place it. She's able to think, but her thoughts don't feel normal. They're shredded, as if those little animal claws are dicing them up.

She sees the driver lift a phone from his pocket to his ear, and realizes the noise was its vibration.

"It's almost done," the driver says into the phone the moment he answers it. "I'm at the house now." She hears another voice clatter through the earpiece. She can't make out the words from the backseat, but can sense the tone. It's panicky. "Wait, what?" the driver asks. "Say that again." The panicky voice courses from the device. "When?" A pause. "Well where is he *now*?" A moment. "Do the police have him?" A moment. "What do you mean? So he's just...anywhere? With your *phone*?" The back of the driver's neck reddens. A vein protrudes from behind his earlobe. "I don't know if they spoke," he shouts. "He's not with me." He glares at the house. "I have to go...I just...I...You let me down, Wade. I don't want to hear it." A moment. "No. I'll deal with this myself." He hangs up.

Shoving the phone into his pocket, he opens his door, then twists in his seat, clasping the gun that's been under him. Jane notices his face. Pupils dilated, his eyes are dark, glossy orbs, reminding her of black ball bearings. Their sight sends the Coke in her stomach halfway up her throat.

He gets out of the car and swings open her door. She cowers across the backseat in the other direction, her back slamming into the other door panel. He clutches her left ankle. She kicks his wrist with her right foot. His grip is tighter than it was when he grabbed her on that hill by the gas station. He seems possessed. He yanks, her little body crashing across the leather seat the opposite way it just cowered.

She screams. He tugs again. She screams again. One more pull, now she plummets out of the vehicle, the asphalt scratching her scabbed knees, the crimson crusts flaking off, raw skin revealed beneath.

He grasps her hair at the crown of her head, a furry blackish-purple clump jutting between his fingers, and heaves her to his side. The stretched hair strands send a ripple of pain across her scalp, reflexively making her eyes water.

Her head in one hand, the gun in the other, he steps onto the driveway.

"Let go of me," she yells.

His grip forces her skull backward at a forty-five degree angle, her eyes stuck on the sky. The muscles along her spine ache with each step she takes in this stance.

They walk as one under the palm trees. Toward the front door.

Forty-One

Danny's mom resurfaces in Buddy's foyer. "Hidden," she announces about the duffel bag. Danny kisses her head.

His phone shakes against his leg. With an excited hand, he digs it out of his pants and flips it open. A text from Monty:

Shouldn't be much longer.

Yes, yes. Yes. That ghost-like faintness in him begins fizzling out. His face, his shoulders, his chest, his legs, all regain a corporeal realness. He feels his blood in his veins. The juices in his stomach. The sweat on his skin.

He slips the phone back in his pocket and goes back to the waiting game. Less than ten seconds into it, he hears a knock at the door.

Danny steps to the tall rectangular window to the left of the entrance. The sight he sees outside isn't the one he expected.

Phil is at the front door. With Jane. And the gun.

The ghostly feeling returns. "It's him," Danny shouts to the room. His voice, audible through the windowpane, seizes Phil's attention. Phil pivots his head right, the black ball bearings in his face honing in on Danny on the other side of the glass.

Clenching Jane's hair in one hand, Phil attempts opening the door with his gun hand. Locked. He points the Sig Sauer at the window.

Danny gets out of the way. He looks back at his parents and Buddy, all huddled by the piano, and yells, "Go in the other room, *go*." He waves them toward the attached study. As his hands flap, the squawk of demolished glass reverberates through the twenty-foot-ceilinged space.

Startled, Danny's mom stumbles. His father catches her and clutches her in his arms. They backpedal into the study, stopping beside Buddy.

Danny remains in the foyer, ready to face whatever mayhem Phil plans to bring in here. A second gunshot blares, the bullet blasting apart a two-foot triangle of windowpane. Phil elbows some jagged shards still standing, breaking enough of a space for a person to step through.

First comes Jane, Phil guiding her by the head. Panting, she tucks her arms tight to her sides, attempting to evade contact with any splintered glass. Once she's in the foyer, Phil pushes her away from him, the forward momentum ramming her into the staircase banister.

Now he enters. Unlike Jane, he isn't mindful of the spiky edges of the shot-out passageway, one of them nicking his head. He doesn't seem to care or even notice. Once inside, he straightens his posture and stares at Danny. The fresh cut somewhere beneath that dyed-black mane releases a trickle of blood past his hairline, down his forehead, and onto his eyebrow.

Jane, propping herself up against the banister, watches the ex-cellmates square their bodies to each other. Danny can hear his mother's terrified voice whispering questions to his father. He doesn't hear his father reply. Likely because he has no way to explain the scene in front of him.

"Where's the money?" Phil asks Danny.

"There is no money anymore."

"Show me your phone."

"Why?"

"He contacted you, didn't he?" Danny stays silent, his gaze steady on Phil's. "What did he tell you?" Danny doesn't answer. "What're you two planning?" Again, no answer, anger showing all over Phil's face.

Danny hears his mom begin weeping. Then hears the clack of footsteps, heavier than hers could be, must be his dad's or Buddy's. The patter veers to his left, into another room. Phil's eyes dart in that direction, then sink back into Danny.

"The money is in this house somewhere, isn't it?" Phil asks. His lips bend into a self-satisfied smirk. "You told me you had it this morning. Which leaves two options. One, you lied. But I don't quite see the point. You knew I'd eventually find out when we arrived. Second option, you were *not* lying about it. Which means it's in here. And now that your friend contacted you and told you he was no longer at

Wade's mercy, you decided you don't want to hand it over. Am I right?"

Danny keeps quiet.

Phil studies his expression. "That's it, isn't it, Daniel? It's in here." Phil takes a slow step toward him. "But you're forgetting one thing." Another step. "Your friend may not be at Wade's mercy anymore...but you're still at mine." He aims the gun at Danny's face. His mom's wailing loudens.

A battle-like howl echoes through the house. Danny hears the same clack of footsteps he heard moments earlier, except faster now. In his left periphery, he spots Buddy charging under an archway into the foyer, a long blade glistening above his head. When Danny's eyes absorb the streaky image, he recalls that samurai sword Buddy always hung over the framed media pieces in the den. It's off the wall, and barreling in his hands toward Phil.

Without the slightest wince, Phil moves the pistol off Danny and onto incoming Buddy. He pulls the trigger.

The bullet enters Buddy two inches above the right portion of his pelvis. The sword falls from his hands, its blade nose-diving into the rustic-stone surface, then vibrating as the handle topples. Buddy's back flattens on the floor around the same time as his unavailing weapon.

"Holy fucking shit," Jane screams from the banister, the powerful, feminine-voiced cry undercutting the low-pitched, low-strength male moan emanating from Buddy's dying lungs.

Phil calmly walks toward Buddy's groveling body, steps in a C-shaped pool of blood leaking from his guts, and lifts the sword from the floor. He carries it to the obliterated window and chucks it into the front yard, bringing the count of available weapons among the group back to one. His gun. Which he now re-aims at Danny's face.

"No," Hannah Marsh screams, running between Danny and Phil, shielding her son's body with her own.

"Back away from him," Phil tells her. She doesn't.

Ben Marsh creeps into the foyer from the study, his hands raised as if to assert he means no harm. He steps through Buddy's pool of blood, which has filled out from a "C" into an "O." As the dying man whimpers nearby, Ben removes a smartphone from his jeans.

Phil whips the barrel of the Sig Sauer onto him and asks, "What do you think you're doing?"

"He needs an ambulance."

"Put the phone down."

"You can't just—"

Phil grabs Hannah's shoulder and shoves her away from Danny. He fastens his left arm around Danny's neck and butts the barrel of the pistol into his temple. He refocuses his gaze on Ben and says, "Put the phone down or I kill your son."

"Okay. Okay." Ben moves it toward his pocket.

"*Down* I said. Not in your pants. On the floor." A moment. Ben complies. Phil bends, Danny lowering with him, snatches the phone with the hand holding the gun, and drops it into the blazer pocket containing Jane's.

He checks his rear, as if to assure Jane isn't up to anything. She's not, hugging the banister in fear. Silence other than Buddy's wispy breath.

"Get me the money," Phil says to Ben, repositioning his weapon on Danny's temple. "I know you brought it here."

Hannah gazes at Ben, then back at Phil. "*You,*" Phil says, nodding at her. "You know exactly where it is, don't you?"

Her face tenses.

"You looked up at him for approval," Phil says. "I saw it. Were you in charge of stashing it somewhere?"

She presses her body into Ben's chest.

"You wanted your husband to consent to you getting it, didn't you?" Phil asks. "Because you know I need that money. And you know I'm not going to take this gun off your child's head until I have it. And you want your child to be safe, don't you? You want to give me the money and protect your child."

"Don't let him get in your head, mom," Danny screams.

Phil tightens his arm's clutch around Danny's neck. Then looks back at Hannah and says, "I'll shoot him just like I shot this one." He gestures with his elbow down at Buddy, who's no longer whimpering. He's still and silent.

"Don't you dare hurt him," Hannah says, tears flowing down her cheeks.

"I don't want to, my dear. I just want that money. Then I'll leave. And give you back your son. That's what you want, right?"

Danny says, "Don't do it mom. You give him that bag and he'll kill all of us."

"So there *is* a bag," Phil says with delight.

Fuck. Danny grunts in frustration.

"Get the bag, mom," Phil tells her. Her face is laced with a muddle of emotion, fear and doubt and hope. "You know you want to. Your husband wants you to as well. He wants what's best for you and your son. I take his silence as consent." The stream of blood from Phil's scalp cut dribbles beyond his eyebrow, down to mid-cheek. "Get the bag and I give you back your boy."

Her lips quiver. Hives dot her neck.

Ten seconds pass.

She steps toward the passage into the den.

"Mom, no," Danny blurts. "He'll kill us all."

She stops under the archway joining the two rooms. "He's more likely to kill you if we *don't* give him what he wants," she replies in a trembling voice.

"Please, mom, listen to me, he—"

"Did you see him shoot Buddy?"

"Yes, but—"

"He has a gun to your head," she yells. "I can't bear this. Why would he shoot you if we give him what he wants?"

"So I don't come after him in the future. Same with you and dad. Listen to me and—"

"How can you come after him in the future if he kills you *now*," she screams, her whole body quivering. "I'll take my chances." She tilts her gaze to the floor, takes a deep breath, and treads to the arch, soon vanishing on the other side.

"Shit, shit, shit," Danny grumbles. Then says to his father, "Dad, stop her. Go. Stop her now."

Ben is silent. "Your mother…your mother has a point, Danny. You're better off giving people like this what they want. Same as the advice about getting mugged. It's best to just hand over the wallet."

Goddammit. The master manipulator meddled with both of their minds to his advantage, just like he did with Danny's in prison.

Danny's heart bangs at an irregular pace, three quick beats, one slow, three quick, one slow. His gaze lasers onto the empty archway as he anticipates his mother's return.

How can he defuse this time bomb of a situation?

He was confident he could jump Phil back in the Buick, take him by surprise and take the pistol off him. But now? In a headlock, the gun barrel on his temple, no more surprise factor. Likely not.

His mother's footsteps tap in some distant room. They grow slightly louder. She's getting closer. The moment Phil sees her emerge with the gray bag he's firing a bullet into Danny's brain, then one into the heads of his parents and Jane.

Only seconds remain. Danny has to do something. He has to get the pistol from Phil. Now.

Just groping for it wouldn't work. For one, the headlock makes it impossible to even see the gun. It'd be hard to get a good grip. Even worse, Phil can see his hands. He'd notice Danny going for it and simply raise it beyond his reach.

Danny needs to disorient him somehow. A punch? No. How could he even land a clean one at this angle? An elbow? A kick? Neither would work, not enough leverage with him inside the headlock.

The thud of the footsteps amplifies.

Poke Phil in the eyes? No, too small a target, he'd likely miss.

He listens to his mom's shoes go *budamp*. She's now in the next room he'd say.

Budamp. Budamp.

Danny's got it. He slips his hand into his pocket and unearths the glass prism Phil gave him back at the schoolyard in
Rene, which he forgot was still on him. Holding it like a stake,
he stabs one of its sharp edges into Phil's right leg a couple
inches above his knee.

Phil screams. His grip on Danny's neck loosens a bit, offering Danny just enough wiggle room to spin around. He wraps
his arms around Phil's waist, drives his shoulder into his chest
like a linebacker, and barrels him toward the pile of shattered
glass at the base of the shot-up window, which Danny assumes
Phil will trip on.

Phil's frame flails as they slash across the foyer. When his
new leather loafers meet the sheeny glass shivers, as Danny
expected, they struggle to find traction and his legs slide out
under him. Danny, holding him, goes down too.

The ex-bunkmates slam onto a bed of sharpness. An ex-
cruciating pain overtakes Danny's right forearm, which is so
overwhelming it strangely doesn't feel like a cutting sensation,
but a burning one, as if he dipped his flesh up to his elbow in
a vat of boiling water.

Phil is flabbergasted, yet managed to hold on to the pistol. Danny reaches for the barrel, but Phil swings it backward, the weapon stretched past his head. Danny leans for it,
but Phil clamps his throat with his free hand, keeping him
out of range.

The skin of Danny's right forearm is studded with shim-
mering crystals of window, at least fifty, red squiggles around
each, which begin thin, then start swelling into dime-sized

dollops, their borders crossing, their fluids coalescing into a sleeve of blood.

Danny hears his father rushing over to help him. But Phil sticks out a foot.

Ben trips over it and crashes headfirst into the staircase railing. He woozily rises to a knee, getting his bearings.

Budamp. Budamp. Hannah's footsteps are at their highest volume yet.

She appears under the archway.

The gray duffel bag hangs from her hand. Danny spots her on the edge of his vision. On the other edge he spots Phil looking at her.

Phil has confirmation to kill. And Danny still hasn't commandeered the gun.

Their gazes meet, Phil's filled with hate. He's ready to murder Danny. However, under the hatred, his eyes are naked and vulnerable, no longer protected by the spectacles Jane kicked in back in Hill Country, something Danny can capitalize on.

He may not be able to reach Phil's gun. But he can reach his eyes.

Danny smashes his window-shard-riddled right forearm across Phil's poorly dyed eyebrows, jamming razors of glass fragments into his dilated pupils.

Phil screeches in anguish. His eyelids snap together. As blood seeps through the sealed lids, Phil sweeps the gun downward from above his head. He points it in Danny's direction. And fires.

But without vision, his angle is off and so is the bullet. Danny slaps the now-closer weapon out of Phil's hand. It bounces along the stone floor and glides into the dining room, attached to the foyer opposite the study.

Phil blinks a few times, reddish glass chunks falling from his eyes. He peeks behind him at the pistol. Ben, still down on a knee, but regaining composure, notices it too.

A moment.

At once the three men, Danny Marsh, Ben Marsh, and Phil Zorn, scramble toward the glistening piece of metal in the dining room.

Phil, the littlest of the three, maneuvers best through the snarl of limbs, and gets out ahead. He dives at the gun. His stomach slides across the floor. He secures the firearm under his palms.

As he curls his finger around the trigger, a voice screams, "Freeze." They all look toward it.

An El Paso policeman armored in SWAT gear leans through the broken window pointing an assault rifle at Phil. Ten other cops, with ten other assault rifles, are huddled behind him.

Phil lets go of the pistol. It drops to the floor. Behind the blood and glass all over his face is an expression of shock.

Danny stares at the team of officers. He doesn't feel shock at all. He feels relief. It was he who decided to call them.

Forty-Two

Danny's hands are cuffed behind him. He sits in a cop car, staring out the window at the scene on Buddy's lawn. Among the palm trees and fountain are five other El Paso police cruisers, parked at a mishmash of angles to each other. Officers yap with each other outside them.

Before they put the cuffs on Danny, a paramedic washed the glass slivers out of his forearm with water, doused his wounds in disinfectant, and swathed them in gauze. Four other paramedics, with much more urgency, tended to Buddy. He's alive, but not by much. Thankfully, Danny overheard one of them tell his former boss he's going to make it. They lifted him onto a stretcher and loaded him into an ambulance, which zoomed down the driveway and onto the street about five minutes ago.

Danny would go to the hospital from here, hang out in the waiting area, and visit Buddy once he was stabilized and permitted visitors. But he can't do that. Danny is going to jail.

And that's okay. It's what he wanted. It's what he had to do. He accomplished his goal. He kept himself alive while keeping Phil from roaming free. Also in the backseat of a cop cruiser on the lawn, also handcuffed, also going to jail, is Professor Predator.

Another ambulance lingers among the police vehicles. Its back doors are open, Jane sitting on its bed, her feet dangling by the bumper, the blood-and-dirt-tarnished laces of her sneakers flapping through the morning air. Her upper half is wrapped in a blanket. An EMT shines a tiny flashlight in her eyes, assessing the extent of her head injury.

Danny reflects on the short-lived, though lustrous, relationship he shared with this hitchhiking, purple-haired girl from the backwoods of Georgia. He wishes he met her under different circumstances. But given the bizarre ones that brought them together, he doesn't think things went too badly.

He did save her life, minutes ago in the house by deterring Phil until the police arrived. And in a way, she saved his last night. If she hadn't kicked Phil's glasses behind the gas station, leaving his eyes unguarded from lenses, Danny wouldn't have been able to land that decisive, shard-forearmed, blinding blow to his face in the foyer.

Danny can't hear her, but watches her mouth move as she talks with the paramedic. She looks a bit bushed, naturally after the last day, but her face has a new energy to it, one Danny hasn't seen since yesterday in Rene when they first picked up the exuberant, California-bound hitchhiker, an energy that dissolved the moment Phil flashed the Sig Sauer at her in the school parking lot. He's glad it's back.

Over the paramedic's shoulder, she notices him in the police car thirty or so feet away. Their eyes meet through the window. Her hand slips out from her red blanket and waves at him. She grins. He's not sure if it's a wave hi or goodbye. But he's happy to see it either way. He can't wave back because of the handcuffs. But he can smile back. And he does.

She's safe from Professor Predator. So are his parents. So is the rest of the population. He has a lot to smile about.

Forty-Three

Monty stands on a wooded hilltop overlooking downtown Rene. The sun is at a late-morning elevation. He's been hiding out in the forest the last few hours, waiting for Sunday church hours to kick in, which in East Texas usually draw most townspeople into pews as opposed to local businesses.

Now is right. Now is when he needs to make his move.

He scopes the names of the storefronts on Rene's main street a distance away. "Nat's Hardware." That should do.

Monty steps out of the tree grove, trots down a grassy slope, and mixes in with the pedestrians on Dixie Street. He keeps his face angled down, shielding it from view. He called the police like Danny requested, and if Danny told them what Monty requested, people shouldn't be looking out for his face. But still, you can never be too sure.

He paces along the sidewalk until he sees the sign of the mom-and-pop hardware shop in his periphery. Peeking through the front window, he notices it's not very crowded.

Church. Perfect. He enters, turning his back to the heavyset man at the register, hooking into an aisle.

Two things. That's all he needs. He'd pay for them, but doesn't have any money on him. He shoplifted a number of times as a kid and knows the motions. Yet, in a predominantly white town like this, deep in East Texas, any black man perusing in a retail establishment for too long without a purchase is bound to stir some suspicion. He has to be quick. And careful.

Sure enough, he hears the voice of the attendant boom into the aisle, "Looking for anything particular sir?"

An old trick comes to mind. Ask if he has something you know he doesn't carry, giving you a reason to leave without buying anything. But make sure it's not so far off it smells like a stunt. "Yes, actually," Monty says over the shelving. "Do you have tents, for camping?"

Monty dips into the next aisle. He spots one of the items he needs. A Phillips-head screwdriver, just like the one that was inside his leg in that Godforsaken basement. He snatches it and slides it in his pocket.

"This is a hardware shop, son," the out-of-view attendant says. "What you need is a sporting goods store."

"Where's the nearest one?" Monty calls out, then scurries into another aisle, where he sees coils of wire on pegs. He takes one and stuffs it in his pocket with the screwdriver.

"We don't have one in Rene. Gotta go all the way up Dixie and make a left on Pallance. Take it until you see the high school. Make another left. Go maybe five or six miles, crossing into Juntonville. You should see a shopping plaza. It'll be there, next to the Arby's."

"Thank you so much, sir," Monty says as he strides out from behind the shelves. Then waves at the man and exits.

He has the tools. Now he needs the target. Peering at the cars parked in the metered spaces on the main street, he reasons they won't work. They're in too plain a view. He needs more privacy. He figures the employees of these little shops park in non-metered private lots behind the businesses. Let's try that.

Monty strolls along the sidewalk, turns at an intersection, and slips into an alley behind the storefronts. He was right. Lots with three or four spots behind each building. Most of the cars, belonging to minimum-wage cashiers, are old. Which is good. He needs old. What he plans to do doesn't work well on any vehicles turned out after the turn of the millennium.

He treads the backside of the business strip, analyzing the parked automobiles. Many are ten years old, but he ideally needs twenty. It takes a couple minutes but he finds one. A beat-up, two-door sedan with a mid-Nineties body style. He checks the view over both shoulders, ascertaining nobody is watching, then removes the ring of wire from his pocket, unravels a two-foot length, curls the end, shimmies it inside the door panel beneath the driver's window, feels around for a few seconds, and pops the lock.

Monty opens the door and kneels on the pavement, looking up at the underside of the steering column. He employs the screwdriver to remove its cover, exposing a multi-hued knot of wires. He grabs them, colored cluster by colored cluster, and discerns where they lead. Once he knows what is what with the wires, he uses the screwdriver to strip the insulation off the tips of a select few. He wraps a couple together. Then touches the end of the starter wire to the end of the battery wires. Between his hands a small spark lights, then the engine comes to life.

He climbs into the driver's seat, revs the motor a couple times, then stabs the screwdriver into a space by the steering wheel and knocks free the steering lock. He closes the door. He puts the car in drive, cruises out of the alley, and onto the street.

"Aha," he shouts to himself in celebration.

The radio is on. He scans through the channels until he arrives at the news. As expected, the latest on the Crick escapees comes over the airwaves. The voice of a male announcer says, "...not certain when the prisoners traveled out of the East Texas area. But it's confirmed two are captured. The El Paso PD was responsible for the arrest. Reports are still coming in, but what we've so far learned is that one of the fugitives, Daniel Marsh, of El Paso, turned himself in. An anonymous call was made to the police, on his behalf, providing an address of a home where he'd be. Apprehended alongside him was Philip Zorn, the infamous professor from Austin. The third inmate, Monty Montgomery, is believed to have died in East Texas. Marsh told officers that Montgomery was badly wounded there and never made the trip to West Texas with the other two..."

Monty smiles. The world thinks he's dead, but he's alive, very much alive now that he's in this car. Since a dead man will be off the radar of the American authorities, Monty figures he can get some fake papers and continue living in the States. But he liked the idea of Mexico. Monty loves his country but, unlike Danny, never had much of a life here. He grew up with shitty parents in a shitty part of a shitty neighborhood with shitty opportunities.

So when he turns onto the highway, he makes sure he's headed south. Likely he'll return to the US someday. But for now, he wants to start anew in a new place.

He assumes he has a few hours until whoever's car this is gets off of work and reports it to the cops. By then he'll hopefully be close to the border, off to a new life. He already knows the first thing he's going to do when he gets there.

See the ocean.

Forty-Four

Danny, back in a white Texas Department of Criminal Justice jumpsuit, sits at a table in a West Texas courtroom, his hands cuffed in front of him. To his left is his lawyer, to his right a prosecutor, across from him a judge, and behind him are a police officer from Rene named Ramos, an official from the Drug Enforcement Administration, and his parents, who paid for his attorney.

Danny's hair no longer has the buzzed look. It's grown out the last nine weeks since Wade cut it in his basement, and is even a little longer than it was prior to the shave.

As the judge pours over a collection of documents, Danny stares at the Texas state seal behind his bench, then the American flag beside it, the red, white, and blue flowing off of a gold pole glinting in the serene indoor lighting.

The judge lifts his wrinkled, though strong-boned face from his reading and peers at Danny. In a deep Southern accent he says, "Mr. Marsh, what you did was despicable. I've spent my life dedicated to the legal system. Prison is the stick that keeps the entire mechanism together. Disrespecting the sanctity of jailhouse walls is like defiling the face of the law, and this very robe I'm wearing now. Do I make myself clear in my utter disgust, Mr. Marsh?"

"Yes, Your Honor."

The judge removes his reading specs, his eyes fixated on Danny. "Given that Mr. Marsh, I must say, after reviewing the statements and materials your attorney compiled for me, I am impressed, to one hell of a degree, by your bravery."

Danny grins, slightly. "Thank you, Your Honor."

"The statement by Miss..." The judge puts his reading glasses on for a moment and scans one of the papers, then removes them, refocuses on Danny, and says, "Miss Pilgrim. Was...just as commendable as it was shocking."

Jane. Danny's lawyer contacted her in California about her offering her account of the events. According to him, Jane lives along the Central Coast and recently enrolled in community college. She had the lawyer tell Danny hi, and assure him he had a standing invitation to visit her out west once he's released.

The judge continues, "What you did by giving up your own freedom to guarantee that a dangerous...a very dangerous...individual isn't free in society is the sort of behavior that makes me glad you're a fellow Texan, and a fellow American." A moment. "That being said...that being said Mr. Marsh. You still broke out of prison. I cannot let that deed go unpunished. It says here felony escape is a charge you're pleading guilty to, am I correct?"

"You are, Your Honor."

The judge nods at Lieutenant Ramos and the DEA official. "If you provide eyewitness testimony in the Rene Police
Department's case against Mr. Wade Lorendinski, as your attorney said you would, I'd be willing to reduce your extended sentence. Is this something you in fact agree to do, Mr.
Marsh?"

"Yes, Your Honor." Danny's lawyer spoke to the various law-enforcement agencies involved with the manhunt,
to put together the pieces of a potential plea agreement. He
learned a man in Rene named Wade Lorendinski was a prime
aiding-and-abetting suspect. After looking into Lorendinski,
he found out the DEA was watching him for over a year as a
player in the East Texas meth trade.

Though the authorities have no evidence for drug charges
against Lorendinski, they do have evidence for a kidnapping
one, which would get him off the streets and back in jail, a big
win for the city of Rene and the DEA. The evidence was found
on the burner phone the El Paso PD confiscated from Danny's
pocket when they arrested him. On it were dozens of photos of
Monty Montgomery chained to a chair in Lorendinski's basement. Danny testifying as an eyewitness to the kidnap should
be enough to put the case over the top.

As for what happened after Monty escaped from the basement, Danny's story hasn't budged. Monty was badly injured
and likely died somewhere in East Texas.

Police still haven't found the body.

The judge says, "Because of Mr. Lorendinski's connection with the Aryan Brotherhood, you'll be serving out the
remainder of your time in a prison without a significant Aryan

population. There's space in the Terotch Unit here in West Texas, where you'll transfer in the morning. Retaliation from a Lorendinski associate will be highly unlikely there. Just to be certain, you'll be placed on a special block with enhanced security. This security will also make another escape attempt virtually impossible." A moment. "But you don't plan on escaping again, do you Mr. Marsh?"

"No, Your Honor."

"Additionally, for your safety, we'll of course make certain prisoner Philip Zorn is not transferred, under any circumstances, into the Terotch Unit while you're an inmate there."

Buddy Chaplin survived the gunshot. It resulted in two surgeries, which he recovered well from, in addition to an attempted-murder charge for Phil. Tacked onto his sexual-assault sentence, the conviction would essentially guarantee the forty-seven-year-old man dies in prison, never to roam the free world again.

Danny's lawyer heard that the whack Danny gave Phil to the eyes caused permanent vision damage. So even if Phil were able to smuggle lab equipment into prison, his marred pupils would prevent him from properly operating it. His science, the only thing he loves, will be forever locked away, just like him.

"Do you have any questions, Mr. Marsh?" the judge asks.

"No, Your Honor."

"For escape, I order three additional months added onto your prior sentence. This is on top of the few weeks you've spent in custody since June. In normal circumstances I would've given you a lot more than three months for a breakout. But this court and I appreciate your cooperation in the

Rene Police Department's case against Mr. Lorendinski. With good behavior, you'll still be eligible for early parole. Thank you, Mr. Marsh." The judge bangs his gavel.

Danny signs some papers. Then a police officer escorts him toward the hallway. He smiles at his parents on the way out. The cop walks toward a squad car parked outside to take him back to the local prison he's spent the last nine weeks.

That wasn't horrible, Danny thinks. He can do an extra three months. He already put in a year and a half. Parole was initially at three. So he's got less than two years to go. Then he's a free man. He'll still be in his mid-twenties when he gets out. He'll have his whole life ahead of him.

The time behind bars seems manageable now, not daunting like it used to in Crick. A lot has changed since then, he supposes. He glances down at his right forearm, eyeing the three tiny scars left by shards of Buddy's window. They're a constant reminder he's not weak, as Phil used to insist. A weak person wouldn't have fought a pistol-wielding psychopath on a bed of cracked glass. And won. A weak person would've run.

Danny has a grit in him he never really needed as an upper-middle-class kid, so never knew existed. But after the incident nine weeks ago, he understands he has this dimension in him. He's a survivor. And if some punk wants to pick a fight with him in jail, Danny is confident he can fend for himself.

More importantly, the ordeal with Phil not only proved Danny is a survivor, but a protector. Yes, Danny did indeed make a mistake one night in 2014. And unintentionally harmed one life. And he'll always live with that. However, when he intentionally made a decision to sacrifice his freedom to keep many other lives safe, he proved to himself he's not evil. This knowledge helped melt away the buried guilt in him, helped evaporate that chunk of ice that's been in his gut for so long.

And he's fine living a bit more of his life in a prison cell now that he's confident he won't end up in that gray box when his life is eventually over.

As the officer leads him outside and Danny sees the sun, he thinks of Jane in bright California. He'd love to take her up on her offer to visit once he's out. And now he could since he won't be on the run in Mexico. He'll be home, in America.

He looks forward to seeing how their time together will play out under different conditions, free from the constraints of Phil.

The world finally feels simple. Contrary to what Phil says, you don't need quantum physics to figure out what life is made of. It's people. Just people.

About the Author

Ted Galdi is the author of two novels, *An American Cage* and *Elixir*. He's a winner of a *Reader Views* Reviewers Choice Award and a Silver Medal in the *Readers' Favorite* Book Awards. Ted has been featured by ABC, FOX, iHeartRadio, and many other media outlets. To learn more, visit www.tedgaldi.com.

CPSIA information can be obtained
at www.ICGtesting.com
Printed in the USA
LVOW10s1507291217

561234LV00010B/865/P

2

9 780989 850728